C000279996

Not Exac

Not Exactly Shangri-la

Martin Moir

Rupa & Co

Copyright © Martin Moir 2009

Published 2009 by
Rupa . Co
7/16, Ansari Road, Daryaganj,
New Delhi 110 002

Sales Centres:

Allahabad Bengalooru Chandigarh Chennai
Hyderabad Jaipur Kathmandu
Kolkata Mumbai

All rights reserved.
No part of this publication may be reproduced, stored in a
retrieval system, or transmitted, in any form or by any means,
electronic, mechanical, photocopying, recording or otherwise,
without the prior permission of the publishers.

Typeset by
Mindways Design
1410 Chiranjiv Tower
43 Nehru Place
New Delhi 110 019

Printed in India by
Nutech Photolithographers
B-240, Okhla Industrial Area, Phase-I,
New Delhi 110 020, India

For Z

CONTENTS

CONTENTS

Author's Note

All the characters and places represented or depicted in this novel are entirely fictitious.

Acknowledgments

I am very grateful to Jackie Moir, Dr Francesca Fremantle, Valerie Phillips, Jonathan Moir, and Dr John Mackrell for reading the text at an early stage, offering encouragement and making valuable suggestions. I also wish to thank Dr Prem Chowdhry, Dr Dominique-Sila Khan, Jonathan Price and Professor John McIlwaine for advice about publication, and Khadija Lalani for typing and reproducing the original text.

The passage from the Bardo prayer on pages 9 and 10 of this book is taken from *The Tibetan Book of the Dead. The Great Liberation through Hearing in the Bardo by Guru Rinpoche according to Karma Lingpa*, translated with commentary by Francesca Fremantle and Chogyam Trungpa (p. 103, Shambhala, Boston & London, 1987).

PART ONE

The Invitation

1

'Though not exactly a part of what geographers call "the Roof of the World", Kalapur may be fairly described as a kind of earthly attic. And, like many such remote rooms at the top of old houses, it is rarely visited, even by those whom you might expect to go there.'

'Not for want of trying!' growled Professor Gabbinger audibly from the front row; his latest application for an entry visa had, as Timothy well knew, recently been rejected like most of the previous ones.

'To be more precise,' the speaker continued, apparently oblivious of the interruption, 'Kalapur is a small Himalayan country of half a million people, situated between four and twenty thousand feet above sea-level at the eastern end of the North-East frontier of India, beyond Sikkim and Bhutan, and to the south of Tibet. Politically it may be described as a semi-autonomous state in treaty relations with the Indian government, which has bound itself not to intervene in the country's internal affairs on condition that Kalapur maintains no formal diplomatic links with any other outside governments.'

At this point Timothy could not resist glancing at Sharir Singh, the representative of the Indian High Commission in London. But Sharir had already assumed that faraway expression which Timothy had come to think of as his 'Himalayan' look, descending over his features like a mountain mist whenever the proceedings of the Royal Himalayan Centre threatened to touch politically sensitive issues. A similar look had also begun to cloud the lined face of Arthur Hoadley, CIE, president of the Centre. As the last British political agent in the area in the late 1940s, he had helped to revise the special protectorate treaty between British India and Kalapur which independent India had later been happy to perpetuate. Perhaps, thought Timothy, there was some elite training school at a place like Dehra Dun where aspiring Indian diplomats were taught a useful repertoire of such expressions by retired officials of the Raj.

'Kept secluded in this way from the rest of the world,' the speaker went on more eloquently, 'Kalapur, "the Land of Time", has been able to preserve the essentials of its own uniquely indigenous Buddhist culture with only minor adjustments to modernity. So its religious leader, the Shar (or Eastern) Lama, believed to be the embodiment or incarnation of the Spirit of Time, still functions as the head of state, though nowadays he devolves day-to-day administrative responsibilities upon the Council of Ministers, in accordance with the terms of the new constitution enacted a few years after the presumed death of the previous Shar Lama in 1944. The country also retains much of the original network of old monasteries, over one of which, Migoling Monastery, I have the honour to preside . . . Some westerners have told me that as they ascend from the Indian foothills up through the Himalayan frontiers of Kalapur, and along the steep road that leads to Himjin, the capital, they feel as if they have stepped on to a kalachakra—a sort of time-machine—gradually drawing them back across several centuries.' The old man paused, as if waiting for his audience to adjust their watches to Himjin time.

Timothy Curtin took advantage of the pause to take stock of the occasion. He had agreed to take over as secretary to the Centre only four months before, after completing his thesis, even though he had suspected that it would involve him in the sort of upfront role that he normally preferred to avoid. In fact, Hoadley had originally got him to take it on, not by direct persuasion or instruction, but by tacitly assuming that he was, of course, going to take over when old Miss Mainwaring had asked to retire. By the time Timothy had realised what was happening it was really too late to refuse without causing offence and disappointment to Hoadley, who was in any case an old man well past eighty whom he felt obliged to support. Besides, Hoadley was rumoured to have kept a personal diary and other papers dating back to his period in Kalapur, and, given the difficulty of gaining admission to the country, Timothy was badly in need of original source material for his post-doctorial study of the final phase of British Indian policy in the Himalayas.

Having now helped to organise the last three meetings of the Centre, he was beginning to think that he might eventually come to enjoy the experience. Along with his temporary post at the university, it had given a slight boost to his minimal self-confidence. He was pleasurably aware too that in materialising Abbot Taranatha in his maroon robes, for this evening's lecture—the first speaker from Kalapur ever to address the Centre—he had actually succeeded in impressing his fellow members. Of course, the coup, if it was one, was partly due to that Foreign Office man, Brian Carstairs, who had originally told him about the Abbot's British Council visit several weeks before. Carstairs, a regular attender at the Society's meetings, was not someone to whom Timothy had naturally warmed. Unlike the fast dwindling older generation of Raj representatives, he appeared to have no personal interest in the history and culture of the Himalayan countries or the condition of their people, and with his tough, no-nonsense air, he had clearly not attended any diplomatic charm school. Still Timothy felt grateful to him for the suggestion, and wondered what he hoped to get out of the evening.

Meanwhile the Abbot had finished his introductory remarks and was apparently approaching the central subject of his lecture. Or was he? The problem was that Timothy was still not sure which aspect of Kalapur the old man was going to talk about. During their hurried and rather confused telephone conversation a few weeks back, it had sounded as if the title he wanted was 'Acorns of Kalapur', but the line had been faint and the Abbot's accent hard to follow. It seemed an improbable topic but one couldn't be sure: it might contain some symbolic allusion, and Timothy was not so well-grounded in Kalapuri culture, though attracted to what he knew of it. He had counted on finding another opportunity to clarify the title beforehand but unfortunately, the Abbot had arrived late and he had been obliged to introduce him and the puzzling subject straightaway, relying on people's polite reluctance to query such things at the beginning of a lecture. But as soon as the Abbot got started, his earlier rather difficult accent largely dropped away, and Timothy listened bemused as the mysterious 'acorns' rationally recomposed themselves into 'accounts', that is, historical accounts of Kalapur.

Gradually recovering from his confusion—or rather putting it on one side to re-evoke later—Timothy began to listen to the lecture with growing interest.

There were, so the Abbot explained, very few important historical archives left in Kalapur. Most of them had originally been kept in several large monasteries close to the capital and had therefore been lost when many of those buildings were destroyed by fire during the nineteenth century. Hence—and here the Abbot was clearly warming to his subject—it was now difficult to find much solid evidence within Kalapur on which to base objective accounts of the history of the country during the past three or four centuries.

'I hardly need to remind this distinguished gathering that major works of history depend on individual documents as oaks depend on acorns,' he added.

Timothy again felt uncomfortable. Though the simile had been delivered with apparently innocent spontaneity, he could not help feeling that it had been meant for him, but whether to help or increase his confusion he could not as yet determine.

The Abbot next described various environmental threats to the historical and cultural heritage, dwelling graphically on the worms resident in the library of his own monastery, which were in the process of devouring a particularly ancient manuscript set of the Tibetan Buddhist canon, the Kangyur and Tengyur.

'Local scholastic opinion,' he observed drily, 'is divided on the issue of whether these tiny creatures will acquire merit from their activities or whether, on the contrary, they will suffer future rebirths at an even lower plane of existence.'

The Abbot's expressionless expression left open the question of how he himself viewed their fate. Most of the listeners, however, chose to laugh, and in the resultant relaxation in the atmosphere, Timothy was again able to look around the room to see how the regulars were taking it.

He was specially interested to observe the reactions of the small group whom he had come to think of as the mystics or Buddhists, for it had not taken him long to discover that most of the Centre's active members could be roughly assigned to four or five major interest groups. Thus, apart from the several retired or serving officials like Hoadley, Carstairs and Sharir Singh, and the academics like Gabbinger, there was also a small band of very elderly ex-Indian Army officers, led by Colonel Fox, an assortment of mountaineers and botanists, and finally, the mystics, of whom Lady Aloysia Scott-Packenham and Serena Gray were the most prominent.

Not, of course, that all these groups were entirely separate from each other. For instance, Lady Aloysia, though primarily a mystic, was also the widow of Sir Granville Scott-Packenham, the early conqueror of several Himalayan peaks, and therefore on friendly terms with some of the older mountaineers. Similarly Serena, an American graduate who was halfway through her thesis on Tibetan Buddhism, moved freely between the mystics and the academics. Indeed, it was on the basis of their shared academic background that Timothy had cautiously attempted to engage her in conversation during the previous meetings. The trouble was that he was so beguiled by the liquid beauty of her eyes that he could find little to say – literally nothing on the last occasion, when she had asked him what he thought of the concept of emptiness in the Mahayana Buddhist texts. Perhaps, he now reflected, his silence had not been such a bad response after all. Anyway, despite the embarrassment with the acorns, he still felt buoyed up by his success in producing the Abbot, and therefore ready to try again with Serena. Maybe he would ask her to come for a drink after the lecture.

Reluctantly, Timothy once more focused his attention on what the Abbot was saying. He had now moved on from the dangers that beset Kalapur's historic manuscripts and was disclosing some of the more positive aspects of the picture.

At least two unique treasures had apparently survived. The first was the so-far unrecorded oral tradition of ballads and epics. The other was the work known as the 'Lives of the Lamas', regularly compiled in Migoling Monastery since the late seventeenth century. Besides recording the spiritual achievements of the great lamas, this chronicle also covered some of the important events of their reigns, often in considerable detail, though interspersed with Buddhist texts and prayers. There was evidence too that, influenced perhaps by the old Chinese historiographical tradition, the compilers of the chronicle had been able to utilise and transcribe some of the official documents from the Lama's chancery. This was obviously of cardinal importance given the loss of many original archives. The chronicle itself now consisted of several dozen separate sections written in an archaic literary form of the Tibetan script. Parts of it, he added, were of such a secret nature that they were written in the so-called 'water-script', which only became visible when the plant-fibre sheets were immersed in water. At this point Gabbinger stared incredulously at the Abbot. But the latter as usual, showed no signs of being aware that such features required explanation.

'So that you may better understand the historical significance of this chronicle,' he announced rather solemnly, 'I have been given permission by the Council of Ministers to read you a rough translation of a short passage in the account of the reign of the Shar Lama for the year 1690:

> In this year another miraculous occurrence was reported to His Holiness the Protector of the Doctrine of the Buddha by the governor of the Western Pass. A shepherd by the name of Norbu had found the deceased bodies of two strange beings at the highest point in the pass. It appeared that these beings had just been overcome by the violent snowstorms and intense cold of this inhospitable region. Their heads were covered in long red hair and their bodies wrapped in unknown woollen garments. The shepherd told the governor that he had found the bodies of two migos or wildmen. However, after examining them, the governor could not decide who or what they were, and reported the discovery to His Holiness. His Holiness declared that they were either wildmen or wandering ghosts and should be treated with compassion. The governor was at once instructed to arrange for a lama to make belated offerings and guide the spirits of the creatures through the bardo (the experience between death and rebirth).

The Abbot then explained that the passage ended with the following prayer:

> When the journey of my life has reached its end
> And since no relatives go with me from this world
> I wander in the bardo state alone,

May the peaceful and wrathful Buddhas send out the power
of their compassion
And clear away the dense darkness of ignorance.

Having intoned the prayer the Abbot removed his spectacles,
straightened up and faced his audience. 'It is my belief,'—his words
were spoken very deliberately to an expectant hush—'that the strange
beings described in this passage were none other than the two English
East India Company merchants, Blake and Arbuthnot, who, you will
recall, disappeared in 1690 somewhere between North-East India and
Tibet on a mission to export broadcloth to the population of these
high altitudes. If I am right, you will appreciate that the "Lives of
the Lamas" has value not only for the history of my country but for
yours as well.'

Timothy, who knew all about the mission of Blake and Arbuthnot,
and their mysterious disappearance, stared wonderingly at the Abbot.
Could this extraordinary story possibly be true? Was there any chance
that the Abbot would help him get permission to enter the country
to examine the chronicle and other manuscripts? Would there be
an opportunity to ask him after the lecture? His spirits began to
soar as the prospects beckoned, and at the same time he could not
help looking hopefully in the direction of Serena. To his surprise it
seemed that she was smiling at him. He smiled back, only to realise
too late that her radiant expression, though it certainly included
him, was almost certainly meant for everyone – like the peaceful
and benevolent smiles of the bodhisattvas that no doubt adorned
the walls of the Kalapur monasteries. Hurriedly he turned away and
gazed distractedly at the high lecture room windows and the cold
darkening winter evening.

Abruptly, he became aware that the lecture had come to an end
and the speaker was being politely thanked by Arthur Hoadley.

The Abbot having indicated his readiness to answer questions,
Timothy listened while Hoadley, in his slow, methodical, rather

concerned way, began to formulate the first enquiry. He had, he said, noted with great interest what the Abbot had told them about the historical sources extant in Kalapur, and especially about the 'Lives of the Lamas'. What he wondered was the position about public access to the chronicle, given the evident secrecy of some parts of it?

The Abbot smiled benignly. 'Until very recently,' he explained, 'the whole chronicle was indeed treated as a secret document which only a few privileged people were allowed to see – that is to say, its compilers, the members of the Council of Ministers, and the Shar Lama himself. However, I am glad to tell you that it has now been decided to open the greater part of the chronicle to established scholars after some essential conservation work has been carried out.'

'May I ask up to what date the chronicle will then be open?' Hoadley enquired, somewhat anxiously.

'Following the best international practice,' the Abbot replied, his earlier naïve air giving way to greater briskness, 'we have decided to keep closed only the last thirty years plus a small group of specially sensitive earlier entries. We also plan to publish selections from the whole work, starting from the 1940s.'

That could open up the period of Hoadley's involvement in Kalapur, thought Timothy, unless those parts have conveniently disappeared in the water-script! That was probably why the old fellow looked distinctly worried as he turned to other members of the Centre for further questions.

Predictably, it was Carstairs who at once waved his arm vigorously. Timothy had noticed before that he always tried to get in first. This time he wanted to know about opportunities for direct British trade with Kalapur. How far—he glared at Sharir—would it be subject to bureaucratic control from India? Retreating back into his original air of archaic innocence, the Abbot disclaimed much knowledge of commercial activities, though he suggested that the programme for preserving the historic heritage of the country could benefit from British chemical products and expertise. 'I can at least assure you,' he added quietly, 'that the new generation of British businessmen who come to Kalapur will not suffer the fate of Blake and Arbuthnot!'

Timothy knew from experience that it was only a matter of time before one of the regulars would spark off a renewed debate on one or other of those specially contentious issues that perennially bothered the Centre. The 'existence or otherwise of the yeti', had not had an airing for the past few sessions, so given the Abbot's story about the supposed wildmen, it was bound to come up soon. Sure enough, Colonel Fox was already looking restive. A large, elderly man, with a rasping voice full of suppressed indignation, he had disconcerted Timothy on their very first introduction by barking at him what sounded like, 'Fucks!'

The colonel now hailed the Abbot with an unexpected degree of respect, as if he were addressing a rather exotic regimental padre.

'Your Reverence referred to the Kalapuris' original supposition that those English merchants were wildmen or yetis, but I noticed that you yourself wisely refrained from commenting on this. May I now ask you, as a learned man who knows Kalapur very well, to tell us what you think of those silly snowmen stories?' .

'In the past,' the old man answered judiciously, 'there were many reported sightings of yetis – we call them migos in Kalapur. Nowadays there are few; in fact most people believe that seeing them brings bad luck.'

Before Fox could react to this cryptic utterance, Lady Aloysia, the Society's yeti champion, had jumped in at top speed.

'Far from being just silly stories,' she stormed, 'many reports of yetis are based on sound scientific evidence. I have here, for example, a photograph showing several human-looking tracks made in the snow in the mountains north of Himjin at the height of sixteen thousand feet. This was taken by my late husband, Sir Granville Scott-Packenham, in 1963. In fact Granny also told me that several of his most trusted Kalapuri helpers had personally encountered yetis on various occasions.'

Lady Aloysia brandished her old photo at the Abbot. But by this time the colonel had recovered his ground, and without giving Taranatha a chance to comment, he again weighed in: 'Those tracks are more likely to have been left by wandering bears or large monkeys. As for those Kalapuris – I well remember them from my Indian Army days. They were courageous little chaps but, my goodness, they would tell you all kinds of fantastic yarns if they thought you wanted to hear that sort of stuff!'

'I must really request members to restrain themselves on this subject, which in any case is hardly central to this evening's topic.' It was Hoadley asserting his authority at last. 'Indeed I see from my watch it is now well past seven-thirty and we must not detain our distinguished guest, who has given such an illuminating picture of his country's historical heritage.'

Colonel Fox and Lady Aloysia reluctantly subsided to join in the polite applause. But unexpectedly, the Abbot rose again to his feet. 'In Kalapur,' he now beamed at everyone, 'we clap our hands when we wish to drive out an evil spirit. Here, I believe, this custom has a different meaning!' This brought him more enthusiastic applause.

Forgetting his own distractions, Timothy tried to make sense of the whole strange performance. The Abbot was certainly a scholar of some kind. But beyond this what sort of man was he? From much of his talk it seemed that he had only had a traditional Buddhist monastic education and had probably not been outside Kalapur before, except perhaps to India. On the other hand, despite Timothy's first impressions, he clearly had an excellent command of English, and had shown by sudden shafts of sophistication that he knew far more about the outside world than one might have supposed. Then there had also been those bizarre moments when it almost appeared as if he himself was deliberately switching personas, fully aware of how they were perceived by his audience, and inwardly amused to juggle with their responses.

As the meeting began to break up, Timothy abruptly remembered that he had two things to do in a hurry: to find a way of sounding out the Abbot about a visit to Kalapur and to ask Serena if she would join him for a drink. Since the Abbot was being monopolised by Lady Aloysia and her photograph, he began looking round for Serena.

'Did you hear what he said about publishing that chronicle?' – Hoadley was standing anxiously but very firmly in front of him. 'That could be a very serious business for us. I suppose you know that our last few years in Kalapur were pretty rough. Some wild accusations were being made against us—against me—which I thought had now been safely forgotten. If this document gets published, the whole thing will get raked over again and British interests will suffer. Timothy, our only hope is for you to go out there to persuade the authorities to drop this scheme or those parts of it that could rebound on us. I can't go—I'm too old—and in any case it would look bad if I did!'

As Hoadley rambled on nervously but inescapably, Timothy caught sight of Serena leaving with Carstairs. 'Oh God,' he thought, 'if she's ready to go out with him I might as well give up.' Hoadley, however, did not give up so easily. In fact, Timothy realised that he was now being invited to have lunch with him next week at his club, 'so that I can put you fully into the picture, and we can tackle this problem together.' He was not at all sure whether he wanted to go to Kalapur now if it was going to mean tackling problems there for Hoadley. Eventually, the latter declared that it was time for him to leave, after reminding Timothy of his official duty to see the speaker safely into a taxi and back to his hotel.

By this time virtually all the other members had also departed, and Timothy looked around for the Abbot. Lady Aloysia, he was relieved to see, was just saying goodbye to him, still waving her photo. He now had the old man to himself but could not summon up the nerve to broach the subject of the visit. It seemed too pushy, and in any case with Hoadley's proposed schemes the prospect was becoming far less appealing.

'Thank you for your most enlightening lecture,' he found himself saying, and 'perhaps you would like to use the bathroom or toilet before I go for the taxi.'

The Abbot nodded, and for the first time Timothy became more aware of his physical presence. He was small but thin and very erect, with a kind of silent dignity – not at all hostile but somehow discouraging further conversation. Probably he was just tired. Timothy led him across the courtyard. It was cold, dark, and beginning to snow. He had to restrain a secret schoolboyish curiosity to see how the old man would negotiate the loo. Would he hitch up his robe or retreat into one of the cubicles? But before disappearing the Abbot slowly drew a large envelope from the recesses of his robe and handed it to Timothy without a word. It contained an official invitation to visit Kalapur.

2

For several days after the Abbot's departure Timothy pondered on the meaning of the invitation. Though hardly conscious of it himself, he had developed a tendency to look for hidden motives behind most official actions, partly as a result of his long immersion in British Indian diplomatic history and partly from a natural sense of insecurity.

The letter itself, signed by the cultural secretary of the Government of Kalapur, briefly invited him to spend two months in the country to give advice on the editing of historical documents to Abbot Taranatha and the other members of the Historical Records Commission. All his expenses were to be paid and it was further proposed that he should start the assignment by the middle of March. It was a smooth-sounding document, with only one mistake: not for the first time he was addressed as Dr Timothy Curtains!

But why on earth had they selected him for this important mission, and not someone far more experienced and distinguished in the field of Himalayan studies, like Gabbinger, who had only recently acted as his own supervisor? The letter itself provided no clue. Timothy tried to picture the Abbot sitting in his remote monastic cell, meditating on that article he had written last year in the *Asia Historical Review* on 'Kalapur and the Raj', and suddenly exclaiming to his monks: 'This is the man we need for our history project!' It didn't seem very likely, especially since before the Abbot had disappeared into his taxi, Timothy had actually managed to ask him more or less directly why he had been chosen.

'It must have been because of the merit you have acquired from your past actions,' the old man had answered with apparent gravity, then adding in his final and most disconcerting switch of tone: 'And please don't forget to bring plenty of warm clothes—it can still get bloody cold in March!'

Clearly, the Abbot was far too unfathomable a character for one to be able to hazard any plausible conjecture about his personal role in the affair. Better to concentrate on certain other individuals within the range of his acquaintance who could well have played some part in the selection process. Carstairs, for example, could easily have been approached by someone in the cultural wing of the Government of India acting on behalf of Kalapur. After all, it was he who had originally encouraged Timothy to ask the Abbot to address the Centre. But if so, why hadn't he said anything about his recommendation beforehand? He had nothing to lose by such a disclosure, unless perhaps he had been unsure whether his advice had been accepted. Maybe—and Timothy suddenly recalled Carstairs' abduction of Serena at the last meeting of the Centre—maybe he had recognised Timothy as a potential threat to his own designs on Serena and had therefore helped to engineer the whole scheme of spiriting him away to the Himalayas!

Realising that his speculations were getting out of hand, Timothy contrived to dispel his increasingly diabolic projection of Carstairs and instead began to contemplate the apparently more amiable figure of Sharir Singh. This almost Tantric feat of visualisation also yielded him the reflection that it was far more likely that Sharir from his official power-base would have put Timothy's name forward to the authorities in Kalapur. Not that he supposed that Sharir thought particularly highly of his abilities. Most probably he saw him as a harmless, fairly competent young academic who was less likely to upset India's historical applecart in Kalapur than Gabbinger, an old Marxist and a well-known champion of the autonomy of the Himalayan peoples. Perhaps Sharir himself would be willing to reveal more when Timothy went to see him about his visa arrangements.

However absorbing though these speculations were, Timothy was all the time uncomfortably aware that they were not the real issues that would eventually confront him in Kalapur, for beyond them lay the far more difficult question of how he would cope with the Abbot's publication plans.

'My dear Timothy, I'm so sorry to have kept you waiting!' Hoadley had come into the club at last, full of apologies for being late, but with an unusual air of briskness about him. Timothy had previously thought of him as an anxious, even bumbling old fellow, but looking at him now, he suddenly perceived that in his younger days, before his precision and thoroughness had become a burdensome concern for the detail he could no longer always handle, he might have been quite formidable. 'Let's have lunch first and then we can talk about our little problem.'

The club lunch was excruciatingly slow in coming, and hard to digest. Timothy had rashly ordered something called 'Special Pizza Oasis', which turned out to consist of a large expanse of uncooked dough surmounted in the middle by a solitary dried-up olive. Since to force the stuff down he had unwisely consumed far too much chianti, he ended up feeling even less confident about his ability to keep cool and avoid committing himself to whatever plans Hoadley had in store for his Kalapur mission. By contrast, the old man, who had drunk comparatively little, appeared even more masterful as he led Timothy towards two deep armchairs at the far end of the club's vast Edwardian lounge.

'You know Timothy, that invitation of yours is a godsend. It provides us with an ideal opportunity to get them to drop the idea of publishing whatever that crazy chronicle says about British policy in Kalapur. I'm sure you will succeed.' Timothy realised that Hoadley was already deploying the same fait accompli tactics he had used earlier to ease him into taking on the secretaryship of the Himalayan Centre.

'But before we talk about that problem,' Hoadley continued, 'I'm curious to know what you made of Abbot Taranatha.'

'To tell the truth,' Timothy replied, 'I couldn't make him out at all. At first he struck me as a rather quaint old monk educated in the traditional way. But then he would suddenly say something that showed that behind that mask he was incredibly alert and knowing.'

'Exactly,' said Hoadley. 'So let me tell you a little more about his background. You see as a young man in Kalapur, Taranatha was considered to be an outstanding student of history and philosophy, and in 1950 (I think it was) he was awarded a special scholarship to study Western Thought at London University. I think he spent about two years here and no doubt picked up a lot. Then, of course, he went back to Kalapur, and slowly over the years rose up through the monastic hierarchy, published several books, and is now apparently considered by the government as an academic pundit. Incidentally, the reason why he was given that scholarship was because we suspected that some of the young Kalapuri intellectuals at that time were being attracted to Chinese communism. So it was politically important that we did our best to give at least one of them a pro-western orientation or perhaps I should say "occidentation".'

'What do you think has happened to his orientation since then?' Timothy enquired.

'It's hard to say. My guess is that he experiences inner tension. Anyway, you will have an opportunity to find out very soon.'

Timothy wondered if they had reached the point when he should begin to dissociate himself from Hoadley's schemes. But before he could say anything, the old man had already launched into a full-scale account of his experiences in Kalapur, and there seemed no point in trying to stop him.

'I expect you already know generally about what was going on in the Himalayas during the Second World War.' Hoadley's voice had descended to a well-practiced confidential murmur which at times made him almost inaudible. 'But I'm sure you don't know much about what actually happened in Kalapur during 1944-45 – almost nobody does!'

'Wasn't the old Kalapur Lama—I mean the Shar Lama—killed in 1944?' Timothy put in with an effort.

'No, not exactly,' Hoadley virtually whispered back, 'or rather that's exactly the point we still need to watch very carefully. You see the old Lama was a bit of a nationalist as well as a socialist, and he got taken in by all that Jap propaganda—"the New Order in East Asia, freedom from western colonialism," and "the shared heritage of Buddhism"—you know the sort of stuff they put out then. Anyway, at the beginning of '44, I learnt that His Holiness was secretly receiving a party of Buddhist monks from Kyoto and I really got quite worried! I suppose in ordinary times we could have lived with that; but you have to remember at that point the Japanese had already swallowed up Burma and were about to launch themselves on India. If they got a foothold in Kalapur things could have gone even more serious. We couldn't afford to take any risks – so you can imagine that for the next few months I kept a close daily watch on the Lama and his movements. One morning in June (it was just after Kohima where the Japanese advance had been broken) one of my Kalapuri informants came to my office in quite a state. He said that early that same morning the Lama had boarded a small airplane (one of two which the Chinese had supplied a few years before with our acquiescence) and flown off for an unknown destination. I immediately reported the event to GHQ India and nothing more was heard of the Lama and his plane.

'Of course, there was a great hullaballoo in Kalapur and we became extremely unpopular. Fiery demonstrations for days on end outside my residency office – I even had to ask for a special force to be sent up from Simla to protect the staff. You see, they thought we had secretly shot down his plane somewhere in the wild borderlands between Burma and China. His supporters also claimed that he had only been on his way to a special rendezvous with the Chinese communists not with the Japanese, as we strongly suspected. It's still not known exactly how, when and where he disappeared and I must emphasise to you'—and he breathed the words into Timothy's ear—'there is absolutely no evidence to support the accusation that we were responsible for his death!'

Hoadley paused for breath before resuming in a slightly louder voice. In fact while listening to him, Timothy realised that his vocal chords had become finely tuned in the course of his career to register the official variations in the classified levels of his message, viz., from top secret downwards.

'The whole episode also resulted in all kinds of political and constitutional crises. In the first place, I had to intervene in the internal affairs of the state (the first time we had done that for decades) by setting up a special Council of Regency while they looked around for the new incarnation of the Shar Lama. My God! That wasn't at all easy. You see on the one side, many of the old Lama's most devoted followers could not believe that he was really dead – they thought he had gone into hiding somewhere to meditate and would one day return. And, on the other side, there were those who, though they accepted that he had indeed come to a sticky end—probably killed by us!—also concluded that the process of reincarnation could no longer operate properly. I remember one particularly fanatical monk who denounced me as "the national and metaphysical enemy of Kalapur"!' Hoadley chuckled at the recollection.

'Well, it took three or four years for things to settle down after that. I myself left the country in 1947 and they still hadn't all agreed upon the new incarnation. Eventually my Indian successor, a very shrewd fellow, managed with the help of the influential Tibetan settlers (who had always been opposed to the old Shar Lama and his policies) to get a new boy Lama installed—who is of course still there—and at the same time converted the old Regency Council into a more modern sounding permanent Council of Ministers.'

Hoadley's saga was drawing to a close and the old man was beginning to look a bit puffy and glassy-eyed with the strain of recalling what had probably been the most difficult time of his life. Reading between the lines, Timothy began to sense that the Raj had probably been none too pleased with his performance in Kalapur. Whatever the truth about their secret involvement in the Lama's disappearance, they would have tended to conclude that the situation should never have been allowed to reach such a point; and Hoadley was at least partly responsible through his initial failure to keep a close enough watch over the Lama's activities. Most probably that was why there had been no knighthood for him at the end of his long career.

Timothy realised that he was now expected to say something. 'What exactly do you want me to do?' he enquired innocently.

'I should have thought that it was hardly necessary for me to spell it all out to a bright young chap like you,' Hoadley replied, a shade testily. 'Obviously you will need to study what the chronicle says about my period very closely. If, in your judgement, it takes a dangerously anti-British line then do your best to get the Abbot and his friends to see sense and at least drop the plan to publish those parts.'

'But wouldn't that look too much like the former colonial power trying to censor an independent primary source?' Timothy tried hard to get Hoadley to appreciate his potential dilemma.

'Yes, I think you are right. There is certainly that danger. That's where I count on you using your discretion,' said Hoadley, firmly missing the point. 'Tell them the Japanese wouldn't like it published, or that it's too recent to be treated as part of history – better to concentrate on the earlier less well-documented periods, and so on. Oh and by the way Timothy,' he smiled, 'when you get back from Kalapur do please come over to see me. I'd like to show you the confidential diary and other papers I kept during my Himalayan service. I think you will find them quite interesting!'

As they walked slowly back to the reception hall, each seemed to be lost in his own thoughts, Timothy feeling he had been out-manoeuvred by the old man, whilst Hoadley was clearly pretty exhausted by his efforts at recollection. But as he took Timothy's hand to say goodbye, he looked as if he still had something more to say but couldn't find the right words. 'Look, Timothy,' he said at last. 'I know you probably think I'm a foolish old fellow worrying unnecessarily about things that happened long ago. But I think that when you have been sometime in Kalapur you will find out that these things still matter there, they matter terribly!'

'As you know, history matters a lot in Kalapur, so I rely on you to use your discretion,' Sharir Singh beamed across his desk at Timothy, his speckled black beard jutting and glistening. There was something almost menacing about his bonhomie.

Timothy had gone to see him the day after his session with Hoadley to try to expedite his application for an Indian visa but also, if possible, to find out more about the origin of his invitation. Sharir had cheerfully obliged on both counts, making it clear that it was indeed he who had recommended Timothy for the assignment on the strength of their personal acquaintance, as well as the feeling that Professor Gabbinger was perhaps a bit too old for this sort of adventure.

But it also soon emerged that Sharir had his own agenda. Touching lightly, but somehow significantly on India's interest in the contents of the Migoling chronicle, he reminded Timothy that India had played an important part in re-establishing stability in Kalapur through the installation of the new Lama in 1948, and the enactment of a new constitution. India, he said, was quite proud of that particular achievement and would be happy for it to be accorded full and proper recognition in the Abbot's projected publication. At the same time he also contrived to convey to Timothy, without actually saying so, that the Indian government would not be so pleased if the chronicle presented a less than creditable picture of the Indian policy. Anyway, as a historian himself—Timothy recognised that the crunch had now come—Sharir looked forward to hearing in advance of publication what the manuscript had to say about that particularly interesting phase in Indo-Kalapuri relations.

Timothy tried his best to break free from the ties of obligation being drawn around him.

'Wouldn't it be simpler,' he suggested, 'if India simply asked the Kalapur authorities to send an advance copy of the proposed publication to Delhi first, especially in view of the close ties between the two countries?'

'That might also be possible,' said Sharir doubtfully, 'but you know India does not like to presume too much on our special relationship. Incidentally,' he added, his beard again glistening ominously, 'for some reason they asked us to find them a British historian to advise them rather than an Indian. But, of course . . .' he did not finish the sentence. Timothy grasped his meaning well enough: if he himself felt any reluctance to fulfil the mission and act as Sharir's confidential informant, it would be easy to withdraw his invitation and substitute any number of young Indian historians more than willing to perform the task.

Whenever Timothy felt sorry for himself he would remind himself that he was an only child and an orphan. Both his parents had died in a car accident while he was still at school, and he had then been looked after by an elderly aunt, who had acted more from a sense of duty than out of affection for him. After sometime he had slowly recovered from the immediate shock, though in a more fundamental way, the loss would always be there, alternately enhancing or diminishing his fragile sense of happiness. Meanwhile he was already able to recognise some of the cruel benefits of his position: being spared the sight of his father and mother growing old, and also in the personal feeling of freedom, of being tied to no one.

Thinking over all that had happened since he had got the invitation, he began to feel that the leading members of the Himalayan Centre, instead of being amusing, almost fictional characters, had become almost too alive, and too close. It was as if they were turning into a substitute family – not benign but sinister and manipulative. Old Hoadley, for example, for whom he had originally felt a mixture of pity and respectful sympathy, had exploited his senior position to protect his own interests and reputation. He had in effect been outwitted and almost bribed by someone he had supposed to be 'well past it'. It was true that the old fellow had revealed a more human side at the end of their meeting but perhaps even that had been a calculated attempt to win him over. More gallingly, Sharir, assuming an avuncular air, had jollied him along with a mixture of banter and veiled threats into tacitly agreeing to act as a sort of historical spy for India. As a result of their combined efforts, the prospect of the trip to Kalapur was becoming increasingly negative.

At the same time he was aware that not all the members of his new Himalayan family were seeking to manipulate him and limit his freedom of action. Serena, for instance—the only one he would have really liked to have been bullied by—still kept her distance. Also Lady Aloysia, when she had heard of the invitation, had made friendly, almost grandmotherly, overtures. She had even asked him to Sunday tea, producing a most delicate apple strudel, and regaling him with bizarre memories of her late husband's mountaineering days in Kalapur. Even she, however, had ended up by entrusting him with her own personal mission: that of collecting up more first-hand accounts of yetis, with which she hoped to confront and overwhelm Colonel Fox at a future meeting of the Centre.

Listening to her stories of Kalapur, the land of Tantric Buddhist mystics and wildmen, also sowed a further seed of self-doubt in Timothy's mind. What exactly would the Buddhists in the Centre, especially Serena, have made of his own conduct towards Hoadley and Sharir? On one level, perhaps they might have conceded that his reluctance to challenge them both openly by asserting his own belief in the autonomy of history and opposition to all forms of official censorship, had in a sense amounted to a kind of selfless act. If, as most Buddhists seemed to hold, there was ultimately no real continuing self in the human personality, could he not claim to have acted, or rather not acted, in accordance with that principle? But as an argument it clearly wouldn't stand up. Buddhists, he knew, also recognised the importance of ethical actions – the Five Precepts and all that! True, he had not actually indulged in 'false speech', but had not his silence in effect given assent to the whims of his manipulators? In any case what about his motives? He had not spoken out against Hoadley basically because he had not wished to face the consequences of upsetting him. Similarly with Sharir, he had been manoeuvred into feeling some kind of obligation and had not wanted to risk losing his invitation. In neither case had he acted out of 'non-self'. On the contrary, it was all too obvious that his attachment to the ego was very much alive – still twisting and turning in his sense of humiliation.

Disturbed by his thoughts, Timothy found it hard to concentrate wholeheartedly on improving his reading knowledge of Tibetan as he had planned to do during the few weeks remaining before his departure. Nor had he contacted Gabbinger since the Abbot's lecture, apart from a brief telephone call. Not only did he feel very uncomfortable that he should have received the official invitation and that his former teacher, his guru really, had been passed over, but he also knew that Gabbinger would strongly disapprove of his entanglement with the machinations of Hoadley and Sharir. Much of Gabbinger's career had been spent in battling with those he referred to as 'bureaucrats and colonialists', and it was he who had first deeply impressed on Timothy the importance of steering clear of all officially inspired or commercially motivated academic projects. 'Official history,' he was fond of saying, 'was a contradiction in terms!'

But there was also another, more deep-seated and personal dimension to his uneasiness about Gabbinger's reactions, and his reluctance to face him, and there was no point in pretending otherwise. Indeed now, as much as at any time during the past two years, he felt the need to go over those past experiences again, depressed yet elated by the recollection.

3

From the very beginning of his association with Eric Gabbinger it had been obvious that the latter was not going to be a conventional supervisor for his thesis: friendly and helpful but essentially remote and impersonal. 'If I am going to be of any benefit to you,' he had told Timothy during their first serious talk, 'and if you are going to help me (for this should be a two-way process), it is vital that we enter into a closer human relationship. Otherwise you might as well engage a computer to supervise your work or do it by correspondence course!'

Timothy could still recall the disquiet triggered by this announcement. What sort of 'human relationship' had Gabbinger got in mind? It was not that he had any suspicions about his supervisor's sexual intentions: all the available evidence, especially that represented by Lucy, the old man's very attractive second wife, seemed to rule out that possibility. No, the real threat arose from his fears that somehow Gabbinger planned to invade the inner recesses of his mind and feelings – to argue him into a corner and force him to commit himself on the great issues of ethical and political life. Still defensively cocooned in the private world of his own youthful imagination and emotions, he was not at all sure he would be ready to cope with such open challenges.

As things had worked out, Gabbinger's demands did not prove as daunting as he had at first expected. Certainly he had more than once forced Timothy to stand his ground in political debate—sometimes injuring his self-esteem in the process—but the long-term effects of these encounters had been generally stimulating, and at no time had he seriously doubted that his supervisor's intentions were fundamentally benign and positive. Moreover, even the more demanding dialectical tussles were often accompanied and balanced by long pleasurable evenings at the Gabbingers' Bloomsbury flat. There he had the opportunity to make friends with several postgraduate students from Asian countries with whom his supervisor appeared to maintain equally close and hospitable 'human relationships'. He also learnt to appreciate the delights of Mrs Gabbinger's Indian cooking.

It was, of course, those meetings with Lucy Gabbinger which were eventually destined to transform an innocently educational and enjoyably social experience into something else. She was, he supposed, in her early forties, more than twenty years younger than her husband and twenty years older than himself. She had a fullish but elegant figure, fluffy blonde hair flecked with grey, and a rather playful manner – not exactly flirtatious but very warm and amusing. 'She's a little bit like a sort of intellectual version of Mrs Robinson', was how Lee, his cynical Malaysian friend, had described her, after he and Timothy had watched a video of *The Graduate*. Timothy remembered that at the time he had been rather shocked by his friend's description.

Apart from her accomplishments in Indian cookery, Lucy Gabbinger also worked as a curator in one of the big national museums, and was unusually perceptive about the history of art, oriental as well as western. In this way she complemented her husband, who freely admitted to having a bit of a blind spot in art appreciation – 'part of the superstructure', he would call it disparagingly, much to his wife's disgust ('Eric, how can you be so one-dimensional?'). Timothy, on the other hand, responded rather more spontaneously to her expressive elucidation of Tibetan Tantric art, than he did to Eric's more cerebral analysis of the political and economic issues facing the Himalayan region.

It had been towards the end of the second year of Timothy's research, just before the summer vacation, that the 'event' had happened. At Gabbinger's suggestion, he had gone round one afternoon to their flat to deliver a draft chapter of his thesis. Gabbinger had been unexpectedly called away to an urgent meeting soon after his arrival, but both he and Lucy had insisted on his staying for tea.

The sitting room had been warm and sunny, with the French windows open on to the small walled garden. He remembered he had been rocking very gently on the old Indian swing chair, which the Gabbingers had brought back from one of their frequent visits to the subcontinent, while Lucy, with her winning eyes, had been sitting on a low oriental stool in front of him, telling him funny stories about how she had managed to persuade an Indian publisher to bring out her book on Himalayan art. He remembered that she had then got up to make the tea, and he had followed her into the kitchen. As she turned round to say something, he had seized hold of her and started to kiss her hard on the mouth. At first she seemed to respond—at least she had not resisted—and he had found himself half-propelling, half-guiding her back into the sitting room, all the while pressing his hand against her breast. Only then had she seriously tried to break free from his grasp, and in the ensuing struggle he had somehow lost his balance and ignominiously tripped sideways through the garden door and onto the grass outside.

Lucy had recovered her self-possession surprisingly quickly – it was obviously not the first time that such a thing had happened. But for Timothy the immediate aftermath had been very hard to cope with. He had begged her to let him go at once but she had insisted that he should still stay for tea. 'These things sometimes happen, especially when one is under the strain of work,' she had told him quietly. 'It was all quite natural, nothing to be ashamed of.' He had sat there listening to her, speechless with embarrassment, but somehow managing to finish his tea. Then suddenly getting up, he had pushed past her and rushed out of the flat.

Nothing like this had ever happened to him before with an older woman. Of course, he knew what his male friends would have said, if he could have brought himself to reveal the secret. They would have told him that it was precisely because of his long personal history of repression and frustration, that he had suddenly broken out with Mrs G (his Indian friends in particular relished that mode of referring to her). Yet, though he could half-accept this sort of explanation, somehow it didn't really help. The shock to his whole conception of what he felt he owed to the Gabbingers was too deep to be assimilated and settled so easily.

Two years had passed since then but he still found it very hard to think about the episode dispassionately, and even to recall how he had managed to cope during the weeks that immediately followed. Though he had no reason to think that Lucy had told her husband, he had still felt compelled to keep away from the Gabbingers' flat for as long as he could, without arousing suspicion. However, this stratagem had not helped to overcome other difficulties. For instance, he found that he invariably became tongue-tied and nervous whenever he went to see Gabbinger at the university, to such an extent that the latter began to notice. 'What the hell's the matter with you Timothy?' he had enquired on more than one occasion. 'Nothing,' he had replied with an unconvincingly blank smile.

Sometimes he had even thought of telling Gabbinger what had happened, internally rehearsing various approaches to the subject, such as: 'You remember what you said at the beginning about the need for us to have a close human relationship. Well . . .' Each time it had been impossible to complete the sentence, even inside his head. So he concluded that there was no alternative to a long and painful silence: 'No, nothing is wrong, honestly!' Meanwhile the slow progress of his thesis conveyed another message only too clearly.

Quite unexpectedly, the possibility of a partial cure for what he saw as Timothy's inexplicable mental block, occurred to Gabbinger himself. 'Why don't you spend six months in India, at the Himalayan Institute in Delhi?', he had suggested one morning. 'I think I can fix it through the exchange programme. It will mean that you will have to put off the submission of your thesis. But at your present rate that's going to happen anyway, and at the very least, a stay in India should wake you up a bit.' Timothy had gratefully accepted the offer and had gone to Delhi soon afterwards.

Looking back on it now, there was no doubt that he had benefited immensely from the experience. India had not entirely done away with his sense of guilt, but it had given him many other things to think about, and to that extent had helped him to put the event into some kind of perspective. When he returned to London six months later he found himself working like a maniac at his thesis. He also discovered that during his absence Lucy Gabbinger had left her husband. The old man—and for the first time he had begun to look like one—never really explained what had gone wrong, and Timothy himself made no attempt to find out what had become of her.

'You've been keeping away from me ever since the Abbot's lecture,' said Gabbinger accusingly, when Timothy had finally summoned up the courage to go and see him but he knew the man well enough to realise that he was only being teased. In fact, much to his relief, he found that Gabbinger was not at all put out or surprised by his own failure to secure the invitation to Kalapur. He had had too many previous altercations with those officially involved to expect that they would forgive him now, and he was genuinely pleased that his former student had been given such a marvellous opportunity to find out what was going on in such an isolated and unknown country.

He was not, however—as Timothy had foreseen—at all pleased to hear about the intrigues of Hoadley and Sharir. The Abbot, he admitted, was certainly a rather mysterious personage, but he was still a genuine scholar and seeker after truth. He and his colleagues should be given the best technical advice and encouragement but they should be left to make up their own minds about which portions of the chronicle should be published, free from outside pressure. Above all, Timothy should have firmly dissociated himself from their plots. 'You used to tell me that you and your generation were intellectually and emotionally freed from our past connections with these countries – that you were post-colonialist. But here you are, apparently agreeing to join in their intrigues!'

Timothy defended himself as best he could. He had not finally committed himself to either Hoadley or Sharir; he had listened to what they each had to say, but had deliberately kept quiet about what he would do when he got to Kalapur. He would have to play it by ear, find a way of avoiding putting any unfair pressure on the Abbot, whilst hopefully not upsetting Hoadley and Sharir too much when he returned. But Gabbinger would not be reconciled: 'When these supposedly civilised officials approach you to do their bidding, Timothy, you should learn from the ways of the Kalapur wildmen—the migos—when confronted by homo sapiens. Aloysia will tell you about their legendary tactics. Either they disappear quickly to hide in the snowy mountains or else they turn around snarling, and frighten their would-be hunters!'

4

'We are now crossing the Kalapur border and are beginning our approach to Himjin.'

Despite the assured and pukka tones of Captain Feroze, most first-time passengers found it hard to believe as the little Fokker plane lurched out of the clouds and slotted its way awkwardly through the closely towering peaks and desolate glaciers. It was not a question of lack of confidence in the pilot's navigational skills or even the capacity of his elderly aircraft to negotiate a safe passage: sophisticated travellers soon get used to such routine miracles. No, the real problem was ontological not technical. How could a complex human settlement—a whole civilisation—possibly exist here in the midst of these solitudes?

Baffled by the conundrum outside, the passengers looked elsewhere for some meaningful diversion. A small party of Japanese giggled nervously amongst themselves. Other tourists bit deeply into their momos snacks – the small round meat dumplings being distributed by the cabin crew. Timothy noticed that unlike the tourists depicted in the Himalayan travel brochures, with their happy munching smiles, the expressions of those around him failed to register unmixed delight at 'the first exquisite taste of Kalapur'. 'Yuck!' snorted a middle-aged American woman from the depths of her dumpling. 'Yak!' corrected her husband, picking more fastidiously at his. Having enjoyed his own momos on principle, Timothy consciously sought to distance himself from his unappreciative neighbours.

Not for the first time the book he had picked up yesterday at the New Delhi Literary Emporium provided a convenient cover for his withdrawal. It was a recently published official handbook for Kalapur which, rather like the momos, proved far more substantial than at first seemed likely. In fact, once you got past the bland foreword contributed by the Indian agent general, the main text was packed with all kinds of interesting stuff, including numerous tables and graphs designed to show the national progress achieved during the last fifty years under the leadership of the present Shar Lama. Amongst the names of the people in the list of acknowledgments Timothy, spotted Abbot Taranatha.

However, despite the wealth of statistics, it was clear that the country's economy was far less developed than those of the other better-known Himalayan states. The main exports still seemed to be honey and rice, and though some mineral resources were thought to exist in the interior, so far no proper survey of their nature and extent had been undertaken. All this helped to explain the current emphasis on giving a modest boost to the tourism industry. Other more puzzling features also emerged from a closer look at the tables and notes tucked away in the appendix. For example, the level of rural crime, reflected in the number of reported murders and robberies, struck Timothy as unexpectedly high for such an isolated and supposedly tranquil country. Perhaps he would have an opportunity to investigate this odd phenomenon during his short stay. Meanwhile, he concluded, whatever the precise socio-economic conditions of the country, it was obvious from the sophisticated character of this publication that the official mind in Himjin had changed considerably since Hoadley's time.

Timothy yawned. The cabin was getting warm and he now felt distinctly drowsy. A picture of the 'Lives of the Lamas' chronicle somehow drifted into his mind. Instead of mantras and invocations, it used smart graphs to demonstrate patterns of spiritual progress based on cumulated totals of prayer wheel revolutions. Altogether too whimsical, he thought, and yawned again. What was it Gabbinger had once told him? 'Imagination and humour can illuminate the historian's art, but they should not be allowed to overwhelm it.'

Slowly the Kalapur handbook began to slip down between his knees and the light in the cabin seemed to dim. At the end of the gangway the familiar figure of Gabbinger himself swung into view – standing next to a blackboard covered with diagrams in pink and white chalk. Timothy noticed with mild surprise that his former supervisor appeared to be wearing a maroon robe and that his hair was closely cropped like a monk's. 'Once you are in this monastery,' he was saying, 'you must enter fully into its daily round. And you must prepare yourself to take the triple vow of poverty, celibacy and history!'

'*Yappo mindoo!*' ('that's not good!') – the Tibetan words, rapped out loudly and repeatedly from inside the first-class area immediately ahead, abruptly terminated Timothy's reverie and the cryptic message of Gabbinger. '*Yappo mindoo!*' The speaker was evidently the tall, disagreeable-looking lama who had boarded the aircraft in Delhi accompanied by two thickset Kalapuri bodyguards. He was clearly a personage of some consequence treated by the cabin crew with exaggerated deference – even the cool dignified stewardess had nervously surveyed her feet when he passed. Timothy, who had a keen awareness of the anger of powerful men, could not make out the immediate object of the lama's displeasure but it was certainly something more than the flavour of his momos.

Meanwhile the window view of Kalapur was gradually changing. They had descended a little from the frozen solitudes to a level where a less awesome type of alpine scenery was beginning to unfold. The snowbound peaks were still visible through the clouds but they were now seen to be fringed with high pasture lands, which in turn spread out over dense forests. It was here, Timothy surmised from his earlier reading—between eleven and fifteen thousand feet—that the few remaining Himalayan yetis, championed by Lady Aloysia, were still alleged to roam, shadowing the snow leopards and wandering herds of yaks, to eke out a precarious existence from the meagre food supplies available. Preferring himself to remain agnostic about the existence of these creatures, it nonetheless struck him that this was the right sort of terrain for semi-human beings to survive in, lying between the icy inhuman peaks they had just left and the warmer human settlements they were about to reach.

The sudden realisation that they would soon be landing caused Timothy to abandon these reflections, and at the same time to reawaken a train of anxiety which had been originally set in motion during his short stay in Delhi. He had deliberately decided to spend a few days there before flying to Kalapur, partly in order to examine some old files about British Himalayan policy held at the National Archives but mainly to see his Indian friends, Shiv and Sonya. Like him they had just completed their theses, and were about to embark on academic careers, but unlike him (as he supposed), they were usually filled with high spirits and bursting with ideas about history, the universe and everything else – just the sort of company he felt in need of, before confronting whatever trials awaited him in Kalapur.

Unfortunately the encounter with Shiv and Sonya had turned out differently. Though they had certainly been glad to see him, there was something curiously subdued about their mood. He had tried his best to revive the exhilaration of their earlier debates but it hadn't worked out, and they had even ended up by having a disagreeably banal argument about the respective merits of British and Indian policies in the Himalayas. He had sensed that they were unwilling to concede the historical evidence for India's neo-imperialist interventions in Kalapur, preferring to interpret these moves as legitimate measures for national defence against possible Chinese expansion. And—for the first time—he had found himself offering some partial defence of British activities in Kalapur during the 1940s, and of Hoadley's latest efforts to conceal what had happened.

After that evening's argument he had stayed awake for hours vainly endeavouring to make sense of his own position, to reconcile his own conflicting reactions. But no clear solutions had emerged from the process, only succeeding questions, jutting sharply into the roof of his consciousness like the frozen mountains they had just passed through. The old Shar Lama had been killed by the British or had he? Hoadley had been a party to the murder, or had he? And even if the answer to both questions was affirmative, was it fair to condemn their actions now, given the extreme circumstances of the war-time crisis? In any case, was it really part of the historian's duty to pass moral judgement on such matters? In London he had hardly been aware of such perspectives: the whole character of the problem had appeared to him in a different light. To put it crudely, the issue had been whether he would have the guts to stand up for an impartial historical enquiry in the face of a combined Indo-British attempt to silence it. That night he had been unable either to find a solution or even to define the problem, and now, as the plane approached Himjin, he was uncomfortably aware that he was still unable to do so.

A sudden startling glimpse of the Himjin valley stretched oblong in the clear sunlight checked the flow of Timothy's anxieties. For an instant, he seemed to be looking down on a giant board of snakes and ladders—a favourite game of his childhood—with a green serpentine river looping its way across the valley and hard-edged paddy fields runged up against its slopes. Inside the plane the passengers came back to life, and the rising hubbub almost succeeded in drowning the commanding tones of Captain Feroze's landing announcement. 'Ah so!' breathed the Japanese party in appreciative unison as they caught sight of the gleaming golden spires and white walls of the Shar Lama's palace. 'I guess we've arrived!' shrugged Timothy's American neighbour.

PART TWO

Migoling Monastery

5

'Welcome to Kalapur!' said Abbot Taranatha beaming at Timothy and gripping his hand warmly. 'I knew you would not let us down. I'm only sorry we could not include a yeti in the reception party – that would have finally settled the sceptics in your Himalayan Centre!' His gap-toothed grin extended further as he motioned towards a respectable-looking monk with a briefcase who was standing by his side. 'So, no yetis yet, but here is Norbu, the treasurer of Migoling Monastery and warden of our guesthouse. He will be looking after your needs during your stay.'

'Welcome!' repeated this functionary in a flat tone that somehow combined formality with doubt.

Sending off the Warden in search of refreshments, the Abbot led Timothy across the crowded little airport lounge and into an adjoining office. Relaxed and open, he seemed quite a different person to the enigmatic figure Timothy remembered from their first encounter.

'You know, Timothy (may I call you Timothy?), when I was a student in London many years ago, I would sometimes discard my monk's robes, put on a pair of blue jeans like yours, and go and sit in one of those pubs near the university. I learnt a lot that way.' He continued to reminisce in this vein until the Warden returned with some cokes. Before drinking, Taranatha playfully sprinkled a few drops into the air, all the time looking quizzically at the Warden. 'How would you feel, Norbu, if we gave up our monks' robes and changed into blue jeans, like Dr Curtin here?' Norbu's face stiffened and he emitted a peculiar clucking sound. 'Don't worry about him,' the Abbot turned back to Timothy, 'he may sometimes cluck a little but I guarantee he will take good care of you.'

The warmth of the Abbot's welcome had at once allayed Timothy's customary reserve, and for a while also dispelled the unease created earlier in his mind by the mysterious delay that had occurred before he and his fellow passengers had been allowed to leave the plane. The captain had put it all down to unspecified 'technical difficulties', but the fact remained that the disagreeable first-class lama and his bodyguards had been permitted to disembark as soon as they had landed. When the rest of the passengers were eventually let out half an hour later, they had noticed clusters of armed police and militia scattered around the airport perimeter. Everything else was apparently normal and quiet as they had walked towards the airport building in the sharp late morning sunlight, but there was also an indefinable air that something had just taken place which they had not been allowed to see – as it were the calm that follows the storm.

'Now,' said the Abbot, suddenly switching to a more serious voice that reminded Timothy of his London lecture, 'this afternoon I have to attend a special meeting of the Council of Ministers—here in Himjin—to sort out some of the details of our history project. So I have arranged for Warden Norbu to take you in an official car direct to Migoling. I suggest you then have a look round, have a nice meal and try to get a good night's rest. I hope to be back at the monastery sometime tomorrow and we can then begin to plan our work. Oh, by the way,' he added casually, 'I might as well tell you now that your old friend Mr Hoadley will not need to worry any more about our publishing the story of his war-time involvement in Kalapur. Fortunately for him, the original manuscript covering that episode seems to have disappeared.' Taranatha's sharp wrinkled eyes glanced swiftly at Timothy, reassuring but also somehow challenging, as he got up to leave.

After the Abbot's departure the Warden continued to sit and gaze blankly at his new guest, as if trying to get used to his alien presence. Timothy's increasingly desperate attempts to engage him in conversation were met by short factual replies which were either not fully intelligible or somehow effective in closing down further enquiry. Sometimes he merely grunted or repeated the question to himself. In fact their whole encounter struck Timothy as rather like what would happen if old Colonel Fox were to finally confront a yeti. At last the Warden got up and beckoned Timothy to follow him.

Outside it was bright and clear and almost deserted, since most of the other tourists had by now left for their hotels in the centre of Himjin. It struck Timothy that whatever the significance of the airport as the major link between Kalapur and the outside world, in itself it was hardly more than a small group of huts in an open field surrounded by mountains, a place which only came to life once a day – in the afternoon for the incoming flight from India and in the following morning for the departure flight. Apart from an empty army truck, there were no signs now of the police and soldiers whose presence had earlier disturbed him – nothing apparently to explain why they had been there or why there had been that delay. Perhaps they had merely formed a kind of guard of honour for the important lama.

As they walked across the rough parking area towards the driver of the waiting car, Timothy noticed two small dogs tussling in the dust for possession of what looked like a sheet of cardboard. '*Khi so gyap gi doo gay?*' (Do the dogs bite?), he enquired not so much because he was wary of the dogs which he saw were only puppies, but because he was still trying to reassure his silent companion that for all his strangeness he could at least muster a little phrase-book Tibetan. But before Norbu could reply, or more probably repeat the query, Timothy suddenly spotted that the placard, now abandoned by the dogs, had something written on it in bold Tibetan script. To his surprise he succeeded in reading it. 'Langdarma Sarpa,' (the new Langdarma), it said, with underneath some kind of painted motif that looked like a banner. He would have liked to have examined the placard more carefully but he was now aware that the Warden was tugging at his arm.

'Dr Curtin we are getting late,' he said anxiously. Reluctantly Timothy let go of the placard and followed the Warden back to the car. As they drove off, the little dogs resumed their struggle.

Although he suspected that he would not get very far, Timothy determined to keep up his efforts to induce the Warden to explain the meaning of the placard. Reckoning that an oblique approach was more likely to be productive, he innocently mentioned that there had been an important looking lama on his plane: did Norbu by chance know who he was? Yes, it turned out he did know: it was the Shar Lama's brother, who was a high official in the government, in fact the man in charge of the Ministry of Culture and Religious Affairs. But why had there been all those soldiers round the airport? Timothy persisted, emboldened by his initial success. This question, however, proved too much for the Warden, who muttered something about security and relapsed into a nervous silence.

They were well away from the airport by this time and Timothy saw that they were following a road which seemed to skirt round the edge of the Himjin valley, avoiding the town itself but yielding a breathtaking view of the long sloping white walls of the Shar Lama's palace, stretched out along the river like some great sleeping animal. As he took in the wonderful sight, it seemed to give him a renewed spirit to put his questions to the Warden head-on. 'Why,' he asked suddenly, 'did that placard refer to the Second Langdarma? Was it part of some demonstration or religious procession at the airport?'

Norbu hesitated: he had clearly not expected Timothy to have been able to read the message. 'Procession,' he said doubtfully, 'only procession!'

Timothy felt no irritation at the Warden's obvious prevarications. It was clear that there had been some sort of public demonstration directed at the lama, and that for some reason he could not as yet fathom, that dignitary was associated with anti-Buddhist policies. Whatever their exact nature, it was also clear that they were perceived as pretty threatening by the demonstrators, to be likened to the persecution of the faith carried out by the infamous Tibetan King Langdarma in the ninth century. Presumably the other placards and the demonstrators themselves had all been seized and whisked away by the militia before Timothy and his fellow passengers were allowed out.

For a few more minutes the Warden continued to say nothing, but Timothy sensed that he felt relieved that his strange foreign guest had somehow penetrated the mystery of the placard. At the same time Timothy also realised that Norbu in fact, had only been trying to protect him from some potentially awkward involvement in local politics, looking after him, as the Abbot had predicted. With these unspoken exchanges, the tension between the two largely disappeared, and for the rest of the journey Timothy found his protector almost overwhelmingly anxious to answer all his questions about the country through which they were passing. Eventually he even went as far as to admit that certain militant groups were strongly opposed to the radical changes in the country's Buddhist traditions now being introduced by the Shar Lama's government, and that it had been their demonstration that had confronted the minister at the airport.

Although he later came to know the route to Migoling quite well, Timothy took in little on this first journey once they began to climb out of the Himjin valley with its fertile fields of barley and small farmsteads. The road itself—which was very narrow—gradually wound its way up through a mountain pass hemmed in by dense pine forests. On these stretches there was virtually nobody to be seen; only once did they pass a rather wild-looking man in a fur-cap standing next to a white horse. Driving slowly because of the dangerous twists and turns, it took them well over an hour to reach the point where the Warden explained it would be necessary to abandon the car, and take the steep footpath that led up to the Migoling Monastery. Throughout the journey their driver had not spoken a word, and even when Timothy thanked him at the end, the man merely nodded.

'Don't worry,' said Norbu, sensing Timothy's slight puzzlement, 'he is dumb, he can't speak!'

The place where the path started was marked by a small stone structure with a wooden roof which—much to the Warden's delight— Timothy recognised as a chorten, a Buddhist monument dedicated to the memory of some important religious figure. This one, it turned out, had been built to commemorate the spot where Padmasambhava, the Tantric sage who had converted most of the Himalayan region to Buddhism more than a thousand years ago, was said to have meditated before commencing a titanic spiritual struggle with Migo Lopen, a powerful local god, also believed to be the tutelary deity of the wildmen or migos who were said to live in the surrounding mountains. This contest, like all Padmasambhava's struggles, ended in his opponent's defeat and conversion into a faithful protector of Buddhism. The monastery of Migoling, the place of the wildmen, was established a few centuries later and put under the special protection of Migo Lopen. Timothy felt a tingle of enlightenment. So this was the connection between Migoling and the yetis which Lady Aloysia had been so anxious for him to investigate. Feeling himself liable to be caught between the mysterious wildmen and the equally mysterious Kalapur police force, he decided that it would be prudent to gather as much merit as possible, and so he too began to follow the Warden and the driver in their respectful progress round the chorten.

The ascent to the monastery by the footpath normally took about half an hour, the Warden explained, but with Timothy's luggage to cope with, it would take a little longer. However, they had hardly begun the climb when two young boys of about nine or ten, wearing novices' robes, suddenly sprang out of the trees ahead and insisted on carrying the cases on their backs. The disparate little troupe, headed by the plump panting Warden, then set out in a single file up the path which led through a dark and mossy forest, enlivened only by the occasional deep red bloom of the early flowering rhododendrons. Winter had not quite ended and it felt increasingly chilly as they climbed higher.

To keep up their spirits the boys improvised a rambling ditty telling of their encounters with fierce old monks, princesses, birds and migos, and even finally with Timothy himself. Each encounter ended with the same refrain, in which they all joined:

Gava drogi yin? (Where are you going?)
Gompa Migoling. (Migoling Monastery)

At last the trees and vegetation began to thin out and they emerged on to a grassy meadow at the far end of which stood the monastery itself. It was not quite as large as Timothy had imagined but imposing enough with its lofty white walls and raised entrance. Outside, a line of white prayer flags fluttered in the breeze – fragile and almost skittish beside the massive bulk of the monastery.

As soon as they had climbed up the steps that led up to the entrance hall, the two boys let go of their burdens and dashed off before Timothy could find a way of rewarding them.

'Don't worry! It's not necessary,' said the Warden in disapproving tones. On the facing wall, a stern-looking representation of one of the Guardian Kings of the Four Directions obviously took the same view. 'This is Dhritarashta, the Guardian of the East – he is also the special protector of the Shar Lama,' Norbu announced. Since some response seemed to þe expected of him, Timothy nodded politely in the guardian's direction.

'And this is Padmasambhava with his two consorts,' added the Warden, introducing three more benign and graceful figures on the opposite wall. 'But where is Migo Lopen?' asked Timothy who had been looking forward to seeing a representation of that tutelary deity. 'You will see,' said Norbu.

Two servants, who had appeared in response to the Warden's call, now took hold of the bags and led the way into the first courtyard. Timothy stopped for a moment to take in the scené. Three sides of the courtyard were occupied by offices, the monks' living quarters in addition to a study area and library. The fourth side consisted of the main temple block. Four storeys high and approached by a steep flight of steps, it effortlessly dominated the whole ensemble without disturbing its essential harmony.

In a funny way he began to feel at home in this strange place, so like the quadrangle of an Oxbridge college with some surrealist touches added, like the cock strutting out towards the temple steps. It was late afternoon and none of the monks were visible, though some deep chanting voices could be heard coming from the classroom across the way. But to his surprise, he gradually made out that it was not Buddhist prayers that were being chanted but an English nursery rhyme: never before had 'Jack and Jill went up the hill' sounded so profound!

'How come they they are chanting that?' he enquired.

'It is the Abbot's wish that all our monks learn English,' Norbu explained.

Meanwhile the servants continued to lead the way round the side of the temple block, cheerfully spinning a line of prayer wheels as they went. They then descended a few steps into a second courtyard, more venerable looking than the first. Keeping close to the outer rim of the courtyard in a clockwise direction—Timothy realised that they were in effect circumambulating the temple—they stopped outside a finely carved and decorated doorway in the far corner of the quadrangle.

'Migoling Guesthouse!' the Warden announced proudly. A short blast from a conch in the first courtyard provided a timely flourish. But Timothy's attention was immediately drawn away towards some freshly painted motifs decorating the top of the doorway, and one shape in particular, which resembled the sign at the bottom of the protesters' placard at the airport. 'What's that, Norbu?' he asked.

'That,' replied the Warden solemnly, 'is the Banner of Victory, the second of the eight Auspicious Symbols. They represent the offerings made to Shakyamuni Buddha after he attained enlightenment.'

The steps leading to Timothy's room on the second floor were more like a ladder than a staircase. He had no idea what sort of room it would be – perhaps no more than a monk's sleeping cabin of the sort he had glimpsed in the first courtyard. He composed his features to disguise his anticipated sense of disappointment. But to his surprise the room turned out to be pleasant and spacious, with a window opening onto the courtyard. True, there was no electric light and no running water but he had been warned about this, and at least there was some kind of stove in case the nights turned cold. The furnishings were simple but adequate: a low table, some Tibetan rugs, a thick mattress on the floor, a cupboard with several silver butter lamps, and a bookcase on top of which stood a small bronze Buddha. All the walls were plain white except for one which was entirely covered by the yellow, blue and reddish outlines of a beautiful fading mandala.

'What a fantastic place!' said Timothy, genuinely happy to express his feeling of elation.

'But there is also something else!' said Norbu, hurrying across to the other side of the room and beginning to fiddle with some rusty latches. After a brief struggle, the two large wooden shutters swung open to reveal the direct overpowering view of a huge snow-topped mountain caught in the shadow of the setting sun. 'The abode of Migo Lopen!' he said darkly.

6

Wrapped tightly in his thick black rugs, Timothy lay on his mattress, sipping his butter tea and munching his rice. To his surprise he had slept soundly throughout the night, comforted and probably even a little drugged by the heat from the charcoal stove. It was nearly eight o'clock but he was as yet in no mood to stir. The little stove had gone out some time ago and the room was distinctly cold. Outside, a thick damp mist hid the view from his window.

As the strong salty tea gradually worked its way through his system, he began to examine the mandala on the opposite wall with growing interest. It consisted of an outer square within which lay a series of concentric circles, which in turn enclosed a tighter sequence of diminishing squares. The whole design was elaborately patterned and multi-coloured with red, yellow, white and two shades of blue. He had no idea what it really signified but it appeared to represent some sort of process of mental penetration, initially attractive and emotionally absorbing but ultimately hard, analytic even limited. His own subject, history, he thought, was rather like this: one started out being caught up in its swirling contours, its broad imaginative appeal, only to end up boring painfully into an ever-decreasing area of ascertainable truth.

Stirred up sufficiently by this effort, he turned away from the history mandala to contemplate his own history project. In suddenly revealing that the more recent parts of the chronicle had disappeared, Taranatha had seemed to imply that they would not after all have to grapple with the problem of establishing the true fate of the previous Shar Lama and Hoadley's possible part in it. At the same time there had been something ambiguous about the way in which the Abbot had conveyed the news. Until he knew more about the background it was too early to feel confident that the issue had gone away, especially as he had an odd feeling that the demonstration he had nearly witnessed at the airport was somehow connected with it. Anyway, he would presumably work it out eventually. Meanwhile he had some time to himself since the Warden had explained on the previous evening that he would be busy with the monastic accounts for most of the morning. After that he would be free and had promised to show Timothy round and introduce him to some of the leading personalities. Hopefully, by the late afternoon the Abbot himself would be back.

Timothy unravelled himself and advanced shivering towards the bucket of water which a silent monk from the kitchen had brought along earlier with his butter tea and breakfast. Its icy contents quickly dispelled the remnants of sleep, and in the same moment he also decided to dispense with shaving; he had for long nurtured a secret desire to experiment with a bearded life and Kalapur seemed a good place to try it out. He estimated that he had nearly four hours before Norbu would be ready. He would use the time to explore the place quietly by himself – surely nobody would object.

Having left his room he made straight for the temple block in the first courtyard. The chances were that most of the monks would now be gathered there in the assembly hall on the ground floor for one of their numerous daily rituals, and he would then have a good opportunity to observe them, and perhaps also catch a glimpse of what the mystic members of the Himalayan Centre called 'their intensely spiritual life'. He hovered for a few moments in the vestibule, admiring the vivid murals, especially one showing an elephant, a monkey, a parrot and a rabbit grouped together like a happy family. It seemed an auspicious image for his stay at the monastery. He knew from personal experience that it usually took more than good intentions to break down the barriers that tended to separate people of different languages and beliefs. But maybe this time he would succeed with these people or they would succeed with him, and together they would make friends – like the animals on the wall.

The entrance to the hall was covered by a long curtain. Very gingerly, Timothy peeped round the edge of it and stepped inside. The place was dimly lit and suffused with a mixture of butter vapour and incense. It took a little while before he was able to distinguish several rows of monks sitting cross-legged on cushions in a small central nave. At the far end of the hall, beyond an altar filled with offerings, he could make out several large gilt images of Buddhas and Bodhisattvas gleaming softly. The whole hall, he also began to see, was swirling with scrolls, scarves and banners, whilst almost all the walls and pillars were alive with painted figures—mostly apparently divine or demonic, fearsome or compassionate—and depicted in a style which, to his western sensibility, appeared to combine the most powerful expressionism with a purified art-nouveau. His friends in London had been right: it was extraordinarily beautiful, mysterious, uplifting even . . .

A moment later, he became aware of other more incongruous features. Most of the monks were not all actually praying, chanting or meditating. Some were lounging about on their cushions, noisily slurping tea or gossiping in whispers with neighbours; others were scratching their shaven heads, yawning or spitting. He had obviously arrived at the wrong moment, during one of the many intervals in their liturgies. Suddenly he noticed that a large burly figure holding a whip, who had previously been sitting near the entrance, had got up, and appeared to be advancing rapidly towards him in a threatening manner. Concluding that visitors were unwelcome, Timothy hurriedly withdrew, pulling the curtain behind him. From the safety of the courtyard below, he looked back up at the frowning figure with the whip – almost certainly the Kudun or Master of discipline. '*Gonda*, excuse me,' he called politely. 'I didn't know it wasn't allowed.'

Turning his back on the temple block, Timothy walked disconsolately towards the outer gateway of the monastery. His earlier buoyant mood had collapsed, leaving only an acute sense of disillusionment – with the dozy monks, their hostile disciplinarian, and with himself, for having failed to stand his ground. As he passed through the gateway, he could not help glancing sideways at the figures of the Eastern Guardian and Padmasambhava, which had so caught his fancy when he had arrived the day before: now they merely looked flat and grotesque.

Once outside the monastery he hesitated. Where should he go? Mostly he felt like getting well away from the place for a few hours, ridding himself of the temple's smell of rancid butter that still seemed to cling to him. At the same time he told himself not to overreact to what had probably only been an unfortunate and isolated experience. He decided on a compromise. He would not leave the place immediately, but begin by exploring the outer boundaries of the monastic buildings to get a better idea of their overall layout.

The way round the monastery wall was more difficult than he had expected since the ground was rough and bumpy, leading him up and down through mud and soggy grass. At one point he noticed a line of monks' robes hanging out over the walls to dry – evidently it was the Migoling washing day! Then, turning a sharp corner, he was confronted by a huge ditch apparently full of mud. As he got closer, he saw it was not mud but turds, hundreds of them, piled up high and distinctly malodorous. Across the ditch stretched a slimy wooden plank leading up to an open hut built close to the monastery wall. He stared at it all in horror and fascination. Was it possible that having finished their morning rituals, those same disagreeable monks would soon be filing their way towards that plank to evacuate their bowels? At least he was lucky to have a separate loo of sorts in the guesthouse. But Nirvana seemed a long way off!

Abruptly he sensed that he was being watched. 'My God!' he thought, almost sliding off the end of the plank in alarm, 'the monks are coming!' It was not so, but sitting on the wall above like Humpty Dumpty, a solitary moon-faced monk was grinning down at him. 'Shit!' said Timothy. 'Shit, shit, shit!'

Looking at his watch, he was surprised to discover that he had been walking fast for more than an hour, following—though with only part of his mind—a track that wound upwards behind the monastery, towards the mountain visible from the guesthouse. Most of his attention had been concentrated on his recent encounters – his failures. In particular, he couldn't help contrasting his own undignified retreat from the assembly hall with the likely reactions of his associates in the Himalayan Centre. Carstairs, he knew, would never have given way, he would have strode forward to meet the Kudun. Even Hoadley, more diplomatic and circumspect, would probably have parleyed with the man in the vestibule to try to ascertain the local rules for foreign visitors. As for the monks themselves, scratching and gossiping, they had hardly looked like human beings on the threshold of profound spiritual experience, as Serena and Lady Aloysia liked to think.

Another familiar voice delivered a different verdict. 'For God's sake, Timothy'—it was Gabbinger at his most iconoclastic—'Stop feeling sorry for yourself because you failed to stand up to the natives. Who do you think you are anyway? One of those nineteenth century British imperialists who stormed their way up into the Himalayas, with their troop escorts, to bully and lecture the local people? And what exactly did you expect to find here in this remote monastery? A band of bloody bodhisattvas? Next time you deserve to fall into their shit!'

He began to feel better. Despite or because of his disconcerting encounters, he was beginning to get a line on Migoling which could be developed later in the letters and emails he would have to send home. It was, he decided, 'the place where all travellers' illusions are quickly shattered.' He also drew some comfort from the thought that whatever he might lose in the telling of his own misadventures, might be balanced by the humour with which he planned to recount them. Even the Centre's mystics might appreciate the story since he recalled that, at their most serious they also believed that confusion would always overtake those who clung too hard to fixed concepts and expectations – even those that concerned the doctrines of Buddhism itself!

He now began to look around more attentively, whistling as he went a familiar hymn tune from his school days. The early mist had now lifted, leaving a cold but bright morning. 'He who would valiant be gainst all disaster . . . ' The track was about to cross another rolling pasture in the middle of which some yaks were grazing – long, dark and formidably horned. He remembered what Lady Aloysia had told him about these beasts, that they had 'an uncertain temper', or, if you inclined to the yak's point of view, that they were 'sensitive and easily upset'. He judged that in his present accident-prone state it would be better not to be too 'valiant'. By taking a side path that branched off from the main track, he could avoid any close contact with these animals. He followed the new path as it first skirted around the meadow on higher ground, and then began to edge its way along the side of a rocky escarpment. Down below the land dropped away into a pleasant wooded valley, not far, he surmised, from the chorten of Padmasambhava where he and Norbu had left the car yesterday.

Now that he was well clear of the yaks, Timothy sat down on a boulder and took a bite from the apple he had saved from breakfast.

It would be sensible, he thought, to try to get hold of a rough plan of the area if he were to go on any future excursions. Perhaps Norbu or the Abbot would be able to provide one. All around there was a deep, natural stillness of a kind that he had seldom if ever experienced. Even the silver-tailed Himalayan crows were nowhere to be seen or heard. He took a second bite from his apple, and to his astonishment the intrusive sound was answered by a cough from further along the path. A thin scholarly-looking monk, holding some twigs, had emerged, it seemed, from out of the escarpment, and was standing a few yards away.

'I hope I did not startle you.' The monk spoke in perfect English, friendly and apologetic. 'You must be the visitor from England the Abbot was telling me about. Welcome to our hermitage!' Timothy greeted the monk warmly; somehow the place was so peaceful and the figure so gentle that he felt no alarm. 'My name is Lama Wangdi, and I am the Tsenyi Lopen, the Master of Philosophy at Migoling.' He sat down on the boulder next to Timothy.

'I am sorry if I disturbed your meditation,' said Timothy politely. But Wangdi explained that this was not the case: he had not been meditating but preparing the cave hermitage further along the path for its next occupant from the monastery.

'I don't expect you know much about the training of our Buddhist monks,' he continued, 'but it is our custom to send the more advanced students for a long period of solitary meditation to complete their Tantric studies. Traditionally that period lasts for three years, three months, three weeks and three days!'

Timothy gasped: 'And for all that time they stay inside the cave and see no one?'

'It depends,' replied Wangdi judiciously, 'there are degrees of seclusion. Here in Migoling we would expect our good students to spend no more than half an hour each day outside the hermitage, and to see nobody, apart from an annual visit from their supervising lama.'

'And what about food?' asked Timothy.

'Well, normally they come prepared with a stock of provisions. Otherwise we send a servant up from the monastery with a simple meal, on the understanding that they do not see or speak to the occupant of the hermitage but only pass the food through a small opening in the door.'

'It sounds a terribly hard life,' said Timothy.

'No doubt,' Wangdi paused a moment – long enough for Timothy to feel again the peaceful stillness of the place, 'but it brings its rewards also.' The Master of Philosophy got to his feet. 'But let me show you the place. After all,' he smiled slightly, 'I am not going to ask you to remain inside!'

Timothy followed Wangdi a few yards till they reached the cave. The entrance consisted of a grey wooden door which, from a distance, could scarcely be distinguished from the rocks and boulders in which it was set. Towards the bottom of the door there was, as Wangdi had said, a small wicker opening through which food could be passed, and to the right of the door there was a tiny window. The cave itself was small and hardly high enough to stand up in but surprisingly well-equipped with all the basic requirements for a prolonged retreat: a straw mattress, a table and chair, and even a small wood-burning stove with a flue pipe projecting out above the entrance. At the far end there was a small wooden altar on which stood a bronze figurine. But although the place had obviously been recently refurbished, an unpleasant smell seemed to pervade it, and Timothy was glad when after a few moments his guide simply murmured: 'This is how it is,' and led the way out into the fresh air.

'I don't think I would be able to survive for long inside that place,' said Timothy, with some feeling.

'It would depend,' said Wangdi. 'But if you prepared yourself properly beforehand by studying our Tantric texts and meditation practices, I see no reason why you should not succeed.'

'Is that all you would need to do?'

'Well, not quite. According to our tradition, you would also need a guru (who could be your lama teacher), and ideally also spiritual communion with a dakini, that is, an enlightened female companion embodying advanced wisdom. You see, together they would help you to discover your own yidam, that is, the embodiment of those Buddha-qualities to which you are most drawn and which you would then strive to absorb.'

For the first time during the conversation Timothy began to feel a little uncomfortable. For a moment he even had the impression that Wangdi was gently, but seriously, seeking to persuade him to try out this extraordinary lifestyle. After all, as Gabbinger used to say, you should never forget that priests and monks invariably seek to convert you if they can: it was part of their profession!

'But perhaps you are wondering what exactly I am doing here,' said Wangdi quietly. To his relief Timothy saw that he seemed to be changing the subject. 'In normal circumstances the Master of Philosophy would not be concerned directly in these retreats: that would be the job of my colleague, the Tantric Master. But since he has been advised by certain authorities to go on a six weeks' pilgrimage to Bodh Gaya in India, it has become my responsibility to deputise for him.' Wangdi paused again. 'But then you may still perhaps find it strange that it should fall to me to carry out these humble preparatory tasks – collecting fuel and so on.'

Wangdi's gentle tone had not really changed but Timothy felt it had somehow entered into another key. And the odd thing was it had not been necessary for him to ask any of these questions himself, though he had certainly wished to do so. Now it seemed all he had to do was to say nothing and wait for the answers.

'The short answer to our question,' Wangdi continued in his academic style, 'is that most of the servants in our monastery are afraid to come to this place by themselves. You see, in the past some of the occupants of the hermitage have claimed that they received mysterious nocturnal visitors, not human beings—at least not in the conventional sense—but migos, wildmen from the mountain heights. Shut up inside the cave, and no doubt very frightened, none of the monks have so far claimed to have actually seen their visitors, only to have sensed their presence outside or heard their cries, and, in one case, felt their breath through the wicker opening. To comprehend the fear that these migos inspire in our people, you have to understand that though Migoling was originally placed under the special protection of Migo Lopen, the tutelary deity of the wildmen, it has always been believed that to meet one of these creatures face to face would bring misfortune, even death. We are, of course, speaking here of peoples' beliefs and not of what your scientists would call objective realities.'

Wangdi again stopped for few minutes, leaving Timothy uncertain whether he should now thank the lama and begin to make his way back to the monastery. But Wangdi had not completed his explanation.

'There is,' he continued, 'one other aspect of the situation which I must leave to the Abbot to explain more fully to you, for it is important that you should understand it properly. Others – I am again referring to "certain authorities", not the simple people in our monastery . . . Others consider that many of the traditional features of the Buddhism of Kalapur are superstitious accretions, taken over from the more ancient religions in these parts, in such a way as to corrupt the purity of the Buddha's original message and to impede the country's material progress. This, they say, applies to many of our Tantric practices of visualisation and meditation, to the respect paid to many of our traditional protectors, like Migo Lopen – even Padmasambhava is now beginning to come under a cloud. The combined effect of these developments is that very few of our younger monks are now prepared to follow the traditional Tantric practice of retreat. In fact, the person, for whom I am specially preparing this hermitage, is not actually a student at all.'

Wangdi's discourse—so unexpected and so revealing—had now apparently ended, and it seemed improper for Timothy to try to press the lama to explain more. Nonetheless he felt he might try one more question. 'Those authorities you spoke of, are they the people in high places who advise the Shar Lama?'

Before Wangdi had time to reply, they both became suddenly aware of two small figures calling and waving to them frantically from the other side of the field. 'Mr Tim! Mr Tim!' the figures shouted, as they ran towards them through the line of grazing yaks. It was not until they were quite close that Timothy recognised the two boys who had carried his bags on the day before.

'Mr Tim,' cried the elder boy who arrived first, 'we were looking for you everywhere!'

'Yes,' said his breathless companion. 'Warden Norbu is very worried. He thinks the migos have got you!'

7

As they all trotted back together along the Migoling path, Timothy told the boys about his adventures and his unexpected encounter with the Master of Philosophy, and how he had almost forgotten about his midday meeting with Norbu. Lama Wangdi's name seemed to have a sobering effect on the boys for it turned out that the Lama was also their personal tutor, who had amongst other things, taught them English during the past two years. 'He is a very good teacher,' said the younger boy, in a surprisingly adult tone.

For the rest of the walk the boys chatted away amicably, occasionally inventing new verses for the Gompa Migoling song they had started the day before. It appeared that both of them came from educated families, and were full of questions about Europe and America, computer games and videos. For his part, Timothy was able to ask if they had actually seen any migos. Not exactly, they admitted, though they claimed to have once found their droppings near a kind of tree nest in the depths of the surrounding forest.

By the time they reached the outskirts of the monastery, Timothy felt he had at least succeeded in establishing some sort of friendship with them. In fact, before leaving, they invited him to join them next morning in a special game called 'Karma' or Rebirth which they claimed to have invented. The only difficulty, they confessed, was something called the Maitreya class at 10 a.m. 'Hadn't you better go to that?' Timothy enquired cautiously, unable to shed his own pedagogic role. But they insisted that they could skip it for once since it was not 'a regular class', only something that the kudun and others were keen on. Recalling the frowning figure with the whip—hardly an enlightened-looking educationalist—Timothy agreed that they could miss it.

As he said goodbye to the boys, he almost collided with the ample form of the Warden who had been anxiously pacing up and down the first courtyard emitting his peculiar clucking sounds. The sounds ceased abruptly as Timothy appeared, and an expression of considerable relief spread over his features. So much so that for a moment Timothy imagined that he was going to be embraced, before realising—to his own relief—that such overt demonstrations of feeling were not part of the usual behavioural repertoire of the inhabitants of Kalapur. It was not that the people were cold or unfriendly, he sensed, perhaps just a little on the old-fashioned English side.

'What happened?' asked Norbu, the remains of his anxiety still flickering. Timothy briefly explained about his excursion to the hermitage, and apologised at length for being late. For the present he decided not to tell his guardian about his earlier more disconcerting experiences. On his side, Norbu also made no mention of having entertained any fears about the migos, leaving Timothy to speculate whether he was merely exercising an equivalent measure of self-protective caution or whether the boys had just made up the story.

Whatever fears Norbu may have had, it soon became clear that he had other reasons for worrying about his guest's late arrival. 'Doctor

Curtin,' he began a little slowly in an effort to appear calm. 'Our high Tulku, Lama Jaya Kumara Rinpoche, has just informed me that he would like to meet you this afternoon. I was afraid you had got lost.' Whoever this Tulku personage was, Timothy perceived that he had certainly succeeded in putting the wind up the Warden.

Responding unconsciously to the other's tension, he now found himself adopting a Hoadley-like diplomatic style. 'I'm sure the Tulku is doing me a great honour but I must admit that I have no idea who he is!'

Norbu smiled: he had now regained his natural good humour. 'Lama Jaya Rinpoche is the resident Tulku of Migoling; he is the reincarnation of one of the leaders sent from Tibet to India more than a thousand years ago to ask Padmasambhava to come to our Himalayan countries to preach the Buddha's dharma.'

'Goodness!' said Timothy genuinely astounded.

'No, not exactly goodness,' said Norbu, misunderstanding his reaction, 'it is really Power that is his special quality.'

'You mean Spiritual Power?' Timothy suggested tactfully.

Norbu hesitated for a few moments. 'Yes,' he said finally, 'Spiritual Power. That's what the Rinpoche himself calls it.' Then leaving Timothy no time for further questions, he quickly changed the subject. 'Now I'm sure you must be hungry,' he said. 'Please to follow me!'

Their lunch was taken in a long low room next to the temple block in the first courtyard. Timothy had earlier surmised that like the Christian monks in Europe, these monks would have taken their meals together at set times in a refectory but this place was clearly organised on different lines. The room itself was more like a kitchen café than a formal dining room, with a take-away and delivery service for the monks attending the temple or working in the adjoining classrooms. The whole business was apparently run by a team of young novices working under the eye of an experienced old cook. On the kitchen side, there were several copper cauldrons and other cooking pots bubbling away above a row of stone-built fireplaces. Every now and then the cook would inspect the cauldrons and if anything was not to his satisfaction, would reach out to rap one of the novices with the end of a long wooden ladle. Norbu explained that this menial work was confined to the poorer novices – those whose families were unable to pay for their upkeep and tuition at the monastery. Boys from wealthy families, like Timothy's two young friends, were excused from these duties. Though Norbu had not explicitly said so, Timothy gained the impression that he considered the boys' kitchen work to be in some sense character-forming, rather in the same spirit as his own unloving aunt had once confided him to the austere regime of a peculiarly atavistic British public school. As the cold memories came back, he could not help putting an extra bit of mental distance between himself and the unsuspecting Warden.

Leaving their order with the cook, they sat down at a long table already occupied by two older monks and a young layman. Norbu introduced them in order of seniority. First came the Migoling Painting Master who was responsible for murals, mandalas, scrolls and images throughout the monastery. He was a tall, rangy man with wide innocent eyes and a whispy grey beard, and though he spoke little English, Timothy took an instant liking to him. After him came a more mysterious late middle-aged monk, who held the position of official Oracle or medium. Barely acknowledging Timothy's presence, he kept his eyes shut and seemed to be entirely taken up with repeating mantras under his breath and counting his rosary. Finally, there was Chana, who in excellent English introduced himself as a lay artist who had studied in India, and was currently assisting the painting master on a special mural commissioned for the temple block.

It belatedly dawned on Timothy after the introductions were over, that these three characters were not there by chance: they had been specially invited by the Warden to meet him, each carefully chosen for his intrinsic interest. He gratefully restored the Warden to the place of honour he had originally accorded him before the unfortunate personal associations triggered by Norbu's apparently unsympathetic attitude to the poor serving novices.

Not surprisingly, the conversation that then developed while they drank their tea—also ordered by Norbu—was dominated by Chana the freelance artist, who not only responded vigorously to Timothy's eager questioning but also contrived to draw in the painting master by keeping up a skilful two-way translation. Even the oracle seemed to participate indirectly with his low, rhymic accompaniment of muttered prayers and mantras.

'You have to understand,' explained Chana, 'that here paintings are not regarded as works of art in your western sense but as religious objects created for purposes of instruction, ritual and meditation.' Timothy could not help feeling a little rebuffed by this rather cold, excluding statement. After all, the few paintings and images he had so far seen had succeeded in making a distinct impact on his sensibility (even though he did not fully understand their meaning) and like many liberal humanist academics, he still preferred to believe that art at least was a universal language. His disappointment must have shown on his face, as the painting master began to laugh and to say something to the others in an incomprehensible dialect.

'He is saying,' said Chana 'that you should be happy that you like our paintings because it shows you are a natural Buddhist.' They all laughed, apart from the oracle, whose eyes remained shut.

'It's not that,' said Timothy, trying to deflect their attention away from himself. 'It's just that you seem to be implying that here all artists are obliged to follow strict religious conventions in their painting, and that there is little opportunity for them to develop their own original styles.'

'Yes, on the whole that is how it is!' replied Chana. 'And the difference between me and the painting master is that he claims to be content with the situation, whilst I am not.' The painting master again interposed but this time his tone was very serious, even severe. 'He is telling you,' said Chana, 'that he seeks to paint always in the spirit of the dharma and for its furtherance.' He paused . . . 'but what he is not explaining is the way things actually work here. If, for example, he gets a commission to paint the portrait of Padmasambhava in one or other of his eight manifestations, he is then obliged to follow precise traditional instructions as regards the colour and shape of the composition, the expression on the guru's face, the robes he wears, the special style of his hat and the symbolic instruments he holds, even down to the detailed appearance of the three skulls to be depicted at the apex of his staff. My own feeling is that it was not always like this in the early history of our art. You only have to look at the power and purity of some of the older murals in Migoling itself to realise this. And equally I feel that things must not be allowed to remain like this – ossified!'

'But surely you still have some freedom?' Timothy put in gently, to cool the argument. 'I mean those scenes showing the four animal friends, I imagine that the religious rules for them must be fairly flexible!' They all laughed again.

'Yes,' said the painting master, wiping his eyes and finally managing a little broken English. 'And like the animals we are still friends, I hope!'

'We should also tell Doctor Curtin,' added Norbu, rather earnestly, 'that here in Migoling, we are lucky to have an Abbot who understands the problems of the artists and encourages them to experiment far more than it is done in other monasteries.' The others nodded in agreement.

The arrival of several steaming bowls of rice, meat and vegetable stew and a mysterious-looking dish called hemadatsi brought their general conversation to an end, and for the next few minutes the Kalapuris concentrated entirely on the food in front of them. Even the oracle opened a wary eye to fill his plate. Anxious to show that he was happy to try all the local specialities, Timothy also helped himself to large portions of everything. Unfortunately nobody thought to warn him about the full fury of the hemadatsi – an unusually potent concoction of chillies and cheese sauce which soon reduced him to choking coughs and streaming eyes. Chana offered no sympathy, and instead suggested that he should take a tough Tantric view of his predicament. 'Through this dish you can experience something of the liberating force of Vajrapani, the bodhisattva of energy and power,' he said, adding that he would show Timothy a fine image of him in his wrathful aspect in the temple after lunch.

Norbu looked reproachfully at the painter. 'I think,' he said, 'Doctor Curtains is more in need of the motherly compassion of Green Tara.'

While these exchanges were going on around him, Timothy began to recover from the worst effects of the hemadatsi. After clearing his throat and sipping some water, he turned with relief towards his hosts across the table – only to find himself looking straight into a pair of strange blood-shot eyes. It appeared that the oracle had been staring at him in this peculiarly intent way for sometime, and he continued to do so for several moments more before abruptly closing his eyes and resuming his muttered mantras. Coming on top of his ordeal with the chillies, the man's stare had a deep unsettling effect on Timothy, and he wondered if the others had noticed it. It seemed, however, that they had all been too preoccupied with their food.

When they had all finished the meal, Norbu and Chana began to discuss what they should do next. Eventually it was decided that whilst Chana would show Timothy some of the murals and images in the temple block, Norbu would go off to tell the Tulku that their guest would be pleased to call on him later in the afternoon.

As they climbed the steps that led up to the assembly hall, Timothy and his new guide were met by the sound of clashing cymbals and honking horns. The place was obviously again occupied by a body of monks deep into the performance of their afternoon rituals – not the right time to go inside, said Chana, rather to Timothy's relief. Instead they stood outside listening.

Timothy had to admit to being baffled by this style of sacred music, ever since he had attended his first Tibetan musical evening in London in the company of Professor Gabbinger and Lucy. Gabbinger had not helped matters by announcing loudly that 'it all sounds rather like a traffic jam in Lhasa'. But then his supervisor had never claimed to have much appreciation of the culture of the Himalayan peoples, despite his unusually sympathetic perception of their political aspirations.

'You mustn't expect to follow the meaning of these sounds at once,' said Chana returning to their earlier discussion, 'anymore than you can appreciate the visual art straightaway.' Timothy again politely protested that though he did indeed find the music difficult, he felt an almost instant liking for the paintings and images. 'On the contrary, I suspect it may really be other way round,' countered Chana, who was clearly the sort of person who liked to challenge the assumptions of others. 'You like the paintings not for their own sake but because they vaguely remind you of something else, one of your many western art "isms" perhaps. Whereas in the case of the music, I predict that you will experience a real breakthrough once you realise that you don't have to like it, just to recognise its power.'

Although one side of Timothy could appreciate the man's perceptiveness, the other felt some irritation at the way in which this stranger presumed to deliver such assured judgements concerning what was after all another's subjective experience. He was tempted to continue the argument but thought better of it once they began to climb the steep ladder-like steps that led up to the next floor. When they had reached the top he saw that the basic pattern of the ground floor was here repeated, with a wide landing fronting a dim cavernous chapel and two smaller side chapels. But whereas the assembly hall below had been jointly dedicated to Shakyamuni Buddha—the historical Buddha—and Padmasambhava, here the main chapel was dominated by three great Bodhisattva images: Avalokiteshvara, the personification of compassion, Manjushri, the representation of wisdom, and Vajrapani, the embodiment of energy and power. These last phenomena, he recalled, had according to his guide, been present at lunch time in the fiery force of the hemadatsi!

The chapel was deserted when they entered, and the combination of the silence, the dim glow of the butter lamps, and the numinous presence of the three images had an immediate effect on Timothy's imagination. He stood for a moment in rapt contemplation, before preparing himself to receive another puncturing judgement from his unsparing companion. But this time it did not happen. Instead he was startled to see Chana raising his hands above his head and slowly descending to a kneeling position, from which he swiftly threw himself forward full length on the floor before the image of Vajrapani. Again Timothy experienced conflicting reactions. One part of him, which presumably had its origin in his conventional Protestant upbringing, felt shocked and embarrassed to see a rational man prostrating himself before a painted clay image – an idol! But another part of his mind was deeply impressed and moved by the other's action. He now sensed that Chana, with his forceful expression of disquieting truths, was spontaneously committing himself to the primary archetype of his being – Vajrapani in his wrathful aspect, the breaker of obstacles, who held aloft the fearful diamond thunderbolt. By comparison Timothy felt small, confused and self-conscious, unable to commit himself visibly and wholeheartedly to a single over-arching value. He gazed in turn at the three images of Wisdom, Compassion and Power. Wasn't there one in which he could recognise his own particular ideal and source of protection?

Meanwhile Chana had got up from the floor and was standing thoughtfully by his side. Timothy fully expected him to launch into a vigorous analysis of the mystical Buddhist land of Shambala, whose verdant landscapes were depicted on the walls around them. But it seemed that the artist's mind was elsewhere, and he was even mildly anxious to leave the chapel without further comment. Even when Timothy attempted to draw his attention to a mandala on the wall of the outer landing, which closely resembled the 'history' mandala in his own room in the guesthouse, even then Chana merely nodded, and murmured that it was indeed called the Spirit of Time. And before Timothy could ask him anything else he had hurried on to the next flight of steps.

The condition of the images and paintings on the next floor was quite different from anything they had so far seen. The main chapel was almost completely bare, with only one very stern-looking image of Maitreya, the Future Buddha, at the far end. An old caretaker monk was pottering around in front of the image, filling up numerous offering bowls of water, rice and ritual cakes. All around the walls and the pillars were covered with what looked like a layer of sandy earth. The whole area, Chana explained, was in the process of being redecorated and rededicated to Maitreya in accordance with the wishes of the Tulku and 'certain authorities' in the capital, Himjin. Previously the walls had been filled with a particularly fine set of murals showing various deities in union with their mystic consorts, including an unusually interesting representation of the first meeting of Avalokiteshvara in his monkey form, with Senma, the lonely ogress, from whose eventual union had sprung the six kinds of beings which now inhabited the universe: gods, demi-gods, human beings, ghosts, animals and sufferers in hell. 'What's more,' he added, 'they also showed a seventh kind of being, the yetis or migos, who according to our local tradition, were also descended from the primal union of the monkey and the ogress. Anyway, as you can see, all this has been wiped away and covered up to prepare the way for more improving subjects, despite strong protests from Abbot Taranatha himself.'

Outside on the landing, there were signs that a more mysterious and violent artistic conflict was in progress. A great painted representation of Migo Lopen, the first protector of the monastery, had recently been almost entirely obliterated by unknown nocturnal intruders. Timothy could just make out the tip of his pointed head towards the top of the wall, and further down part of the hunter's bow which the figure must have been carrying on his right arm. On the other side of the landing, next to the chapel entrance, a space had been cleared for the erection of a new clay image of Lama Jaya Kumara, the spiritual ancestor of the Tulku of Migoling. Chana looked back into the main chapel where the caretaker was still busy with his bowls: 'Apparently the authorities decided to station that guy here to keep an eye on things after the recent intrusion. The fact that he himself is virtually blind and deaf doesn't seem to bother them!'

They stood together in silence for few moments watching the caretaker. Then Chana suddenly turned to Timothy in a quizzical sort of way. 'Why,' he asked, 'do you think that Norbu was so happy to go off after lunch and pass you over to me?'

'I don't really know. I expect he wanted to go back to his accounts,' said Timothy, a little taken aback.

'No, that is not the reason,' Chana continued. 'He went off because he wanted to spend the afternoon with his wife and family down in the village.'

'Good heavens!' said Timothy. 'I thought he was a celibate monk.'

'Why? Did you ask him?'

'No, I suppose I just assumed it.' Timothy answered a trifle lamely.

'Dr Curtin, here you must take nothing for granted! Let me ask you another personal question,' Chana persisted. 'Why do you think the oracle suddenly stared at you in that peculiar way?'

Timothy began to feel distinctly uneasy: 'I really have no idea . . perhaps he had never seen an Englishman before.'

'Perhaps . . . ' Chana echoed his words doubtfully. 'Dr Curtin, I can see you are a very innocent and trusting person – someone who doesn't like conflicts. But you have to understand that this country is full of conflicts, so deep and so strange, that as a foreigner you can hardly begin to comprehend them.' He came up close to Timothy, looking straight into his eyes. 'And precisely because you are a foreigner, you must be always on your guard. You see, in our culture, the man from the West has a special status, arising from his power and wealth, which can easily make him a target for intrigue and exploitation. For us, indeed you are like beings from the mythical land of Shambala, which we just saw in the chapel below, destined perhaps to redeem or replace us.'

He paused again before putting a final question. 'Why do you think the Tulku here wants to meet you this afternoon when you don't even know who he is, and before you have had a proper opportunity to talk with the Abbot who invited you?'

Timothy looked at his watch. 'Well,' he said nervously, 'I suppose I will soon find out.'

8

The private quarters of Lama Jaya Kumara Rinpoche were situated in the first courtyard of the monastery. From the outside there was little to distinguish them from the other apartments that made up the lhabrang, the main residential building for the senior members of the establishment, including the Abbot. It was only after Timothy had been admitted by a deferential servant and conducted along a winding corridor filled with stuffed birds, and then into a richly furnished sitting room, that it became apparent that the place and its owner were really rather different. For one thing, the apartment was much larger than the exterior view had suggested, extending back on several levels deep into the outer walls of the monastery. But there was another far more remarkable feature that only dawned on Timothy after he had been waiting there tensely for several minutes. The lamps which he had first taken for rather elaborately shaded butter lamps were in reality cleverly disguised electric lights, whilst the glowing red embers in the fire place also proved on closer inspection to be electrically simulated.

These discoveries helped to dispel the state of apprehension induced by his earlier talks with Chana. He began to notice the elegant furniture around him, especially the deep, maroon-coloured armchairs which blended nicely with the chic cane tables and fine hanging scrolls. Meanwhile, from somewhere outside the monastery walls came the steady chug chug of a distant electric generator – a sound which had puzzled him earlier. It certainly seemed that the Warden had been right the first time about power being this Tulku's special attribute.

Meanwhile the voice of the master himself, also sounding a bit like a generator, could be heard from another room along the corridor, issuing instructions to some subordinate. Timothy was even able to make out certain words which kept being repeated, such as chang (beer), sha (meat) and momos (dumpling). Evidently some sort of feast was being planned. Since the tone of the talk also suggested that it was likely to continue for a few more minutes, he began to examine the odd selection of books displayed on the shelves above the Tulku's desk. These included an old biography of Moshe Dayan, and a journalistic study of the first Gulf War. There was also a large glossy book entitled *Treasures of Kalapur*, apparently written by the Tulku himself, next to a slim black volume entitled *Maitreya's Mandate*. The rest of the shelves were largely filled with back numbers of the *Wall Street Journal*, each batch stacked horizontally between finely carved wooden boards in the traditional Himalayan style.

'Good to meet you, Professor. I'm J. Kumara!' Timothy spun round nervously to greet the Tulku, who had somehow managed to enter the room swiftly and soundlessly behind him. Though he had already guessed the man could not possibly be an ordained monk, nothing had prepared him for this commanding, middle-aged figure arrayed in a scarlet dressing gown over a smart American suit – more like a flamboyant international businessman than a mystic Himalayan lama. Taken aback by the Tulku's appearance, he almost failed to notice the small fat man hovering in the doorway: it was the cook whose treatment of the novices had earlier upset him. 'Dismissed!' shouted the Tulku in English, without turning round. 'And don't forget what I said!'

'Rinpoche!' muttered the cook, sucking in his breath respectfully as he backed out the room.

'Now what would you like to drink, Professor, a whisky?' Timothy observed that even before he had time to reply the Tulku had already reached for the decanter behind him.

'Yes, please. That would be very nice,' said Timothy, beginning to revert to the formal Hoadley-like style that seemed both to protect and restrict him on these occasions.

'Here's to a happy holiday in Kalapur!' boomed the Tulku, clinking his glass with Timothy's, while his sharp eyes passed swiftly over his guest's appearance, sizing him up and down with a practised authority. 'And now,' he announced, 'the first thing I have to tell you is that my colleague, the Abbot, has had to stay on an extra day in Himjin and will not be coming back here till tomorrow. In such circumstances I felt it's my duty to take the initiative in welcoming you on behalf of the monastery, as well as in my official capacity as the chairman of DDB, the Dharma Development Board.'

It was at once clear that the Tulku was the sort of man who preferred to be left to steer the conversation very much as he chose, though with due regard for the necessary polite formalities. Thus he first wanted to be assured that his visitor was being properly looked after in the guesthouse ('a rather gloomy hole') and introduced to the 'right people'. To all such enquiries, Timothy found himself responding with equal old-fashioned courtesy and a liberal sprinkling of Rinpoches. Yes, he said, the Warden was certainly looking after him well and he had already met a number of interesting people, like Lama Wangdi ('a very sincere fellow, no doubt,' murmured the Tulku), the painting master ('a good old-fashioned craftsman') and the oracle ('a curious chap, really something of a relic from the past and a believer in the old gods').

'But what about your cash access?' the Tulku put in suddenly with a more obvious glint of personal interest. 'If you have any problems with travellers' cheques or credit cards—any problems at all—you must let me know at once. It is very important now, while the dollar and the yen are playing hide and seek with each other, that you get proper value for your money!' Timothy, for whom international finance was hardly less esoteric than Tantric Buddhism, tried his best to sound knowingly grateful.

But, on the whole, he felt the interview was not going too badly, though he could not help remembering Chana's warning that he should look out for the Tulku's real purpose in inviting him. If there is an ulterior motive, he thought, it has not yet emerged – unless it was all merely some kind of public relations show. Anyway, emboldened by his host's generous supply of whisky, he decided to try to reverse the conversational flow and offer the Tulku a slight 'lead' of his own devising.

'Rinpoche,' he began hesitantly. 'I would be most interested to learn a little more about your own spiritual lineage, if it is not improper to ask you?'

'No, not at all,' replied the Tulku breezily. 'In fact, I'm very glad you have asked me this question.' He stopped to finish his second glass.

'I am sure you yourself must already be knowing a good deal about the original Lama Jaya Kumara.' Though he spoke excellent English, there was a slight Indian lilt to his expression, and this, combined with his physical appearance, convinced Timothy that whatever his spiritual lineage, he almost certainly belonged to the so-called "Bharati" community in Kalapur, well-to-do Indians who had been settled there for several generations and also kept close links with the mother country. 'But on the other hand,' the Tulku continued steadily, 'I can perhaps bring you up-to-date with our most recent researches on his life, which are really quite significant.'

'You see, according to our traditional accounts, the original LJK (as I call him) was one of the Tibetan emissaries selected in the eighth century to go on a journey to northern India to invite Guru Padmasambhava to come back with him to Tibet to help spread Buddha's dharma in these Himalayan regions. Although the subsequent story of Guru Rinpoche's mission to these parts is very familiar, next to nothing was known about LJK until very recently. Now, thanks to the discovery of some old manuscripts, which lay hidden for centuries in our Kalapuri monasteries, we know a lot more about him.

'Briefly, Dr Curtin, it transpires that far from being just a messenger, LJK was a very powerful influence on the Himalayan mission, in some ways more significant than Padmasambhava himself. Not only did he plan the details of the whole conversion enterprise but he also did his best to curb what we can now see was Padmasambhava's mistaken tendency to go too far in placating the old gods of the Himalayan peoples (giving them the status of 'protectors of Buddhism' and so on), and incorporating some of their primitive practices and beliefs into the new faith. Of course, I am not denying that Guru Rinpoche was a remarkable and charismatic figure. But like many charismatics'— Timothy noticed that he pronounced the word in such a way as to suggest sick people, like asthmatics—'Padmasambhava's success really depended on the unsung efforts of a cool manager with his feet on the ground, and the ability to secure the essential practical support and funding for the mission. That man, Professor, was LJK!'

The Tulku's eloquent presentation seemed to have reached its climax but he chose to add a further illustration of his thesis. 'You remember what Mrs Naidu said about Mahatma Gandhi never realising how much it cost others to keep him in poverty. Well . . . history now shows that in a rather similar way, Padmasambhava never understood that his spiritual flights were in fact prepared and powered by LJK.'

A confused feeling of unreality had begun to spread over Timothy as he sat there politely listening, as much induced by the whisky as by the bizarre nature of the Tulku's monologue. At the same time he also felt curiously invigorated and determined to seize this opportunity to penetrate further into the secrets of Kalapuri historical revisionism.

A sharp crash from the corridor outside roused Timothy from his reflections, and sent the Tulku striding angrily to the door. A large crate of beer bottles just delivered had been dropped too hard on the stone floor outside. Fortunately nothing had been broken but this discovery was insufficient to mollify the Tulku, who proceeded to berate his servant loudly and at length in a local dialect best designed to convey the full force of his feelings. Timothy found himself recalling the angry face of the kudun, the disciplinarian, who had opposed his presence at the morning service. Out of fairness, however, he also strove to visualise the gentle image of Lama Wangdi, with his quiet sympathetic insight. Was there something about the character of the monastic life here which somehow brought out these conflicting personalities? And if so, was this why the temple murals so often chose to juxtapose vivid representations of wrathful beings with equally vivid images of their peaceful counterparts?

'What was I saying?' The Tulku, now calm and composed, had quietly returned to his seat. 'Oh yes,' he said. 'I was going to tell you a little more about our national reform programme.' Timothy sat up to face him more attentively. Not for the first time since his arrival at Migoling he felt that his questions were being anticipated.

The Tulku took another deep sip from his glass. 'Let me put it this way, Professor: you are privileged to arrive in this country at a time of unique spiritual and material renewal. It is as if we have just woken from a long sleep – the same sleep in which you Britishers found us three centuries ago, and, I am sorry to say, which you helped to prolong for your own interests.' Timothy felt a momentary twinge of irritation, not so much on behalf of Hoadley, but out of respect for earlier more notable agents of the Raj, not all of whom had been arrogant John Bull 'Britishers'.

'Yes, I know I am making you feel uncomfortable,' said the Tulku, now openly grinning at him. 'But when you come here you must try to see the past a little more from a Himalayan perspective.' Timothy felt like saying that such a view was not actually so difficult for him; it was after all also one of Gabbinger's favourite themes, recurring in several of his recent articles. Maybe the Tulku had even found it there. However, sensing that his host was poised to continue his discourse on reform, and hopefully reveal more secrets, he refrained from commenting, and instead smiled encouragingly.

'I must first explain to you that our reform programme, as it effects individuals and society as a whole, is essentially based on what we call the Triple Vow to Maitreya, the Future Buddha, whose advent will signal the end of the present age of spiritual and material decline.'

The Tulku's voice was now achieving a sort of magisterial power which swept on undiminished for several minutes. The Triple Vow, he explained, was normally taken at the end of an individual's pilgrimage to the sacred spots of northern India, the places associated with the life of the historical Buddha. Not only did each pilgrim then solemnly swear to recommit his life to the Buddha's dharma, but he also promised to help to purify the corrupt religious practices of Kalapur, and to work selflessly for the future good of the country. These vows, said the Tulku, were dedicated to Maitreya because they were each designed to create the right conditions for his appearance. And, since the teachings of the historical Buddha were held to be essentially identical with those of the future Buddha, the pilgrim's first commitment to the former also amounted to an invocation to the latter. Similarly, the second vow of purification both flowed from the first vow of personal commitment but also prepared the ground for the advent of Maitreya. Finally, the pilgrim's third vow—the personal dedication to the greater good—embodied the traditional compassion and altruism of Mahayana Buddhism in the form of a dynamic programme for social and economic progress. These ideals had also been implicit in the original dharma, but they were destined to be more fully manifested in the final mandate of Maitreya.

Having finished his lecture the Tulku sat back rather grandly but also expectantly. It was obviously not the first time he had delivered this polished performance, and he was clearly accustomed to handling questions with equal assurance. Timothy wondered how to respond. Although he could not help admiring the man's verve, he found the tone and content of his exposition pretty alarming: a mishmash of medieval sounding logic and modern evangelism, spiced with business rhetoric. Resisting a strong desire to enquire innocently whether the Tulku's private electricity supply was part of the dynamic national programme, he decided instead to ask about the Shar Lama and his embodiment of the Spirit of Time, to which the Abbot had made an intriguing reference in his London lecture.

'Professor,' said the Tulku, a shade reluctantly, 'this is a very complex and evolving issue, and I must be the first to admit that I myself am no philosopher, and that one really needs to be one to do justice to the subtleties of this concept. All I would say to you now is that as part of our creative reappraisal of Kalapuri Buddhism, we are trying to build on the traditional metaphysical idea of the Shar Lama as embodying the compassionate principle of time and progress to provide a national focus for our development plans. This also means that we must all accept the overall policy directions of the Shar Lama, and particularly what he tells us about what has happened to our community in the past and what direction it should take in the future. Basically, it's a question of creating national symbols and dynamic leadership using the grass roots of our religion and culture.'

'And, of course, I don't have to tell a scholar like you that the Spirit of Time concept in Kalapur has nothing to do with the Kalachakra or Wheel of Time practice followed elsewhere in Tibet and India.'

'My God,' thought Timothy, 'this sounds even worse than I expected: a gross distortion of Buddhism, almost fascist! Whoever could have conceived of such a grotesque thing?' But at the same time he could tell from the Tulku's expression, that for whatever reason he was reluctant to say more on this subject. Instead he was busy extracting a spare copy of *Maitreya's Mandate* from his book-shelf, and writing something inside the fly leaf in a bold hand.

'Professor, I would like to present this to you. I think you will find that it explains what I had been trying to summarise in more illuminating detail.'

'Thank you, Rinpoche,' said Timothy weakly. The book, he saw, had been inscribed, 'With Kind Regards from LJK'.

After this little ceremony, the Tulku rose from his chair to indicate that the audience was about to end. But not quite. 'Before you go, Professor, I would like to give you a word of advice,' his paternal tone was now tempered by a touch of confidentiality. 'As I said earlier, you have arrived in Kalapur at a time of immense change. And, as a historian, you will appreciate that such changes invariably provoke opposition from all kinds of vested interests. It is quite possible that during your stay here you'll meet people who criticise the Reform Programme openly in your presence, some of whom may even try to win you over to their way of thinking.

'Now I'm not, of course, suggesting that you should not listen to what these people may say; in fact as an intelligent man with an open mind, you should certainly listen to them. But, Dr Curtin, there is a vital difference between listening impartially, and committing yourself personally to another's cause . . . But then I don't really need to tell you this, do I? A moment ago I poked a little fun at you Britishers for prolonging our Himalayan slumbers, but I am also the first to recognise that there is another very positive side to the character of the British abroad: fair play, impartiality, no local entanglements . . . Stick to that line and we won't go far wrong, isn't it Professor?'

The Tulku held Timothy's hand in a strong farewell grip. As if by magic, the deferential servant noiselessly entered to show him out. As they passed through the corridor with the stuffed birds towards the outer door, the Tulku's voice rang out powerfully behind him: 'Have a nice stay Dr Curtin!'

9

Timothy woke up suddenly to find himself engulfed in darkness – such darkness that there was no point in trying to look at his watch, even if he had been able to find it.

Fighting back a rising feeling of panic, he tried to recall what had happened after he had left the Tulku's apartment. That must have been some time after eight-thirty. He could vaguely remember climbing unsteadily up the stairs to his room in the guesthouse, and collapsing on to his mattress. Gradually other things came back too. Someone had lit his stove so that the room had been warm when he arrived, also a tray of snacks had been left on the table for his supper. The Tulku's whisky had been far more potent than he had realised – so powerful that he must have been sleeping steadily for five hours.

He had also been dreaming intensely. In fact part of his mind was still taken up with the events in the last and most vivid dream. He had been wandering about in the dark chapels of the temple block, talking animatedly to the Warden. He remembered asking him about his wife and children, whose unexpected existence had been earlier revealed by Chana. He had also been telling Norbu something about his own recent experiences with women, especially with Lucy and Serena. Norbu had clucked sympathetically and led him towards a large thangka hanging in one corner of the chapel.

At first he had been unable to make out the subject of the painting, beyond seeing that it contained three figures depicted in harmonious but very sombre tones. Gradually he had come to recognise that the central figure, with its startled eyes and princely bearing, was none other than Padmasambhava, the charismatic missionary; and that the two women on either side were his consorts – the same trio depicted on the wall inside the entrance hall. But while the Warden had been telling him the story of the consorts, the thangka itself had suddenly dropped to reveal the stiff, mysterious figure of the Migoling oracle, his wild red eyes staring straight into Timothy, exactly as had happened during their encounter over lunch. It was then that he had woken up.

The dramatic shock of the dream and the absolute darkness that now surrounded him intensified Timothy's fears. It seemed to make little or no difference whether he kept his eyes open or shut. Blindness, he thought, must be like this. And he himself was hardly more than a blind man in this bizarre country. Fragments of his conversations with Chana and the Tulku now came back: 'Here you must take nothing for granted . . . . Dr Curtin, I can see you are a very innocent and trusting person . . . . Fair play, impartiality, no local entanglements . . . isn't it Professor?'

What on earth had made him think that he could ever succeed in carrying out any serious historical research in this kind of place? He had started out supposing that his only problems would be those conjured up by Hoadley and Sharir, and their attempts to use his visit for their own personal and political ends. He had had absolutely no conception of the peculiar situation that would confront him in Kalapur: that he would arrive in the middle of a sinister state-engineered revolution officially predicated on the Advent of Maitreya, the future Buddha, and apparently subject to the infallibly prophetic will of the Shar Lama. In such an atmosphere it seemed highly improbable that he would be able to pursue the delicate threads of the historical project he had been asked to assist, particularly as he had a growing suspicion that the same threads were in some as yet undiscovered way directly linked to the current politico-religious situation. No wonder a detached observer like Chana had laughed at his naivety, and even the powerful Lama Jaya had felt obliged to warn him of the dangers of getting involved. Meanwhile it seemed that even Abbot Taranatha himself, the man originally responsible for his visit, was being mysteriously delayed in Himjin . . .

Timothy let out a long, hopeless sigh. Though it made little difference, he now decided to keep his eyes firmly closed. In the end, the fears created in his own fertile imagination seemed preferable to the panic induced by an impenetrable outside darkness.

Three long, loud blasts from a conch in the first courtyard brought him back from his second bout of sleep. Throughout the monastery the monks were stirring, summoned to the usual dawn assembly. Although his room was now very chilly, he got up and went across to the window to see what was happenng.

It was still quite dark outside but already he could see a number of shadowy figures, some with cloaks wrapped round their shoulders. For a while they seemed to hover at the several doorways before scuttling off in the direction of the temple block. He also noticed that a large figure was standing by himself in the middle of the courtyard, evidently calling and cajoling the monks to hurry up and finish their ablutions. Almost certainly this was the same kudun who had challenged Timothy in the assembly hall the day before. He had a strong urge to pick up his bucket of water and pour its icy contents down on the man's head.

Despite the doubts and fears that had assailed him during the night, he now felt surprisingly fresh and very hungry. Although the cold soup and rock-like cubes of cheese left for his supper were hardly appetising, he set about consuming them with a frantic zest, before returning to the warmth of his blankets.

It was becoming lighter by the minute, and as had happened on the previous morning, his gaze was drawn towards the mandala on the opposite wall. But whereas yesterday he had been initially intrigued but ultimately baffled by the hard, cold geometry of the design, now he became aware of other more hopeful features, heightened by the streaks of sunlight that played across its surface. He noticed that almost all the spaces enclosed within the succeeding squares and circles were filled with tiny kaleidoscopic shapes, representing such things as gateways, lotus plants, animals and groups of dancing deities. This transformation in his perception of the mandala also seemed to reflect his own changing personal experience of the monastery itself. On arrival it had been a totally mysterious and alien place, but now at least it was beginning to acquire some of the qualities of a human community, inhabited by individuals, a few of whom he could recognise and even relate to, however tentatively.

But that was not all. There was also the curious way in which his earlier perception of the mandala as somehow symbolising the quest for historical truth, had turned out to be more than just a subjective fancy. It was after all, as Chana had told him, the representation of the Spirit of Time, and therefore perhaps in some sense as yet to be disclosed, the key to the Kalapuri concepts of past, present and future.

Feeling slightly ashamed of his unbridled imagination, he sought to bring himself back to earth. He could almost hear Gabbinger's voice again telling him that he was in danger of being carried away by a pretty pattern on the wall. By way of administering himself a stern, kudun-like rebuke, he picked up the book which Lama Jaya Kumara had given him on the previous evening. Here, at least, was some sort of basic text which might throw further light on what was happening.

Sometime later, Timothy was interrupted in his study of *Maitreya's Mandate* by a light knock on his door. The two boys, Chime and Pema, had arrived to remind him of his promise to play the rebirth game with them. Since there was no sign of the Abbot nor even of Norbu, and he had had more than enough of LJK's evangelical prose, he was quite happy to join them. Looking rather mysterious, the boys asked him to follow them to what they described as 'a special place' where the game could be played to maximum effect, and hopefully, safe from discovery by the organisers of the Maitreya class. Having himself just wrestled for too long with the new conceptions of Maitreya, he found himself sympathising even more closely with their point of view.

The boys led him to the other side of the courtyard towards a rather derelict-looking tower at the end of one of the monks' accommodation blocks. The Warden had told him that this was the oldest part of the monastery and was now only partly occupied. Together they entered the tower and began to climb the steep creaking stairs.

Inside it was dark since most of the shutters were closed, and Timothy could not easily determine what, if anything, the place had been originally intended for, though it was important enough to contain a number of ancient but dramatic murals. A large painting, occupying most of the second floor landing, particularly caught his attention. It showed some cave-like places in which various people, whom he deduced to be the souls of the dead, were being roasted or stir-fried in deep cauldrons by devotedly attendant demons. 'The eight hot hells!' said the older boy, contorting his features into a suitably demonic grimace.

Timothy stopped to examine the mural more carefully. He was reminded of how the Buddhist members of the Himalayan Centre, including Serena herself, used to maintain, somewhat defensively, that such illustrations were only to be taken metaphorically. The essential purpose of the dharma, they had said, was to provide a way out of suffering by recognising its origins in human attachment, which in turn was the product of illusion. But looking at these scenes, metaphorical or not, it was clear that the suffering depicted was meant to be seen as real enough, if only to remind those who saw it of the value of adhering steadfastly to the path that led to its cessation. At times like this, Timothy felt himself becoming unexpectedly unsympathetic to the claims of religion in general. All too often, the basic technique seemed to resemble the classic salesman's pitch: first try to convince people that there was something utterly wrong or seriously lacking in their lives; then offer them the one and only solution.

When they reached the top floor the boys began to giggle uncontrollably – the sort of giggle that suggested that they were beginning to get frightened, whilst clearly enjoying the sensation. As Timothy peered cautiously through the main door that led off the landing, he began to understand the reason.

Ahead lay a dark and cavernous chapel, dimly lit by a few butter lamps. The walls and the ceiling were all painted black, and there was an unpleasant musty smell pervading the whole place. As he stepped inside, and turned towards the right, three huge images seemed to rear up in front of him. Though all were draped with numerous ceremonial scarves, he could see that the two outer images had very fierce expressions and were armed with ropes and choppers. But it was the giant central figure that at once seized his attention. It wore a high pointed helmet from which some sort of spiky red hair protruded to frame a massive mask-like face, whose features seemed to combine human intelligence with animal ferocity. There could be no doubt about this figure's identity. 'Migo Lopen!' Timothy gasped as much to himself as to the boys who were still hovering nervously round the entrance.

Though the chapel was very eerie, Timothy did his best to retain an observant and academic approach to its contents. There was little doubt that he was now in the gonkhang, the special sacred area set aside for the monastery's most potent and fearsome protectors. Apart from the three big images, he saw that the place was filled with dark hanging scrolls showing the wrathful faces of the same protectors, accompanied by their several retinues. Similar figures were painted on the central lines of pillars. Away in the far corner, beyond one of the images, he noticed a pile of ancient weapons, mostly shields and swords, apparently treated as the personal property of the protective deities. As he moved forward in the dark to investigate, his foot struck against something hard. It was a round, cage-like container made of thick glass, with what looked like a model boat inside. Bending down to get a closer look, he saw that it was not a boat but an enormous stuffed foot. 'Migo! Migo!' shouted the boys, who had now advanced a few steps nearer. Suddenly feeling slightly sick and dizzy, Timothy backed away from the strange object. He needed to get away from the gonkhang and take in some fresh air.

'Let's go. Let's get out of here!' he called back to the boys, trying to sound quick and cool like the cops in the American movies from the 1940s which he and his friends in London used to enjoy watching.

As they sat down on the landing outside the chapel the boys could tell at once that their foreign visitor was not feeling well. 'Many people feel sick in gonkhang,' said the elder boy sympathetically, while his companion dug out a dried-up fritter from a small purse and cheerfully offered it to Timothy. Gradually he began to feel better, all the time watched expectantly by the two boys. 'Now we start the game,' they announced.

The board on which the game was played was about two and a half feet wide, and covered all over with squares painted in a range of different colours. There were also a series of ladders leading up and down. The point of the game, as the boys explained it, was to try to make your way as quickly as possible from the bottom of the board up to the line of silver squares at the top which represented Nirvana, each player's progress being determined by the throw of the dice. The coloured squares, through which they had to pass on the way up, stood for the six possible realms of rebirth: as gods, *asuras* or titans, humans, animals, ghosts, and sufferers in hell. There were also various intervening white squares between the main realms. Depending on where you landed, your progress would be impeded or advanced: on the three lower realms you lost a turn, whilst the three higher realms gained you an extra move. Similarly, ladders could help or hinder, depending on whether you landed at the bottom or the top. The boys admitted, that a much simpler version of the game had been played in Kalapur for many generations past.

Much to his own surprise, Timothy's token soon established a clear lead. Whilst his young competitors were still crawling their way through the realms of animals and ghosts on the lower half of the board, he had leapt forward to the higher realms and was fast approaching Nirvana. The boys, however, kept warning him against over-confidence, gleefully pointing out a particularly long and fatal ladder a few squares ahead, which could all too easily consign him back to the lower depths or, more precisely, to an intermediate zone between human and animal kind. 'With the Migos!' was how the boys put it.

Just as Timothy was poised to make the fatal throw, the sound of heavy footsteps mounting the stairs below jolted them all out of their concentration. If it was only the old caretaker, the boys whispered, it would be OK, but if . . . To be on the safe side they hurriedly covered up the board with a piece of cloth and pulled Timothy back inside the gonkhang. Meanwhile as the steps were coming higher and higher, the boys decided to hide just inside the chapel door, leaving Timothy standing awkwardly on the other side. Almost at once a powerful figure appeared at the entrance: it was the kudun! A moment passed before he spotted the boys and rushed forward to seize them. Then dragging them along behind, he turned swiftly back towards the entrance and came face to face with Timothy.

A sort of scowling smile spread across the kudun's features – not unlike the expression on the face of the Migo Lopen image behind him. 'Boys, late for class,' he snarled. 'Very bad boys!'

'It's all right,' replied Timothy with as much dignity as he could muster, 'they are with me!'

The kudun hesitated only for a second – enough time for him to dispel the scowl from his face. 'Please, this is not a right place for us,' he said more politely. 'Please follow me, Sir.' Disarmed by the man's skilful switch of tactics, Timothy felt he was in no position to refuse. However, as they passed by the Rebirth board on the landing, the kudun gave it a sharp rap with his cane which sent it spinning down the stairs despite the boys' cries of protest. For Timothy, already deflated by the kudun's successful diplomacy, the tumbling board seemed to symbolise his own defeat.

When they reached the bottom and stepped out into the sunny courtyard, the kudun's face stiffened. Making no further attempts to explain or parley, he took hold of each boy by the ear and began to march them towards the temple block. Timothy realised that unless he managed to stage some kind of diversion, the boys would be dragged along to the Maitreya class and no doubt punished as well. Seeing that the kudun's grasp of the boys' ears had obliged him to relax his grip on his official cane, he seized hold of it and dodged round in front to bar the way into the temple. '*Yappo mindoo!*' he shouted, remembering the lama's words on the plane. It was a risky step to have taken: what if the kudun chose to challenge him, as he had every right to do.

'No, that is not good!' said another familiar voice behind them. It was the Abbot, who coming from the direction of the main entrance, had almost collided with the contestants. Both Timothy and the kudun were completely taken aback by his unexpected arrival, but Taranatha grasped the situation very quickly and immediately took control of it. 'Kudun!' he said a shade wearily. 'You know that the Maitreya class is not compulsory, even for novices. So why detain these boys if they want to go elsewhere?' Pema and Chime at once ran off, leaving their would-be disciplinarian helpless before the Abbot.

'As for you, Dr Curtin,' said Taranatha with an air of severity that might have been genuine or again might not, 'you may have been a prefect at your English boarding school but here in Migoling you have no official standing. Kindly return that cane to the kudun. Oh! And another thing! Please meet me at the entrance hall in half an hour. We are going to Himjin.'

10

'So, Timothy, what do you make of it all? Is it the Shangri-la you were expecting or something else?' The Abbot's eyes flickered a little and then screwed up, as if he himself found the subject too perplexing.

This, at last, was the opportunity for which he had been waiting – the moment when he could begin to ask all those questions that had been accumulating and bothering him since his arrival. But where to start? He gazed uncertainly down at the Himjin valley several thousand feet below, verdant and peaceful.

It seemed that Taranatha had decided that this was as good a place as any for their first serious encounter. Only a few moments before he had told the driver to stop, and had led Timothy off the road and up through some bushes on to a high grassy mound from which the best view of the valley could be obtained. Far away in the distance they could just see the Shar Lama's palace some miles away at the river's edge, and there too were numerous neat little white houses with dark wooden roofs, dotted around the landscape like the characters of an unknown script. It was strange how the scenery had begun to take on the colours and contours of the murals and scrolls he had seen in the monastery. Even the distant mountains which framed the valley had begun to resemble its Tantric protectors: powerful, bluish black beneath their icy summits, and beyond human reach.

'It certainly looks very peaceful and sheltered from up here,' he said, 'but it's not exactly Shangri-la. In fact,' he added with a sudden surge of insight, 'as far as I can see, there has been no real peace here for many years.'

Taranatha opened his eyes and stared at his guest for a few seconds. 'Now,' he said quietly, 'now we can begin our work.'

The sudden clink of glasses caught them both by surprise. The driver, who had remained behind in the car, had appeared carrying what looked like several picnic baskets. The Abbot's mood and expression changed immediately. 'This is very good!' he almost shouted. 'I had almost forgotten about our lunch.' The driver, a burly young man with an inquisitive air, spread out an orange cloth and two cushions on the ground and then placed the small conical baskets between them.

'You must try our local beer,' said the Abbot with a mock guilty expression. 'And since I am such a duplicitous old lama and this is after all a special occasion, I will ignore my vows of abstinence and join you. And look, here is something else I hope you will like.' He seized hold of one of the baskets, releasing its lid to reveal a dense mass of soggy chips. 'You must be getting tired of our Kalapuri food, so I told our cook to prepare these English chips for you. He was a bit reluctant to interrupt what he was doing: preparing some enormous feast for that rascally Tulku of ours. But, as you see, he has done his best to follow my instructions.' He beamed proudly at Timothy. 'But I assure you, this is still going to be what your Mr Hoadley would call a working lunch.' Then noticing that the inquisitive driver was still hovering a few feet away, ostensibly waiting for more instructions, the Abbot briskly dismissed him.

Timothy had not thought about Hoadley for some time, so it came as a bit of a shock to hear his name invoked now, the more so as he realised that the whole situation—waiting for what the Abbot had to tell him—had a curiously formal resemblance to that fateful lunch at Hoadley's club when the old fellow had first confided his version of events. At the same time, he himself felt quite different than he had on that occasion: sitting now in the sharp sunlight with the chang and chips. Taranatha, he supposed, could only have been a few years younger than Hoadley, but he did not deploy his age in the way Hoadley did: as conferring a special kind of superior status to which Timothy was obliged to defer. The Abbot, by contrast, seemed like a man who just happened to be old, whilst retaining a strength and vivacity that induced a sense of camaraderie and defied the years between them. Also, he no longer felt that Taranatha was playing some kind of game with him, as he had seemed to be doing when they had first met in London. In fact, he now perceived that the man's whole personality naturally embraced an unusual range of expressiveness: from the cryptic to the boisterous, from theatrical self-mockery to a disconcerting capacity to unmask the hidden thoughts of others. Only very occasionally did a slight feeling of uncertainty still enter into Timothy's mind, as he glimpsed, or thought he glimpsed, that beneath the Abbot's natural exuberance lay a deep weariness and sense of isolation.

'You are right to say there has been no real peace here for many years,' said Taranatha. 'I don't know how you have discovered this but it is absolutely true!'

'I don't know why I said it either,' said Timothy, modestly flattered. 'But I think I was just trying to make a connection between what Hoadley and others have told me about the old Shar Lama's disappearance in 1944, and what I can see of the present crisis: I mean the government's reform programme and the popular resistance.'

'But you don't yet know the exact nature of the connection?' Taranatha asked him.

'No,' Timothy replied slowly, choosing his words, 'but I somehow get the impression that some people may still not have accepted that the lama did die in that presumed air crash fifty years ago, while others—or perhaps the same people—are bitterly opposed to the new reform programme.'

'Well,' said Taranatha with the air of someone coming to a decision, 'since you have found out so much already, you deserve to know more! But first, do eat some of those chips! And one thing more,' he said, scrambling to his feet and looking in the direction of the road. 'Yes, it's all right. I can see him dozing inside the car.' He turned back towards Timothy. 'As you already know so much, you perhaps also know that here everything is not always what it seems, and that official drivers can even turn out to be spies!'

'But surely,' said Timothy quite unprepared for this possibility, 'this man hardly understands a word of English . . . '

'Perhaps not, but we don't know for certain do we? We don't even know if he is really a native of Kalapur. Later on we will try a little experiment.' The Abbot peered into his cupped hand as if looking through a microscope.

'But now, Dr Timothy,' he said, formally settling back on his cushion, 'where shall I begin?'

'Well, I remember that when Hoadley gave me his version of events he started with you!' Timothy was now feeling very relaxed.

'Did he indeed? And what did he say about me?'

'He said that around 1950, you were an outstanding young Buddhist intellectual likely to be attracted to Marxism of the Chinese kind, and that he and the Government of India thought it would be good for your soul and their interests to bring you to England on a scholarship to learn about western liberal values.'

'Yes, all that is quite true,' said Taranatha. 'But you shouldn't laugh at Hoadley too much. It was not exactly brainwashing he was aiming at but something far more dangerous, something which even he did not perhaps fully understand: he wanted me to fall in love with liberty!'

'And did you?' asked Timothy.

Taranatha helped himself to some more chang. 'Yes,' he said, 'you can see that in a sense he was very successful.' He paused before adding: 'except that no one who recognises the full claims of liberty can do so without some prior personal constraint, some prior commitment . . . but let us leave me out of this. At what point did Hoadley begin his account of Kalapur?'

'He started in 1944 with the disappearance of the Shar Lama.'

'That's a good moment,' said the Abbot. 'I shall follow his example!

'You see the flight and disappearance of the old Shar Lama opened up a conflict in our society which has widened ever since. The origins of that conflict go back a long way however, at least back to the eighteenth century when large numbers of dissident Tibetan lamas and their supporters began to settle here to escape the enmity of the Geluk establishment in Lhasa. These settlers and their descendants, who were highly educated and often wealthy people, soon acquired positions of power and privilege in our country. They became the heads of monastaries and their Tibetan language gradually became the language of government and higher learning. And so, though they no doubt brought us some cultural benefits, they also generally aroused the resentment and hostility of the local population, who belong to a different ethnic group.

'You know, Timothy, many people in the West have a rather rosy view of the peace and compassion that has prevailed here in the past. They think we are all gentle mystics who resolve our conflicts peacefully according to Buddhist principles. But I'm afraid it has rarely been like that and certainly not now.

'I know you are dying to ask more questions, but it's better that I press on with the story since there is a lot to tell you.

'So, the reign of the last Shar Lama marked a turning-point in our history. You see, though he was of Tibetan origin, he came to identify himself not with his elitist compatriots but with the people of Kalapur as a whole. He had his faults, of course, and was rather too naive about the intentions of the advancing Japanese, but he was still a genuine nationalist leader whose Buddhism was tinged with socialism.

'Naturally enough all this did not endear him to the settler class, any more than it did to the British imperialists in India who for many years had controlled our foreign relations through their local agents – men like Mr Hoadley and his predecessors. So the lama's mysterious disappearance in 1944 was really most convenient to all these people, as well as to the Indian successors of the Raj a few years later. And you can understand why many people here still think the British were responsible for bringing down his plane.'

'And were they responsible?' Timothy managed to put in.

'No, I don't think so. Anyway, as you know, a long and disturbed period followed his disappearance and it was not until 1948 that the leaders of the pro-settler group, acting with powerful Indian support, finally succeeded in having the two-year old boy they had recognised as the newly incarnated Shar Lama formally installed in the palace in Himjin. But, of course, this did not settle the issue: far from it! On the one side, the adherents of the new Shar Lama categorically asserted that the old lama's plane had crashed soon after leaving Himjin, probably somewhere in the wild regions of the Chinese border, and that he and his few companions had all been killed in that crash. On the other side were those people, mainly from the indigenous population in the eastern part of the country, who, right from the start, claimed that the old lama had not only survived the crash (they agreed there had been some kind of crash), but had lived on for several years after, hiding in the wild borderland in the guise of a religious hermit and protected by a few faithful followers. These people thus regarded the new Shar Lama as an illegitimate impostor.

'Since then, the attitudes on both sides have only hardened. The government maintains that its version of events has been independently confirmed by a special Government of India enquiry—without producing the evidence—and has issued orders that anyone spreading rumours to the contrary will be executed on the grounds that such assertions threaten the security of the Buddhist dharma in Kalapur. Meanwhile the supporters of the old lama have responded by forming their own shadowy resistance movement, operating in the inaccessible eastern border area, and over the years claiming responsibility for the occasional assassination of government supporters in that area. So though both sides call themselves Buddhists, they both threaten to kill each other rather than seek a peaceful solution to their conflict.'

'These rebels – these are the people known as the Migos?'

Taranatha nodded.

'Why are they called that?'

'Because it is said that when the old Shar Lama hid in the border regions he was at first protected by the migos or wildmen (what you, of course, call yetis) who are supposed to live there in the mountains. In fact today there is a whole folklore tradition surrounding the old Shar Lama's fate. Some people even believe that he was really the ruler of the legendary land of Shambala, who was driven away by evil forces, but whose successors will one day return with a powerful army to restore law and tranquillity.'

The Abbot abruptly broke off his discourse and began to look again in the direction of the road. 'I think,' he said, slowly getting up, 'this is a good moment to try that experiment.'

To Timothy's surprise he at once began to move forward very quietly but with gathering speed, taking care to conceal his advance from the occupant of the car by taking a roundabout route that led towards the road through a line of bushes. Within seconds he had covered the ground and was already speaking animatedly to the driver, who had obviously been taken quite unawares. It was not only the old man's remarkable swiftness that had astonished Timothy but the peculiar manner in which he had appeared to glide soundlessly over the ground. In a funny way, he was reminded of his earlier experience while waiting for the Tulku the evening before, and how that personage had contrived to come up suddenly behind him also without making a sound. There was something eerie about the way these old lamas seemed to be able to glide about with such silent speed.

'Here you are,' said Taranatha returning from his rapid excursion and carrying a small basket. 'Have one of these apples! They are called "Wonders of Kalapur" – very nice and crisp!' He looked down at Timothy with a triumphant air. 'Yes,' he continued, 'it was just as I had thought. When I reached the car that scoundrel was sitting there reading some Hindi comic, which he then did his best to conceal. So despite his dress and his local accent he is an Indian all right, almost certainly in the pay of their agent general! He probably knows English too. Nowadays there are many such people in Himjin.'

He sat down again next to Timothy, took a small knife from his purse and began to slice his apple. 'In fact,' he mused, 'this experience provides a good illustration of what I was about to tell you about the current political situation here. You see, Timothy,'—he spoke between munches while Timothy watched spell bound as the old man's single remaining front tooth delicately negotiated each bite—'to get the full picture here you have to understand two other developments of the more recent past.' His dental difficulties halted the narrative but only for a moment.

'The first of these things is the tightening of India's grip over our affairs which has taken place since the Sino-Indian war and the Chinese occupation of Tibet. To put it crudely, India fears that China has a vested interest in promoting political instability in Kalapur, and that it does so by covertly supporting the Migo guerrillas. And from my own researches, I know that the Chinese reference books regularly refer to the indigenous inhabitants of Kalapur as their "cousins", quite unlike the rather contemptuous way they treat most of the ethnic minorities within their own dominions. So because of the fear of China, India always keeps a large body of troops stationed near our border, and has recently helped to construct a road from that border to Himjin. And as you will see very soon when we ourselves meet the authorities in the capital, the Indian agent general is constantly in touch with the Shar Lama's ministers and his office is a far more important place than it was in Hoadley's time.

'And this brings me to the last point you need to grasp. Until about five years ago, the Shar Lama's government was itself divided into two main factions: those who, though they certainly represented the interests of the Tibetan settlers and their Indian supporters, did so in a moderate way and were aware of the dangers of provoking a full-scale civil war. And on the other hand, there were the extremists, led by the Shar Lama's brother, who have invented a peculiar neo-Buddhist ideology linked to a secret programme to suppress and marginalise the indigenous people and flood the country with Tibetan and Indian immigrants. Thanks to a skilful exploitation of an alleged guerrilla attempt on the life of the Shar Lama in 1985, this latter party has succeeded in ousting the moderates and now dominates the counsels of the Shar Lama. And it is these men who are planning to publish the last part of the Migoling Chronicle and related material, and you will probably meet them tomorrow.'

'But what do they hope to gain by this?' asked Timothy.

'That will probably become clear at our meeting. Their basic plan is to present and edit the documents in such a way that they would seem to corroborate their version of the events of 1944 and after. That is to say, they will try to prove beyond doubt, that the old Shar Lama definitely died in 1944. Because, as I'm sure you appreciate, any evidence that the previous ruler survived for a few years after 1944—perhaps even dying after his supposedly reincarnated successor had been born—would totally destroy the present regime's claim to legitimacy.

'I think they will call this "advancing the Spirit of Time to bring the past and the present into union"; in other words, what you and I would call rewriting history! And at the same time, they will try to convert the Shar Lama's traditional symbolic representation of the value of coming to terms with past human experience—which is really what is implied in the notion of his embodiment of the Spirit of Time—into a kind of superhuman knowledge, which allows him to declare what did or did not take place in the past with absolute authority.'

Having finished his lecture Taranatha started to gather up the baskets and cushions. As Timothy got up to help him, he realised that he had hardly moved at all while the Abbot had been talking and that his face felt quite sunburnt. Suddenly he also became aware that the Abbot was smiling at him, as if another idea had just struck him.

'I hope,' he said, 'you enjoyed my expert stalking of the driver. It's something I learnt to do when I was your age – a special technique which was developed here long ago by our monks. According to legend, they got the idea by watching the way the migos used to glide over the snow in pursuit of their prey or simply to escape their own hunters.'

The image was so diverting—as indeed had been the Abbot's whole account—that it was sometime before Timothy realised that though during their long talk Taranatha had illuminated many important things about the past and present of Kalapur, he had not actually said what he himself believed about the fate of the last Shar Lama. To that extent Timothy felt that he was no further forward and that the Spirit of Time had not yet revealed all its secrets.

PART THREE

Huma's Story

11

The room where Huma did her conservation work was on the ground floor of the Ministry of Culture and Religious Affairs, one of several dull concrete office blocks in the centre of Himjin which had been run up a few years earlier by Indian contract workers. These buildings stood out awkwardly against the traditional architecture of the city, with its harmonious painted woodwork and elegantly sloping roofs. Both outside and inside, the place was already beginning to look shabby and neglected, and the only way in which Huma could inject a little life and colour into her own workroom, was by regularly bringing in flowers and plants from the garden of the Indian family with whom she lodged on the outskirts of the city.

It had not at first been easy for her to do this, not because her landlady, Mrs Shah objected, but because since her childhood she herself had felt strongly that flowers should be left to grow and bloom in situ, undisturbed by predators, however appreciative of their freshness and beauty. Such love, her mother had impressed on her, was like the love of men for women, usually more concerned with the immediate satisfaction of their own desires than with the true interests of those they professed to care for. But in the end she had succumbed and abandoned her principles in an effort to challenge the deep dreariness that clung to her place of work. Today it was the turn of several bunches of early white magnolias to sacrifice themselves gracefully to the fulfilment of this vital objective.

Huma was only too aware that not all sacrifices were of the graceful kind. In fact, she had just been reminded of this by the arrival of another letter from her elder sister Gulshan, which beneath the surface had breathed unspoken reproaches. Guli had said how happy she was that at least one of the family was having a good break. What she really meant, of course, was how could Huma have taken herself off to Kalapur for this six months' conservation jaunt, leaving her mother and sisters behind in Lucknow, to cope by themselves with the troubles that continually beset them? Just a week ago, Guli had written, their landlord had talked ominously of how only his deep sympathy for Professor Hassan's deserted family had for so long persuaded him to keep their rent so low, even though his own interests suffered as a consequence. They all knew that this was only a prelude to another increase in his demands and, of course, to their debts.

Huma inwardly cursed her father again for having walked out on her mother when they were all so young – left them, as the English graphically put it, 'in the soup', with the largest of promises and the minimum of material help thereafter. Since then, he had only returned half a dozen times and for long intervals the only evidence they had of his continued existence had been occasional letters and postcards written from a variety of academic centres on the west coast of America.

At the same time she could not help feeling guilty at her own reactions, partly because in leaving her family now, if only for a few months, she seemed to be following in her father's footsteps, and partly because she knew that his original departure had not been entirely his own fault. Others, especially her aunts and cousins, had hinted that her mother had been too joyless and fatalistic for such a courtly and ambitious fellow. Men, they said—or rather they had not said, only assumed it—had the right ultimately to do as they liked. 'Rest is all OK,' her sister's letter had ended with the usual lazy formula: something which never failed to excite Huma's irritation.

No, despite the dingy ministry building there was no doubt in her mind that she was glad to have got away from home. Occasionally, of course, she longed for the warmth and the food (the naan here had a very peculiar taste), and she also missed her younger sister's company: Rukhsi, with her eternal Indian rap, was even more cheerfully rebellious than Huma herself. But apart from these things, she found she could cope surprisingly well in Himjin. She liked the local people, finding them for the most part intelligent, humorous and stoical-qualities she particularly admired. The women also, in some respects, seemed to enjoy a greater degree of freedom and independence than she herself was used to among her own Muslim community in Lucknow. Not only did they inherit and manage the family property, and command social respect through their craft skills, but in some cases they even had several husbands – a practice which her mother and her elder sister had predictably found especially shocking when she reported it in one of her letters.

Now, having spent over two months in Kalapur, Huma was also very conscious that the country was undergoing some kind of radical, but mysterious change in its political and religious direction. There were no independent newspapers to explain what was going on, but the resident Indians, including the diplomatic family with whom she stayed, were always passing on disturbing rumours about the Shar Lama's neo-Buddhist revolution, some of which were probably true since there were often sizeable groups of alert-looking militia stationed near the main government buildings, including the Indian agent general's office. All this lent an atmosphere of some expectancy to her life in Himjin, which contrasted strangely with the drabness of her immediate work environment.

Even her special assignment to conserve the Migoling Monastery manuscripts appeared in some ways to be connected with the new reform movement: part of the Shar Lama's effort to confer final historical legitimacy on his regime, by preserving and publishing the documents on which it apparently rested. Abbot Taranatha, the chairman of the Historical Records Commission, whom she had come to like, was nominally in charge of this project but it was clear to her that the real pressures for the completion of her conservation work were coming from the ministry and the Shar Lama's palace. Taranatha would encourage and joke with her when he was around but she could tell that his heart was not really in it.

Huma's awareness of the political and personal undercurrents in the office was constantly sharpened by the physical arrangements in her own area, which served not just as a workshop for her, but also as a kind of ante-room to the office of the Secretary to the Historical Records Commission, an anxious little man called Kelsang. On the side nearest the window and her row of flowers, she had her table and sink, a small guillotine and press, her storage cupboard for paper and chemicals and the small stove which she used when mixing flour paste or making tea. The rest of the space was occupied by chairs for the secretary's visitors. The result was that she was constantly distracted by a succession of official callers, many of whom pestered her with silly or inquisitive questions and requests under the impression that she was some sort of secretary to the secretary. She had now evolved two techniques for dealing with the more persistent of these intruders: either she would turn up the volume on her sister's rap cassettes till the visitors became visibly jittery, or she would point politely to her jar of orange bookworms (extracted from one of the older manuscripts and christened 'the Monsters of Migoling' by Abbot Taranatha), and murmur that she was engaged in some secret biological research for the ministry, which was . . . yes, just a little dangerous . . .

It was late in the afternoon and beginning to get dark when Huma completed her repair of one of the more recent Migoling documents—a property deed from the 1930s—which for some reason the ministry officials were particularly anxious for her to finish quickly. She had had a good working day with no interruptions, mainly because the secretary had been away from his office attending various outside meetings. As there was still a little time left, she decided to amuse herself by looking through the earliest section of the 'Lives of the Lamas Chronicle', which dated back to the seventeenth century.

This was the other part of her assignment but it had been impressed on her from the start that she should give higher priority to repairing and conserving the more recent loose materials connected with the chronicle. She herself found it hard to accept this ruling, for although she could not read the script of the older manuscript, apart from a few letters, she felt sure that it was of far greater historical and cultural value than the more flimsy modern papers on which the officials were so keen. Moreover, whilst some of the pages were remarkably well-preserved, others which had been badly wormed and affected by mould, were in urgent need of attention. There was also something altogether special about this archaic chronicle, so simple yet majestic, with its wide-spanned, heavy paper sheets, made from the pulp of local shrubs, and very clearly inscribed on both sides in a stately calligraphic hand. Bundles of these sheets were not bound but kept carefully pressed between two wooden boards, ornately carved with mythological or religious scenes.

The upper board she was then looking at was especially intriguing: it showed several wild-looking, naked figures dancing round together and watched by a stern group of lamas, wearing high diamond-shaped hats, flowing robes and curiously elongated boots, like skis. She liked the quaint carving very much, and unconsciously began to sing an old Indian film song: '*Mera juta hai Japani*' (My slippers are Japanese). But before reaching the next line she was suddenly aware that somebody had entered the room behind her. Expecting to see one of the ministry officials, and mentally preparing to rebuff him, she was surprised to find herself looking at a tall, thin young man, with glasses, probably English or American.

'*Meri pataloon Inglistani*' (My trousers are English) he recited the next line of the song with an amused but half-apologetic air.

'*Sar pe topi* . . . *Hindustani*' (On my head is . . . an Indian hat): Huma completed it, laughing loudly. Then recovering her caution, she said: 'You did give me a start. May I ask who you are?'

'I'm terribly sorry,' the young man replied. 'I'm Timothy Curtin from England.'

'Well,' said Huma, 'I'm Huma Hassan from India, and I'm terribly sorry too, but the secretary, whom you no doubt want to see, has been out all day.'

'Actually,' said Timothy, sounding a little sheepish, 'I'm not sure who it is I'm supposed to see. Abbot Taranatha was called away at short notice and just told his driver to leave me here for the time being.'

'Ah! Now I know who you are!' said Huma. 'The Abbot told me about you. You are going to help him translate and edit the "Migoling Chronicle", aren't you? He is counting on you a lot. He says Englishmen can seem rather quiet and ordinary, but they have the capacity to rise to great heights if challenged in the right way.'

The visitor blinked nervously. 'I suppose that Migoling Monastery must be pretty high up—about ten thousand feet above sea-level—but I hope he is not planning any special challenges for me, to test his theory.'

Huma smiled: 'Anyway,' she said, concluding that this man was harmless enough, 'you had better sit down here and wait until the Abbot or someone comes to fetch you.'

Huma went back to examining the chronicle whilst the young man lapsed into a slightly awkward silence. Like many Englishmen, it seemed that after a promising opening he had probably exhausted his conversational skills. 'Is that it?' he said eventually, 'I mean is that the chronicle that I'm supposed to work on?'

She nodded. 'Haa (Yes). Would you like to look at it? In fact,' she paused for a second, 'would you like to see if you can translate some of it?'

Timothy looked alarmed. 'Goodness!' he said, evidently facing a moment of truth. 'How am I going to feel if after coming thousands of miles to do this job, I can't understand a word of it?'

'Challenged! I expect!' said Huma cheerfully. 'But don't worry! You'll find it much easier to have a go with only me here than you would with Abbot Taranatha standing over you!'

'That's true,' said Timothy in a resigned tone.

'Here, try this bit,' said Huma, incisively lifting the top half of the stack of sheets lying on her table. 'Look, it's opened at folio eight, a lucky number in Kalapur. *Inshallah*, you will succeed!'

While Timothy poured over the manuscript, Huma busied herself in preparing her next day's work, checking through the condition of the next priority document and planning the kind of repair each page required. But all the time she was also aware that her English visitor was engaged in what looked like a desperate struggle with the palaeography of folio eight. She began to feel sorry for him: it hadn't been very kind of her to plunge him headlong into this ordeal. On the other hand, she was genuinely curious to get to know the flavour of the manuscript, and she knew that most men liked to show off their skills before women. So, if he managed to decipher at least part of the text, it would probably boost his self-confidence – a quality she intuited he appeared to lack.

Sure enough, after a tense twenty minutes or so, Timothy looked up with an air of modest triumph. 'You won't believe this,' he said excitedly, 'but this bit seems to be about three mice!'

'Not three blind ones,' Huma giggled, for like a surprising number of Indians she had been brought up on English nursery rhymes.

'Not exactly,' said Timothy. 'It seems that through somebody's curse, three lamas living near the Indian border were turned into mice, and the spell could only be broken if a new monastery was built nearby. Eventually some obliging local ruler did build a monastery, and the mice at once changed back into lamas.'

'That's very clever of you to make all that out,' said Huma, impressed and happy at his success. 'I never imagined that this solemn-looking chronicle would contain such lovely stories. I thought it would be all about prayers and monastic revenues.'

'It seems to be about them too.' Timothy grinned back at her.

'Anyway,' said Huma, 'it only goes to show that our Abbot was right about Englishmen: you do rise to occasions!'

'If challenged in the right way,' said Timothy, looking chivalrously at her. It was now her turn to be silent for a moment. She was used to nawabi-style compliments, but this felt slightly different. Then suddenly recalling her surprise when, coming through the door, he had joined in her old song, she enquired how he had come to know it. He explained that he had spent six months in Delhi at the university, so knew India quite well and had developed a liking for very old film songs.

Huma began to laugh again. 'I'm going to tell my great uncle about you,' she said. 'He goes to London quite often and he is always saying rude things about the English nowadays, how they are nothing like the sahibs he used to know: how they used to take away our wealth and freedom, but now they only take away our curries!'

'Well,' said Timothy hesitantly, 'I'm also very fond of curries, especially when they are home-cooked.' She noticed that he coloured slightly as he said this, as if remembering some personal experience.

'I am sorry Dr Curtin but I am not equipped to provide curries here: I wish I was . . . But I can offer you a cup of tea after your brilliant success, especially as the Abbot seems to have forgotten about you.' Then, feeling she was beginning to sound like her mother, she added: 'though it may taste a little like flour paste!'

When she had made the tea they sat down together at her work table. Despite his occasional moments of diffidence, she found him very easy to talk to, and began to describe her experiences with various officials in Kalapur. 'You know,' she said, 'I wish someone would turn Lama Jaya Kumara into a mouse.'

They soon established that their respective impressions of LJK more or less coincided, though Timothy, rather to Huma's annoyance, seemed reluctant to condemn him entirely on the basis of only one encounter. She pointed out that her own unfavourable opinion was based on a number of meetings she had had with him since her arrival in Himjin. Invariably, she said, he had either been very nosy, wanting to know about her family and her father in particular, or plain disapproving, implying that as a good Muslim girl she should not be gallivanting round the Himalayas by herself but helping her mother at home in Lucknow.

'Perhaps it's because of his Indian origin,' Timothy suggested, teasingly. 'He feels protective of you in this alien world.'

'He may be originally Indian,' she retorted, 'but he also claims to be one of the chief pillars of the Shar Lama's new reform movement here through that extraordinary spiritual pedigree he is always boasting about. But he has no business criticising me . . . Anyway,' she added cryptically, 'that pedigree of his is going to be his undoing. He may be clever but he has one fatal weakness: conceit!'

'What do you mean exactly?' asked Timothy, clearly intrigued.

She laughed. 'You'll find out tomorrow at the meeting of the Records Commission. The Abbot has asked me to come, so I'm sure that, as the resident western expert, you will also be invited.'

At this point Huma glanced at her watch. '*Bapre!*' she said. 'It's already five-thirty. I had no idea it was so late. I'm afraid it looks as if they have definitely forgotten about you, Dr Curtin. But it doesn't matter. If you are staying at the Himjin Himalayan hotel (Timothy nodded), I can walk part of the way with you. It's not far.' He happily agreed to this suggestion, and as they prepared to go, remembered another old Indian film song: '*Aao hamare hotel main*' (Come to our hotel), he chanted. '*Khanna khao garam garam*' (Eat the food piping hot!), said Huma.

12

Not for the first time in her working life, Huma found herself the only woman at the meeting, sitting with eight men round the long table in the secretary's office, and waiting for the arrival of a ninth, the Minister for Culture and Religious Affairs. All the regular members of the Records Commission were already there: Mr Kelsang, Lama Jaya Kumara and Abbot Taranatha, as well as two officials she had not seen before, and the specially invited foreign advisers: Timothy Curtin and an elderly Japanese professor. They all sat there silently waiting, not in a relaxed way but decidedly on edge, or so it seemed to her. The room itself did not help: it was cold and drably furnished, with no decoration apart from an austere silver figurine of Maitreya Buddha on the secretary's desk, and on the opposite wall a large framed photograph of the Shar Lama, a mournful looking, thin-faced man with heavy spectacles, who was seldom seen in public.

Earlier on it had seemed touch and go whether Huma was actually going to be allowed to attend the meeting after all. Originally it had been the Abbot who had informally told her a couple of weeks back that she should certainly come, and might even be asked to make a statement about the age of the document referred to the commission by Lama Jaya at the previous meeting. No formal invitation had been issued by the secretary but she had assumed it would probably arrive at the last minute. She had accordingly thought carefully about what she would say at the meeting about the lama's document, and that morning in honour of the occasion, had decided to discard her usual garb-jeans, sweater and overall – in favour of an elegant light green salwar kameez. Contrary to her usual style, she had also applied some pink lipstick; she was not sure why, except that it helped her feel more bright and confident, and better able to face LJK.

When she had reached the office around nine there seemed little point in getting down to serious work as the meeting was scheduled for nine-thirty. So she had been pottering around for a few minutes, watering her plants with the jug she had brought from home, when Mr Kelsang arrived. Instead of greeting her politely as he normally did, he seemed oddly disconcerted to see her standing there with her jug, and with only a slight nod had rushed past into his office.

'*Kya baat hai*?' (What's the matter?), she thought. Has he decided not to invite me after all and is too embarrassed to say so? Or is he just more nervous than usual because his boss, the minister, is coming?

One by one the others had also arrived, as she sat there awkwardly by the window. Lama Jaya had ignored her totally; the Japanese professor seemed too bemused to notice her, whilst even Abbot Taranatha, looking very absent-minded, could scarcely manage a toothy grin. Only Timothy, who followed behind him, seemed happy to see her. '*As salam alaikum*,' he said in a way that somehow combined formality with a touch of familiarity.

What to do? She sat there feeling foolish and indecisive. The door to the secretary's office was not exactly shut but pulled to, and although she had learnt to stand up for her rights in a man's world, she felt she could not just barge in and sit down without being asked. It really was up to Mr Kelsang to invite her in, but so far he had said nothing and in his present mood, for whatever reason, was hardly likely to do so now. Besides it was already past nine-thirty, and the minister would presumably be here soon. She was just on the point of deciding to give up, when LJK of all people appeared at the door, beckoning to her. 'Please come in, Miss Hassan,' he said with a forced joviality. 'We are looking forward to your report on my manuscript.'

Relieved of her own dilemma, Huma was now able to sit back and observe the tensions of those around her. The basic scene was only too familiar from her experiences of Indian bureaucracy: it was a question of waiting for the 'bara sahib' – something that never failed to put a damper on the spirits of those compelled to endure it. And, of course, the bigger the boss, the longer would be the wait, and the more uncomfortable they would all become. Also, since the minister was indeed a very potent force in the country, a senior lama and the brother of the Shar Lama himself, she suspected that the atmosphere would only worsen when he finally arrived, with the secretary and other officials rendered tongue-tied, their initiative sapped by the overwhelming presence of their powerful superior. It was true that with Abbot Taranatha here, one could never be sure what might happen, but looking across the table, he seemed unusually old and frail this morning, his eyes screwed up as if in another world.

To Huma's dismay, it appeared as if the subdued atmosphere had even infected Timothy Curtin, who sat there mute like the rest of them, with his eyes lowered. Feeling that she had somehow helped him on the previous evening to face the responsibilities that had brought him here, she hoped he would be able to stand up for himself now if any of the high officials turned nasty. She noticed that he was growing a beard, and the skin on his face was blotchy and peeling badly, evidently the result of sitting too long in the easily underestimated Kalapur sun. It all gave him a rather forlorn, out-of-place look – like a bashful dervish who had somehow strayed onto a government committee. South Asian governments, she reflected, were full of such incongruous types: poets who sat on revenue boards and mystic policemen.

Lama Jaya was the first to break the collective silence. Turning to the secretary, who sat beside him, he began to describe very loudly in English, making sure everyone else heard, how he had recently discovered yet another manuscript account of his august spiritual ancestor, the lama who had helped Padmasambhava. According to this account, so he claimed, Guru Rinpoche had once been asked by a certain king who his teachers were, and had replied: 'Lama Jaya was my first teacher. And Lama Jaya was my second teacher' – a line which he kept repeating contentedly. Mr Kelsang listened very stiffly and respectfully, politely repeating the key phrase in the story, whilst covering his mouth with his hand for fear of defiling the air in front of the Tulku. At the same time, Huma was amused to see that the latter's projection of high dignity was somewhat diminished by his having to fiddle continuously with the arm of his chair, which had become loose and wobbly. Noticing the Tulku's difficulty, Mr Kelsang had jumped up to help him fix it, ending up by kneeling on the floor beside him in an effort to force the arm firmly back into its socket.

He was still down there when the door was suddenly flung open to admit the minister, accompanied by an armed guard. Faced with this more potent apparition, Mr Kelsang immediately slid forward on to the floor in full length prostration, with the result that the minister, who hadn't noticed him, barely avoided treading hard on his back as he swept across the room to his place of honour. Instead of showing concern, he looked rather angry as Mr Kelsang scrambled nervously back into his chair and began shuffling his papers.

'May the Lord Maitreya come!' said the minister formally inaugurating the meeting in a harsh voice that reminded Huma of the ever-present Himalayan crows. A confused murmur greeted his words. Most people round the table were still startled by the secretary's narrow escape.

'In opening this sixth meeting of the Historical Records Commission,' the minister wasted no time in getting down to business, 'it is my pleasure to welcome our two distinguished foreign advisers, Professor Minamoto from Japan and Dr Curtains from UK. I hope you will both enjoy your stay here, and I look forward to meeting you more informally at the special reception to be held tomorrow evening at the Himalayan Hotel.'

Huma looked across to see if Timothy had registered the peculiar rendering of his name but he still seemed to be in a withdrawn state. In some ways, she thought, Curtains is quite a good name for him.

The minister meanwhile had paused to consult Abbot Taranatha before continuing. 'It has been suggested that as a courtesy to our foreign guests, we should try to use English throughout this meeting. So unless there are any objections'—there weren't any—'we shall stick to English.' Huma next saw that LJK was leaning forward to tell the minister something. 'Ah, yes!' said the latter. 'We must also welcome Miss Hassan, our project conservator.'

As she smiled back sweetly, Huma studied the minister carefully: she had never seen him so close up. She particularly noted the way he had rapidly recovered from the undignified episode with Mr Kelsang, and was evidently adept at projecting an urbane image at the world. At the same time, there was a peculiar brisk coolness about his manner which, to her, simultaneously seemed to cover up and yet reveal an underlying spirit of intolerance. He was clearly not the kind of person to cross, if you could possibly avoid it, and yet she felt strangely tempted to find an opportunity to induce him to drop his diplomatic mask.

'I see,' said the minister, 'that the first item on our agenda calls for a technical statement from Miss Hassan, but before I ask her to speak,

I will call on the Venerable Rinpoche Lama Jaya Kumara to remind us of the details of the manuscript he has asked us to examine.'

LJK then spoke with his customary confidence, explaining how at the last meeting of the Commission he had presented a newly-found manuscript genealogy of his spiritual lineage, which appeared to be of great antiquity – so much so that apart from its personal value to him as the present representative of the line, it seemed only proper to offer the document to the new national museum and archive which the commission had been charged to establish. As a formality, he added—and at Abbot Taranatha's specific request—the commission had agreed that the age and authenticity of the manuscript should first be confirmed by Miss Hassan, the conservator working on the chronicle project.

As he finished, the minister and all the men around the table turned expectantly to Huma. Although she had prepared herself for this moment, she had not expected it to come so soon, or so abruptly. Why on earth had Lama Jaya not come and spoken to her quietly beforehand about the results of her tests? The obvious explanation was that he was far too proud and confident to do so. Well, though he certainly irritated her, she had not deliberately set out to humiliate him in public with her analysis of his precious document. But what else could she do but apply the chemical tests? All the male eyes were fixed on her; she could not falter now.

'I have carried out two tests on this document,' she said calmly and clinically, 'to determine whether the paper contains any alum or lignum such as is found in modern, especially twentieth-century paper manufactured in India . . . but not of course in earlier paper made here in Kalapur. The results are positive and I can confirm, with ninety-five per cent certainty, that the document is written on modern Indian paper.' She felt it sounded better to put it like this, rather than say bluntly that the genealogy was not old and almost certainly a forgery. And, indeed, most people round the table did not seem to grasp the point immediately. But, of course, Lama Jaya did.

'But it looks so old!' he stammered. Then, recovering his self-possession, he began to address his colleagues in a rising crescendo. 'How can this girl be so sure? . . . This manuscript was found in a sacred spot near the ancient Migoling Monastery.' Under the weight of his growing indignation, the whole arm finally detached itself from the rest of his chair and fell to the floor with a crash, watched in horrified amazement by Huma and the other members. Mr Kelsang leapt up and flew to the ante-room in search of another chair. The minister however kept his cool – indeed, Huma thought she detected a touch of suppressed mirth in his expression as he firmly took charge of the situation.

'Rinpoche,' he addressed the lama respectfully. 'I think we must conclude from Miss Hassan's report that your document is probably a later copy of some original and far more ancient manuscript which has not yet come to light. With Maitreya's blessing, I am sure you will soon find it.'

'May Lord Maitreya come!' murmured a breathless Mr Kelsang, carrying a whole new chair for the Tulku. That one will never forgive me for this, thought Huma.

'We now come to the main business for today's meeting: finalising the text and introduction for the Commission's publication dealing with the life of the late Shar Lama.' As the minister's rasping voice announced the new topic, Huma could sense that the state of shock and confusion engendered by Lama Jaya's sudden discomfiture had already given way to a new air of expectancy. And feeling herself that some puzzling aspects of her own work might now get clarified, she listened carefully to what the minister was saying.

He began by summarising the history of the project: how it had first been decided some five years ago to publish materials for the late Shar Lama's reign as the first stage in a long-term plan to produce a scholarly edition of the whole Migoling chronicle – perhaps the most important single source for the history of the country. But whereas in the case of the earlier lamas, the chronicle had provided an interpretative narrative of their lives based on an accumulation of contemporary evidence, for the Tenth Shar Lama there was no such narrative in existence, due to the disturbances that followed his death and the long illness of the monk originally appointed to compile it. Fortunately, however, there was at least the collection of documents and notes assembled at Migoling during the late lama's reign upon which the chronicle entries would have been based, and it was this material, supplemented by other archives and testimony subsequently gathered in, that the commission had decided to edit and publish, along with a historical introduction written by its chairman, Abbot Taranatha. Huma noticed that at the mention of his name the latter for the first time opened his eyes and gazed blankly at the minister.

Amongst the supplementary materials for inclusion in the publication, the minister singled out three items of exceptional interest for the light they threw on the Shar Lama's last days. The first was a copy of a secret telegram sent by the British agent in Himjin to New Delhi reporting the Lama's sudden disappearance for an unknown destination; this had been unearthed from the agent general's own archives. The second important piece of evidence consisted of an interview with the former Shar Lama's private secretary, now an old monk of over ninety, who testified that during the last few days before his mysterious departure, the lama had several times spoken of soon starting a new life – obviously a clear reference, said the minister, to his foreknowledge of his impending death and reincarnation. Finally, the minister was pleased to announce that the Indian government had now given permission for the commission to reproduce the full text of their previously classified report on the lama's disappearance and death – a masterly assessment of the key evidence.

'To complete our review of the material for publication, I will now ask our guest, Professor Minamoto, whether any more relevant documents have come to light in Japan.'

'Your Excellency, Venerable Lamas and friends,' Professor Minamoto spoke in a gentle and hesitant whisper which contrasted strangely with the powerful decibels commanded by the minister and Lama Jaya. Yet to Huma it seemed for the first time she was hearing a truthful voice.

'No more historical documents about the Tenth Shar Lama,' he said, 'have been found in Japanese archives, so I regret there is nothing more I can add to the commission's project. But I have been asked by my government to take this opportunity to say we are very sorry for the suffering and dislocation which some of our forces inflicted on the people of this region during the Second World War.'

Professor Minamoto paused and the men around the table smiled awkwardly. 'For a long time,' he continued in a voice that was scarcely audible, 'I hesitated to convey this message, since my own father died fighting for the Japanese army not far from here, and I know that the consequences of suffering and loss cannot be washed away by a bland apology. Also, as a Buddhist, I am conscious that the effective moral continuity of the Japanese state, presupposed by this message, is even more uncertain than the links that are said to hold together our personal identities over time. But in the end I decided to make the statement I had been asked to make, because . . . because it is at least one of compassion, which is the only true link between past, present and future . . . between you and me.'

Two small tears slipped down the professor's face, and to Huma it seemed that the sound of his words hung there for a moment in the air before disappearing into emptiness.

'Thank you,' said the minister briskly, less affected by the gentle message than concerned with checking that Mr Kelsang, who had been writing frantically throughout, had managed to get it down correctly. '*Yappo mindoo!*' he said angrily in Tibetan, as he spotted a mistake in the secretary's notes. 'He said it is compassion, not passion, that is the only true link between me and you. Please pay more attention!'

Huma guessed that it would now be Timothy's turn to be interrogated, and she saw from his anxious expression that he also realised it. She smiled an encouraging smile but he failed to see her.

'Dr Curtains,' said the minister, 'we all know that the British took a close interest in the Tenth Shar Lama's mysterious flight and disappearance. I wonder if you could offer us any further evidence from your side.'

'No,' Timothy replied, in a voice almost as small as Professor Minamoto's. 'I'm afraid I can't. Certainly no more documents have been released by the government.' He seemed uncertain whether to go on, before adding: 'and Mr Arthur Hoadley has also personally assured me that the British authorities in India had no involvement in his disappearance and presumed death.'

A buzz of interest rippled round the table: Huma knew that it was widely believed by many people in Kalapur that the British must have had a hand in bringing down the lama's plane as it flew towards its secret destination.

'Come now, Dr Curtin,' said the minister, almost leering at Timothy. 'Don't be shy. You are an experienced historian who has studied this problem. What do you personally believe happened to the lama?' Timothy coloured but remained silent. Huma could tell that he was deeply troubled, before help came from an unexpected quarter.

'I don't think we should press our British guest for his personal opinion on this issue,' boomed Lama Jaya.

The minister shrugged. 'You are right, Rinpoche,' he deferred. 'It's just that this is a matter that deeply concerns our country. But . . . yes you are right. I was perhaps being too inquisitive.'

'But now,' he said, turning rather formally from Timothy to Taranatha, 'it only remains for me to request the chairman of the Records Commission, Abbot Taranatha, to complete his study of the materials for the Tenth Shar Lama's reign, and to submit the historical introduction which will accompany and interpret those documents. We look forward, Venerable Lama, to a final account of these momentous events.'

The Abbot took his time before replying to this challenge, for Huma could tell that, despite the minister's respectful approach, it was a definite challenge. But when Taranatha did eventually speak it was as if he was thinking out loud and talking to himself.

'Let us be clear about what the commission is asking,' he said dryly. 'It is asking me to confirm what it already believes about the Shar Lama's life and death, particularly his death. It is asking me to produce a comprehensive account of his reign partly on the basis of an assortment of minor legal documents preserved at Migoling, and, partly from various odd supplementary materials – an isolated and inconclusive British agency telegram of uncertain provenance . . . the uncorroborated and incoherent reminiscences of a semi-senile monk . . . and the report of an interested foreign government deeply involved in the immediate aftermath of the events it purports to uncover. Am I to be a historian or just a story-teller?'

Several dark shadows appeared to pass rapidly across the minister's face, but he retained his air of formal politeness. 'We have entrusted this very difficult but important national task to you, Your Reverence, precisely because you are our foremost historian. As for the rest, as the members of the commission know, we have already thoroughly discussed and dealt with the points you have raised on several previous occasions. Five years have now passed since the commission was first asked to complete this project, in time for the fiftieth anniversary of the Eleventh Shar Lama's accession. We cannot delay any longer.'

Well, thought Huma, that's it. Taranatha is not going to be allowed to escape his task, though she admired his courage in standing up to the minister. Meanwhile the latter, still keeping his cool, was formally asking if there any more questions before the meeting was closed. Suddenly Huma saw the chance for which she had been looking.

'I hope you will excuse me as an ignorant outsider for asking what is probably a very silly question,' she looked innocently at the minister. 'But when and where did the late Shar Lama die?'

The room at once became very quiet, and even the Abbot seemed to come out of his trance. The minister gave her a sickly smile.

'In the deep sense,' he began quietly, 'the Shar Lama is the embodiment of the Spirit of Time in the bodhisattva form, and therefore never dies but eternally dispenses compassion and wisdom, preparing the way for the advent of Maitreya. But in this phenomenal world of our experience,' his voice began to rise, 'the Tenth Incarnation of that power died in an air-crash over the Eastern Himalayas in June 1944, to be reincarnated two years later in the present Shar Lama.'

Now finally dropping his diplomatic mask, he stood up and stretched his arms out wide like a giant crow. 'But to those who choose to remain ignorant of these events,' he rasped, 'or worse still deny them, the Spirit of Time presents another and terrifying aspect, as it moves forward to crush them!'

'The minister is of course speaking metaphorically,' said Lama Jaya hastily. But Huma, and she guessed the others, were left in no real doubts about his meaning.

13

'Enjoy yourself but don't stay out too late!'

Huma found it hard to cope with Mrs Shah's moderately maternal attitude towards her. It was not so flagrantly bossy as to justify a full-scale counter-attack but nor was it so modest in its assumptions about their relations as to be comfortably ignored. The general effect now was to take the wind out of her sails as she stood in the hall of Mrs Shah's bungalow, defiantly wound up in the unfamiliar patterns and textures of the kira, the tube-like Kalapuri skirt and the short jacket she had chosen to wear for the minister's reception. She knew that Mrs Shah would find her choice of dress bizarre; for her it would be inconceivable not to appear for such an occasion in either a sari or a salwar kameez. She had not actually voiced her disapproval but the dynamics of her expression when she first caught sight of Huma made words redundant. Perhaps her decision to keep quiet had something to do with a desire not to lose face since her husband, a middle-ranking accountant in the agent general's office, had not been considered important enough by the government authorities to merit an invitation.

Huma said goodbye to Mrs Shah and set out in search of a motor rickshaw to take her to the Himalayan Hotel. At six-thirty it was already quite dark but fortunately she spotted one hovering near the entrance to the Indian residential colony.

'*Gava drogi yin?*' (Where are you going?), asked the Kalapuri driver in Tibetan, apparently not realising she was Indian. The unexpected success of her disguise exhilarated her, coming as it did after Mrs Shah's 'put-down' look and maternal admonishment. She sat back and enjoyed the sensation as the shaky little vehicle bumped and twisted its way towards the city centre.

At the same time Huma did not feel quite happy about her own motives. In some ways it was perhaps, rather adolescent to try to pretend she was something other than what she really was: a middle-class Indian Muslim girl from Lucknow. But it was not just that. Behind it lay all her growing dislike of the role that her fellow countrymen and women were playing in Kalapur, and the way they lent support for the Shar Lama's repressive regime. She had had a nice talk about this with her new friend Timothy after yesterday's meeting, but he had been whisked away by the Abbot before they had really finished. Anyway he had promised to be there at the reception this evening and she looked forward to seeing him again. No, she said firmly to herself, her decision to don local dress was not just a piece of youthful bravado or play-acting, it was a political statement as well! *Mashallah*, she giggled, if the clothes don't make you feel good, the right words certainly do!

The Himalayan Hotel was the only western-style luxury hotel in Himjin, and for Huma it had been a case of hate at first sight. All that fancy woodwork and those wide whitewashed walls – a phoney version of the Shar Lama's palace designed to present a chic traditional facade for a lifestyle that was totally alien to the indigenous people! She knew too that it was Indian-owned – part of a chain of similar places beginning to skirt the southern fringes of some future Himalayan theme-park.

An Indian flunkey also dressed in Kalapuri costume, bowed extravagantly as she passed through the main entrance. The irony of her own attire gave her a nasty jolt.

Once inside the hotel, she had to admit that the atmosphere had a pleasantly soothing effect. The quiet music, a subtle commercial blend of Indian and Himalayan styles, combined with the subdued lighting of the scarlet and gold décor—deliberately evoking the rich interior of a monastic temple—all helped to put Mrs Shah and the Indian doorman behind her. The several touristic venues, the Tenzing Bar and the Yeti Inn, were already beginning to fill up as she made her way towards the Potala Room where the reception was being held.

On entering, she found herself part of a queue of people waiting to be received by the Minister of Culture and Religious Affairs himself. Mr Kelsang had the unenviable task of effecting the introductions and making sure that no one lingered too long. This he characteristically accomplished with a range of jerky hand movements and much nervous whispering in the minister's ear. When it came to her turn it seemed at first that both men failed to realise who she was, before the minister himself at last gave her a sidelong look of recognition. 'Yes, of course, Miss Hassan,' he rasped quietly. 'And how much longer do you plan to stay in Kalapur?'

'About two more months, according to my contract,' said Huma trying to smile lightly.

'Good!' said the minister, leaving Huma uncertain whether his approval related to the length of her stay or the not-too-distant prospect of her departure – probably the latter, since he had certainly had sufficient time to reflect on the undesirable effects of the undiplomatic outburst into which her apparently innocent enquiry had led him at yesterday's meeting.

The large reception area was already occupied by the usual crowd who attended these functions: Indian diplomats in smart creamy jackets, their wives immaculately turned out in fashionable silk saris; small clusters of Kalapuri women in their long harmonious kiras, chatting amicably together, in marked contrast to their sober-suited husbands, most of whom either stood around awkwardly by themselves or gathered to pay court to one or other of the distinguished lamas who had consented to grace the occasion. Though several faces were familiar to Huma, there was nobody whom she knew well, no signs yet of Timothy or Taranatha, and fortunately no sign of Lama Jaya Kumara either.

'*Keerang kanay ray?*' (Where do you come from?), asked a plump grandmotherly figure hovering before her in a cloud of smoke, like a benevolent genie.

'India,' Huma replied, aware that with her inadequate grasp of Tibetan she could hardly hope to sustain her Kalapuri disguise.

'My dear,' cried the old lady joyfully, and at once breaking into English. 'I am so happy to meet you. You are the first Indian girl I have ever seen who deigns to wear our national dress.'

Huma now began to take in the human aspects of the apparition: the broadly smiling Mongolian features, the layers of diaphanous silk garments that enveloped her figure like a balloon, the small capable hand clutching firmly at a smoking cheroot.

'Please don't misunderstand me,' the old lady went on. 'I love Indian people, and India is my second home, but the women who come here do tend to be a rather conservative lot!' She gestured eloquently towards a nearby group of matrons in saris.

'You don't have to apologise,' said Huma. 'I know exactly what you mean.'

For a moment the old lady's attention seemed to wander, till Huma realised that she was actually in the process of attracting the attention of a waiter carrying drinks. 'I'm going to have a large whisky,' she announced. 'Will you have the same, my dear?'

Huma agreed. 'After all,' she found herself saying, 'tonight I'm supposed to be an emancipated woman of Kalapur, not a Muslim girl from India.'

'Bravo!' said the balloon lady, taking another puff at her cheroot. 'But I am sorry to tell you that the women here are not all as free as you may have imagined. For instance, if you go out to any of the villages near here, they will tell you—I mean women as well as men—that it takes a woman nine lives before she can be born as a man. And to tell the truth,' she came closer to Huma, 'as long as we are ruled by this bunch of India-backed celibate lamas, nothing much is going to be done for women . . . And it is really such a waste!' She turned towards a cluster of Kalapuri women. 'After all we are so much more balanced than men are!'

Huma found the old lady so warm and convivial that she had no hesitation about sharing her own personal feelings. 'The trouble with me is,' she said, 'that although I have no sympathy with our male oppressors, I have an almost equal lack of sympathy for the women who just sit down and accept that oppression as a fact of nature or a matter of faith, or—worse still—actively collude in it.'

'That's no good in this part of the world,' the older woman countered. 'That way you will end up having to fight both sexes!' She puffed reflectively at her cheroot. 'Of course, there are other possible solutions to your dilemma . . . You could try to sidestep it by living in the West – the alleged happy home of emancipated women. Or you could try to transcend it by following our Buddhist dharma, the way of meditation and religion. But I can tell you that both these paths are full of risks. If you go to the West, you may suffer rejection and disillusionment. And if you stay here and meditate, you may get nowhere fast, simply because, as our teachers tell us, you are starting out on your journey without compassion.' She began to laugh again. 'In any case I'm afraid the lamas here are not what they used to be. Any moment now, I expect they will declare that in future Lord Maitreya's heaven is only open to them and their born-again male cronies!'

'You must tell me who you are,' said Huma. 'I've never met anyone like you here!'

'You can call me Deche Dekyi, if you like.'

'You are really a princess then! I might have guessed.'

'Not exactly,' said the old lady, 'but since I am somehow descended from the old Buddhist kings of Kalapur, people here like to call me that. It's all rather exaggerated really, but it comes in quite useful at times. You see, I'm almost the only person left in Kalapur who can tell the bastards who rule us what I think of them and their policies!'

At this point Princess Dekyi began to look over Huma's shoulder.

'My dear,' she said, 'I can see a young man over there who has been trying to catch your eye for the past five minutes. So I'd better stop monopolising you and go and pay my customary "respects" to that demon minister. So goodbye Huma – it is Huma isn't it? And if you ever need my help, here is my card, or you can ask Abbot Taranatha where to find me.'

Huma watched as the small balloon-like figure bobbed and puffed its way through the encircling crowds – past the lines of saris, and in between the kiras, until, beyond the ancient lamas in their maroon robes, she disappeared from view. Huma finished her whisky, now feeling rather self-conscious. Had the Princess really been there talking to her? Or was she the product of her own imagination, perhaps even her wish-fulfilment? In this country, she thought, you could never be quite sure.

14

As she lost sight of the Princess, Huma turned eagerly towards Timothy whom she knew had been waiting patiently for her to finish her conversation with the exotic balloon lady. But to her disappointment, Timothy himself had by now been caught up in an animated talk with a middle-aged American, almost certainly some kind of diplomat, and it was some minutes before he succeeded in extricating himself and finally made his way across the crowded room to join her.

'Huma, I'm really sorry we couldn't finish our talk yesterday.' Timothy's apologetic tones sounded rather unexciting to Huma after her bracing dialogue with Princess Dekyi, and she also sensed within herself some slight resentment towards him for allowing himself to get distracted when she had been bursting to tell him about the Princess. He, of course, was totally oblivious of all this, and naturally wanted to tell her about what had happened to him the day before.

'The trouble was that the Abbot wouldn't stop talking. It was two hours before I got away and you had disappeared by then. I never imagined that Taranatha could get into such a state.'

'I'm not surprised,' said Huma. 'I mean that one'—she gestured towards the Shar Lama's brother, still suavely greeting his guests—'that one was virtually threatening to have him eliminated unless he produces the history they want.'

'Yes, that's right.' Timothy smiled. 'Anyway it was terrific the way you got him to reveal his true colours. At least we now know what we are up against.'

'Did the Abbot say what he was going to do?'

'Not really. Most of the time he was just telling me how he got landed with the job of writing the history. It seems they were very crafty about it. At first they just asked him to edit the chronicle, beginning with those beautiful early volumes you are so fond of. But then they gradually made it clear that he must start at the end, with the last Shar Lama's reign. For a while he still thought he would be able to control the project and keep it on an objective historical basis. But they soon made it obvious that they were not interested in that sort of history. What they wanted was a carefully doctored narrative which would suppress all references to doubts about the old Shar Lama's death, and bolster their own legitimacy.

'Now he says that if he doesn't produce the goods on time they will almost certainly sack him from his position in the monastery, just as they are apparently getting rid of other abbots and key officials who refuse to cooperate.'

Timothy paused. 'And the awful part of it is that he seems to think I can somehow help him to get out of this mess!'

'That's because he has these strange ideas about Englishmen rising to challenges,' said Huma grinning. 'Anyway,' she added, suddenly recalling her previous encounter: 'who says you won't succeed with me to help you – me and my new friend Princess Dekyi!'

'Was she that extraordinary woman you were just talking to?' Timothy asked.

'Excuse me for interrupting,' said a tall Indian diplomat confidently addressing himself directly to Huma. 'But aren't you Professor Ali Hassan's daughter?'

Although she had not spoken to him before, she at once recognised Ahmed Sherwani, the Indian Agent General. But she didn't like the way he had just barged in, so instead of answering his question immediately, she began to introduce Timothy. The agent general quickly flashed his teeth in Timothy's direction before returning to Huma.

'I think you had better ask Professor Hassan yourself,' she said. 'I haven't seen him for nearly three years!'

Mr Sherwani didn't seem to want to take in this news. 'I have been a great fan of your father's,' he continued undeterred, 'ever since I studied History with him at the university. He is such a remarkable scholar and has contributed so much to Indian history.'

'Perhaps. But he hasn't contributed much to his own family,' said Huma bleakly.

The agent general laughed awkwardly. 'Now then, don't be too hard on your father; he really is a great man in his field. And I must also tell you it was your father who first inspired me to start collecting historical manuscripts myself. My friends tell me that I now have a rather fine collection. And you can imagine that I am sometimes even tempted to work on them here, and neglect my official duties!'

'It's good to give way to temptation sometimes!' said Timothy trying to break into the conversation. This only secured him another fleeting smile from Mr Sherwani.

'In fact Miss Hassan, almost the only thing that keeps me from working on my manuscripts is their very fragile condition . . . some of them would literally fall apart if you touched them!' At last, Huma realised, he was coming to the point. 'So since I know you are a conservation expert, I was hoping you could spare some time to advise me on what to do about them.'

'Certainly,' said Huma sweetly, 'but I'm not sure it would be right to deflect you from your official duties.'

'Good, that's settled then,' said Mr Sherwani with an air of brisk satisfaction. 'Please telephone my PA for an appointment . . . Now I really must go and rejoin the minister. Goodbye. Oh! And Mr Curtains, you too should come and see me sometime. My colleagues in London have told me about your mission.'

Not very convincingly, Timothy tried to emulate the agent general's practised diplomatic smile.

'Was I sufficiently off-putting?' Huma asked as soon as Mr Sherwani had left them.

'No . . . I mean . . . yes,' said Timothy obviously confused and a little crest-fallen. 'Actually, I was rather surprised that you agreed to go and see his manuscripts. I know these sort of guys and they usually have some ulterior motives.'

'Ulterior motives? You mean he has taken a fancy to me?' There had been something disapproving, even a little possessive about Timothy's tone which had slightly disturbed Huma. 'In any case,' she added, not wishing her feelings to show, 'perhaps I also have a hidden motive: like wanting to see if Mr Sherwani knows anything that might help us rescue Taranatha.'

Whether it was the effects of the whisky, to which she was unaccustomed, or whether it was just that the room was becoming too hot and stuffy, Huma felt the need for a change of atmosph‿e. So, with Timothy trailing awkwardly behind her, she began to make for the door.

Though it was cooler and quieter in the corridor outside, she still felt slightly flustered and was conscious that Timothy also had become silent. They began to walk up the corridor not knowing what to say or where exactly they were going. Somewhere ahead the sound of music could be heard; and as they got nearer, they realised it was coming from the direction of the Yeti Inn. It was not, however, the usual hotel music but a plaintive tune from another world: 'Home

Sweet Home,' but there was also something indefinably different about the way it sounded.

Inside the dimly-lit restaurant it was at first difficult to make out what was going on. The whole place was filled with giant artificial plants like a jungle, with a clearing in the centre for an array of huge pots, containing the remains of a vast buffet dinner. Away on the far side of the room, a long trestle table was just visible at which a group of men and women were sitting, having apparently just finished their meal. As Huma and Timothy got used to the light, they saw that it was a Japanese party and that they were all singing together, accompanied softly on the harmonica by a man standing at one end of the table.

'There's no place like home . . . ' As the poignant voices rose and fell to the familiar strains of the old melody, all Huma's earlier bad feelings seemed to float away, leaving not exactly contentment but a kind of void. She noticed too that her companion seemed to be transported somewhere else as he too listened equally intently. Both strangers in a distant land, and beginning to sense the presence of threats they could scarcely comprehend, they instinctively drew closer together. 'What a sad song!' she whispered.

'Such a sad song,' said another gentle voice, 'and universal in its appeal.' Neither of them had noticed the small figure of Professor Minamoto standing in the corner behind them, partly hidden by the plants. They greeted him warmly. 'Somehow it became very popular with Japanese soldiers in Burma during Second World War,' he said. 'My father told us in his letters home that they sometimes used to sing it in the jungle at night, before going to sleep.'

'What you said yesterday about Japan was very moving,' said Timothy, now visibly revived. 'I think we all feel the same way not only about the war but about the Kalapur history project. What do you think we should do about it?'

Professor Minamoto blinked. 'Thanks to Miss Hassan,' he said, 'we now know the true situation here. The government is not seriously interested in history but in making propaganda. As historians we can no longer support their project. On the contrary, I think we have a duty to try to subvert it.'

'But how are we going to do that?' asked Timothy, surprised by Professor Minamoto's sudden firmness.

The latter considered the question for sometime before replying. 'I think it is becoming increasingly clear that the late Shar Lama did not die in that air crash in 1944, but somehow survived for a few years more in the wild border regions with China in the guise of a religious hermit.'

'That's what the Migo guerillas say, I know,' said Timothy. 'But is there any concrete proof of his survival?'

Professor Minamoto again thought for a while, apparently trying to find the right words. 'Dr Curtin, you must have heard of the Japanese monks who visited the Shar Lama in 1944.'

'Yes,' said Timothy, 'Mr Hoadley told me about them.'

'Well, one of them stayed on in Kalapur until 1948, studying at various monasteries before returning to Japan. Unfortunately he is now dead. But a few years before he died he told me in strict secrecy that while in Kalapur he met several reliable men who claimed to have seen the Shar Lama in his mountain hiding-place, as late as 1948. They said that he was then a very sick man, about to die, and that he was looked after by five faithful followers, known as the Five Protectors. Apparently he had no further desire to exercise power in the world.'

'Did the monk know what happened to those protectors?' asked Timothy.

'No, he didn't. As I said, he returned to Japan soon afterwards.'

'What do you think happened to them?' asked Huma.

'My belief is that soon after the new regime had established itself in 1948 they would have hunted down and killed most of those men, leaving perhaps one or two who escaped to set up the Migo resistance movement. By now I expect they are all dead.'

'So if the monk's story is true, it means that the present Shar Lama cannot possibly be the legitimate successor to the Tenth Shar Lama because (as the minister told us yesterday) he was born in 1946?' said Huma, wanting to get the position quite clear.

Professor Minamoto nodded.

'But where can we hope to find any hard evidence?' asked Timothy.

Again Professor Minamoto seemed uncertain how to reply or rather, how to convey the essential features of the situation. 'As you know, the Buddhist intellectuals of Kalapur,' he said finally, 'take history very seriously since they hold that in the form of the Spirit of Time it is the medium by which all beings will eventually be brought to enlightenment. So I feel sure that somewhere they will have kept a true account of these events. Besides, we have no reason to believe what the minister told us earlier about the monk deputed to write the last Shar Lama's life being prevented from doing so by illness.'

'You mean we somehow have to search for a manuscript in one of the monasteries, starting presumably with Migoling?'

'Yes, Dr Curtin,' said Minamoto, no longer hesitant or blinking, 'especially since I have been reliably informed that the late lama himself used to spend much of his time there.'

'But if there is a manuscript hidden somewhere in Migoling, surely Abbot Taranatha would know about it.'

'Perhaps, Dr Curtin. But perhaps he prefers to keep it secret for his own reasons; or perhaps he is waiting for the right time to reveal it. That is the way things are decided here. But given the mounting crisis in Kalapur, I don't think we can afford to wait for him.'

15

During the days that followed the reception Huma's life largely reverted to its regular pattern, but she also sensed that its tempo had somewhat quickened. In her workshop at the ministry she was able to make steady progress in her repair of the Migoling documents, whilst Mr Kelsang, apparently recovered from the traumatic attentions of the minister, once more acknowledged her efforts with little bursts of polite appreciation. Away from the office, Mrs Shah continued to project her special brand of maternal solicitude but this no longer seemed to grate on Huma as it had before. It was as if their silent confrontation over Huma's dress that evening had cleared the air between them, at any rate for the time being. Even the small bunches of flowers, which Mrs Shah now pressed on her more warmly, seemed to exude a more powerful scent, and create a fresher, brighter look within the dull confines of her workshop.

At last, she thought, spring is coming to enliven this cold, little country, with its strong but disturbed people. In recognition of this she gave up her previous habit of taking a rickshaw to work in the morning and instead got up earlier so that she could walk across the city, enjoying the growing variety of birdsong and the spreading signs of greenery. After a while, she also began to recognise some of the people whom she passed on the road: the women carrying their babies on their backs, and the old men standing in the sunlight near the open market, with its pungent smell of spices mixed with tobacco and petrol. Even the dark gaunt mountains which encircled and compressed the Himjin valley, began to take on a softer, greener look, their peaks hidden by the rising mist.

In this new mood of confidence she had decided to respond positively to Mr Sherwani's invitation, and had telephoned to fix an appointment. She felt she had been rather too hard on him that evening, mainly because of his ill-judged mention of her father. And on reflection it occurred to her that since he evidently belonged to her own Shia Muslim community, it was unlikely that he would try anything on, as Timothy had at first suspected.

Meanwhile Timothy, who had been temporarily installed by the Abbot in a small room at the top of Huma's building to help the old man with some translation work, had become a regular visitor to her workshop, which he flatteringly referred to as her studio. He would punctually arrive at the end of the afternoon at four-thirty, by which time Mr Kelsang had gone home and Huma herself was beginning to pack up her things. They would then leave together and go and sit in a nearby Indian café, where they could talk more freely about the mysterious politics of Kalapur, the likely fate of Taranatha, and the tantalising possibility that somewhere hidden in the monastery at Migoling, they might find a true account of what had happened to the previous Shar Lama.

In the course of these talks, she also discovered that Timothy liked to ask her all kinds of other more personal questions, mostly about her family and social life in Lucknow. Did her sister Rukhsi show any signs of being interested in boys, and if so, how did her family react? Did any of the women in the family visit the mosque or did they pray at home? Was she herself a practising Muslim and would she ever agree to an arranged marriage? Huma did not mind these questions; on the contrary she rather enjoyed them, especially listening to the answers she gave him. It was as if feeling herself the object of the sympathetic attention of an outsider, enabled her to discover new things about herself, and at the same time to rediscover a warm feeling about her life at home, something she had not expected to experience. In some ways, it also reminded her of the conversations she used to have with her cousin brother Jamil when he would bring round to their house the first good mangoes of the season, and then proceed to cross-examine her about her feminist ideas. But whereas she could tell that Jamil invariably felt threatened by her views, and wished to persuade her that in her heart of hearts she didn't really believe what she told him, Timothy's attitude seemed quite open-minded, and it was only once or twice that she half-glimpsed that his questions were not totally inspired by a spirit of friendly abstract enquiry. But far from making her feel awkward or suspicious, this perception lent a touch of underlying excitement to their meetings.

Rather to Huma's surprise, Timothy also showed himself especially sensitive to the problems she regularly faced with her father: her need for his love baffled by his constant failure to provide it, as she put it to him. Somehow Timothy seemed to grasp intuitively exactly how she felt and why, even though, as he explained to her, he had lost his own father when he was only a boy. He was also able to offer his own tentative explanation of her father's recurrent behaviour, viz., that he sounded like the sort of man who had in some sense not fully grown up, and therefore found it hard to shoulder the responsibilities that had come to him with family life. Precisely, thought Huma; why didn't I think of that? It all made her feel closer to Timothy, almost as if he were the brother she never had, or was it something else?

Today, she knew, would be his last visit before he returned to Migoling to join the Abbot, and it bothered her a little that he had not arrived at the usual time. Turning absent-mindedly over the pages of the old chronicle, she wondered whether something unexpected had happened. But in any case he could have easily come down to tell her if he was going to be delayed. The result was that when he did finally appear around five-thirty—full of apologies—she angrily blurted out: 'You're late!' In the circumstances it was a natural enough response, but somehow the accusing tone she had used—and the sense of dependency she felt it implied—made her feel more uncomfortable, and from then onwards their talk in the café was not as relaxed as it usually was, with Timothy's unnecessarily extended apologies only adding to the tension between them. She could see that he also sensed this, and was trying his best to steer the conversation back to the familiar tracks they normally both enjoyed. But this time it didn't work: whatever he said, sounded banal and artificial while her own replies became increasingly cold and monosyllabic.

When it was finally time for Timothy to leave, though she knew he was dying to kiss her, she deliberately distanced herself and awkwardly stuck out her hand for him to take. 'When will we meet again?' he asked anxiously.

'I don't know,' she said blankly, then adding in her mother's resigned voice: 'If it happens, it will happen.'

By the time Huma had walked back to her home on the other side of Himjin, she was beginning to regain her composure. The whole episode with Timothy, embarrassing and depressing though it had been at the time, had gradually made her more conscious of her growing feelings for him. Sensibility was succumbing to sense – or was it the other way round? – she wondered as she fumbled for the key to the Shahs' bungalow.

Inside, on the hall-table, she almost failed to notice the letters waiting for her. One she recognised from the envelope as the monthly newsletter of the Uttar Pradesh Working Women's Association, the other was from her sister Rukhsi. Since Rukhsi, unlike Guli, was not a regular correspondent, Huma was impatient to see what it was that had moved her to write. But conscious that Mrs Shah was hovering expectantly in the background, and suspecting that the letter might not contain the sort of news she would wish to share, Huma retreated to her own room to read it.

To her surprise, Rukhsi's letter was mostly taken up with an account of her father's unexpected visit to Lucknow some two weeks before. Apparently he had just turned up there out of the blue, and then spent hours closeted with her mother. Neither of the two daughters had been taken into their parents' confidence, and Rukhsi's suspicions had been further aroused the next day by the arrival of her *taya* and *phufi* (her father's elder brother and sister) – a sure sign of trouble, said Rukhsi darkly. All the 'old people', as she called them, had then gone into an extended secret huddle, drinking endless cups of tea and consuming vast quantities of halwa. Desperate to find out what was going on, Rukhsi had finally managed to overhear two giveaway remarks. 'It's a marvellous idea and most fortuitous,' her aunt had told her father as she was about to leave. 'And in the long run I'm sure Huma will thank you for making such excellent arrangements for her future.' And again, a little later on, Rukhsi had clearly heard her uncle say amidst loud laughter: 'The best way to get her to agree is to make her think she has chosen the man herself!'

Huma sat back on her bed shaking with emotion. It was quite obvious that the whole family, including her father, had joined forces to plot some kind of marriage for her and that they were carefully laying their plans well in advance. And all this despite the fact that she had always made it absolutely clear to all of them that she had no intention of entering an arranged marriage, and that if she ever felt like getting married it would be to someone of her own choice. How dare they conspire behind her back! And above all, how could her father, who claimed to be a liberal in social matters, allow himself to be a party to such plots?

In an effort to calm down Huma threw aside her sister's letter, and began to flick through the pages of the Working Women's newsletter. This, however, only made her feel worse, since as usual it was largely filled with stories of child brides, dowry murders, and women wedded to the Quran.

She felt like crying. Why had her father always been such a washout at the very times when she needed him most? And, worse still, why did she still retain the vain hope that one day he would act differently? It had always been the same story, as far back as she could remember.

One particular episode from the remote past now came back to taunt her. She had been about eleven at that time, attending the local convent school in Lucknow, run by the Sisters of Inordinate Mercy – a misnomer if ever there was one!

'I must not ill-treat little boys.' Sister Caritas had written the words at the top of Huma's exercise book, telling her she had to copy them out five hundred times. Only then would she be allowed to go home.

'It's not fair!' Huma had yelled back. She had repeatedly tried to explain that she had only smacked the boy because she had caught him bullying little Rukhsi in the infants' playground. But Sister Caritas had refused to listen to her side of the story.

'You are a wilful girl Huma and you must learn to do what you are told!' And with that she had locked the door of the punishment room firmly behind her.

The deep convent bell struck five. All the other children had long since gone home, but Huma had not yet written a single line. Suddenly she had heard adult voices in the corridor outside. Sister Caritas was talking to someone. She was sure it was her father, come at last to fetch her, to set her free.

'I'm afraid Huma has been rather naughty today,' Sister Caritas was telling him. 'So I had no alternative but to keep her behind for an hour. As you know, Professor Hassan, we always try to enforce strict discipline in this school in the interests of children and parents.'

Huma waited expectantly for her father's voice to be raised in protest. He must, he would tell Sister Caritas to release his daughter. But what she then heard was very different.

'I quite understand Sister,' her father said meekly. 'I will wait outside till you are ready for her to leave.'

Huma felt tears of rage and despair pouring down her face. '*Abbu! Abbu!*' she cried, hammering on the door with all her strength.

Huma dried her eyes. Her father had taken no notice of her cries then, and no doubt he would be just as reluctant to hear her protests now. It was not that he lacked eloquence or powers of persuasion when he chose to exert them, just that he always seemed to cave in when confronted by strong but narrow-minded people like Sister Caritas or his own brother and sister. Anyway, she reminded herself, she was no longer a little girl and would have to summon up those reserves of strength which her father lacked. Secretly, she suspected, he would eventually be glad if she did. She also comforted herself with the thought that her family would hardly be in a position to implement their plans before she herself returned to Lucknow, by which time she would be more than ready for them.

Security at the agent general's office was very tight. Not only was Huma thoroughly searched on entering but she was also kept waiting for another half hour while those ahead of her in the queue were obliged to complete lengthy forms stating the purpose of their visit, their father's name and profession, etc. It was strange how Indian bureaucrats everywhere liked to collect such absurd details, as if they still felt themselves to be the agents of an occupying power which—in the case of Kalapur—they were rapidly becoming. Huma wondered if it was all a hangover from the British Raj, and made a mental note to ask Timothy what he thought.

When she was eventually shown into Mr Sherwani's large office she was surprised to find him looking slightly nervous as he rose from his desk to greet her.

'It's so good of you to come, Miss Hassan . . . Really a great pleasure.' She had the impression that he was resorting to a highflown Urdu style in an effort to cover up some lingering personal anxiety. In fact, on closer observation, he struck her as considerably younger and more vulnerable than he had appeared at the reception. Perhaps his tension represented some sort of reaction to the excessive security that surrounded him; after all, she herself—a mere visitor—had already begun to feel slightly jittery while waiting outside to see him.

While Mr Sherwani busied himself ordering tea through his secretary, Huma had a quick look around his office. On one of the walls she spotted a large print of what looked like Martiniere, the famous boys' school outside Lucknow. Yes, he confirmed, it was indeed that school which he had attended as a boy . . . It had been a most happy time in his life. And after that he had gone on to Delhi University, where he had studied under Professor Hassan, and really started to learn about History. This time Huma carefully refrained from reacting sharply to the mention of her father. Mr Sherwani was not such an insensitive man as she had previously supposed; and it was hardly his fault if history was more real to her father than his own family.

As they sipped their tea, he went on to tell her about his diplomatic career. He had already had four foreign postings—in Kuwait, Cairo, Canberra and Paris—besides a spell in the research department in Delhi. Paris, he said, had been his favourite place, and when visiting Versailles had even been reminded a little of Martiniere! The only unfortunate thing about the Paris period had been that he had then had to separate from his wife. Huma noticed that his eyes registered a genuine sadness as he spoke. No, he added, by way of explanation, there were no children.

Huma began to feel restive. Why was he going into all these personal details? It was interesting in a way, but she had not come here merely to make friends with him. In an attempt to change the subject and steer the conversation on towards the real purpose of her visit, she enquired how he found his present assignment in Kalapur.

'Very interesting,' he had replied, reverting to a more guarded professional tone. 'You see, Huma, what is happening here today is very fascinating because the changes that are in motion could so easily swing the country in opposite directions. Putting it crudely . . . either the place could soon take off economically, and eventually becoming a new little Asian tiger cub—with some help from India of course—or it could retreat into factionalism and bitter religious strife.'

'From what I can see,' said Huma, trying to draw him out further, 'it's more likely to produce the second scenario.' She then described her recent meeting with the minister at which, she said, he had displayed distinctly fascist tendencies.

Mr Sherwani looked disturbed. 'If I may give you a word of advice, Huma'—there was a warning note in the way he now addressed her—'don't express your own views too publicly here, and whatever you do, don't try to interfere in their internal affairs . . . Quite apart from anything else, it could make things difficult if you wanted to stay on longer.'

Huma wondered for a second why she should want to stay on, but she let that thought pass. Instead, she decided it was high time to ask him about those fragile manuscripts he had told her about at the reception. After all, that was why he had invited her in the first place. But when she raised the matter, it seemed almost as if he had lost interest in that subject.

'But I tell you what,' he had added, suddenly brightening up. 'Why don't you come round to my official residence next weekend. You can see the manuscripts then and also meet my father and mother who are coming up from India to stay here for a few days.'

For a moment Huma didn't know how to respond. It seemed that Timothy had been right about these fellows having ulterior motives. With an effort she kept cool, and politely explained that that would not be possible as she had already been invited to visit Migoling Monastery that week by Abbot Taranatha, as part of her conservation work (she hadn't actually, but it was the only excuse she could think of on the spur of the moment).

Mr Sherwani appeared completely nonplussed by this reply. 'But Huma. . . .', he stammered. 'You must come . . . Didn't your father tell you? It's about the marriage proposal!'

PART FOUR

Debate and Stance

16

It was not apparent that the forest track was going to lead anywhere in particular. Timothy was not even certain that it was a track, since at times it seemed to lose all definition and offer little more than the possibility of some sort of forward progress through the enveloping trees. But it suited his mood to keep going, unsure whether he was following or inventing the path.

Things had not gone well since he had returned to the monastery after his stay in Himjin. Immediately on his arrival he had been told that the Abbot was seriously ill. Nobody seemed to know what exactly was wrong with him except that he was being treated by a local doctor who had forbidden all visitors. Timothy couldn't help wondering whether his condition was psychological – some sort of depression triggered by the minister's ultimatum to him to produce the official history or face the consequences. But whatever the nature of Taranatha's indisposition, it meant that Timothy had had no real work to do for the past few days since none of the documents he was supposed to study had as yet been passed over. In theory, he should have welcomed this as an opportunity to start the search for the missing manuscript chronicle which Professor Minamoto believed to be hidden somewhere in Migoling, but somehow his last meeting with Huma had taken away his zest for that adventure. It had after all been originally planned as something they would try to do together, but for reasons that he could still not quite understand, she had been so cold and distant on that last occasion that he almost felt that their earlier warm relationship had now virtually dissolved. Attempting to escape this negative memory, he tried hard to conjure up a happier image of Huma smiling across at him in the Indian café but somehow the picture wouldn't stay.

In desperation he had sought to keep up his commitment to the project by trying to enlist the help of Chana, the artist, who was still engaged in restoring the temple murals, especially the giant figure of Migo Lopen which had been earlier defaced by unknown intruders. Timothy had read somewhere that important religious texts and prophecies in Kalapur were sometimes hidden inside the heads of statues, though other accounts had suggested that they might be concealed at their base, wrapped around the wooden core of the image, the so-called tree of life. With his bold and independent spirit, and knowledge of the numerous images scattered throughout the monastery, Chana should be an almost ideal partner in this search, someone whose presence in the various shrines and temples would not arouse suspicion.

But Timothy's efforts to persuade Chana to join him in his search had not succeeded. Far from being a remover of obstacles in the spirit of his master Vajrapani, he had seemed on this occasion to take a delight in creating them, and—from the top of his ladder in the semi-darkness of the Maitreya temple—had subjected Timothy to a barrage of questions designed to demonstrate that the whole idea of a search was preposterously flawed: that there was no evidence for the existence of the manuscript other than 'that Japanese guy's hunch', that absolutely nothing was known about the monk chronicler who was supposed to have compiled it, that Timothy had been given no permission to embark on his investigations which in any case were strictly illegal and subject to severe penalties. And even if against all the odds, he were to succeed in finding the elusive manuscript, it would be promptly denounced as a forgery by the Shar Lama's men and nothing would come out of it. Timothy had felt distinctly battered, rather like he used to feel after surviving one of Gabbinger's critical onslaughts on the chapters of his thesis. 'Oh well,' he had sighed, 'I suppose you're right,' adding vaguely, 'I'd better think of something else.'

Having walked for some time through the forest, he had now become less bothered by the existence or otherwise of the path, and more conscious of the atmosphere around him. Though it was cold and quiet, there was something almost warm about the freshness and audible in the stillness. It was as if the whole forest was alert and watchful, like an elaborately realistic stage set awaiting the arrival of actors. This odd sensation became so powerful that he felt impelled to stop, to stand still for a moment and feel himself part of the landscape, ready for anything that might happen. Of course, he soon reflected, it was probably all a trick of the imagination, or more likely a natural response to a peculiar moment in the Himalayan cycle when winter was poised to slide into spring.

Finding this objective-style explanation seemed both to diminish the total experience whilst increasing his awareness of particular aspects of it. He began to see that though the prevailing tone of the forest was set by the green pine trees, there were here and there flashes of other colours: red and yellow rhododendron bushes, half-hidden between the trees, and isolated bluebells standing stiffly in the scanty grass. Even the trees, he now noticed, were far from uniform. Some were festooned with moss and lichen which gave them a ghostly, almost prehistoric look. And to his surprise there didn't seem to be many birds around – apart from an occasional pheasant rustling in the undergrowth. Nor were there any obvious signs of animal life: no squirrels or monkeys, such as he had seen earlier on the lower slopes.

But what about the famous migos? In a funny way he recognised that they had been present somewhere at the back of his mind ever since he had watched Chana working on the huge figure of Migo Lopen. Perhaps that lingering image had even informed his perception of the forest as gathered in readiness for the appearance of something or someone. Unlike his earlier explanation in terms of the climate, this new idea was somewhat disturbing. He began to hurry forward again along the supposed and tantalising path.

He had, he realised, so far failed to get to grips with those elusive creatures, failed to take them seriously. Back at the Himalayan Centre meetings they had, of course, provided a regular source of entertainment through the weekly duels of Lady Aloysia and Colonal Fox. But the idea that he would one day be standing here in this primeval forest, nervously contemplating their existence, would then have seemed totally absurd. At that time the issue had not been whether the yetis were real or not, but who would win the next round in the ultimately unwinnable contest between romantics and realists. Even during his short stay in Kalapur, the original yeti or migo question had further faded into the background, or rather it had given place to the far more pressing problem of the identity and activities of those who had appropriated the migo name in their shadowy resistance to the Shar Lama.

But suppose the original migo did actually exist – and it was hard to dismiss all the reported sightings and folklore as so much baloney or fraud. Suppose one appeared before him now, with that curiously conical head, bristling red hair, and glaring eyes, how would he respond? Would it be like meeting another human being, ineffably wild of course, but intelligent and potentially rational, like a sort of relict Neanderthaler? Or would it be more like encountering a gorilla or an orang-outang, fierce and brute-like, facing him from the other side of an unbridgeable evolutionary divide?

As he posed the question, the distinction on which it was based seemed to crumble. Animals after all could be gentle and playful, and incredibly quick-witted too, just as people were sometimes brutal and stupid, overwhelmed by fear and passion. If, for instance, he were suddenly to come across another man here in the deep forest, his first reaction would very likely be one of fear – a feeling that the man might wish to harm him. And what of his own nature? Much of the time he was deeply baffled by it – as fearful of what might happen if he gave way to his semi-conscious impulses as he was of what would not happen if he held them in check. The migo, if it appeared, had almost certainly more to fear from him, or, if not from him personally, from his fellow humans. Most probably, the creature knew that already: knew that contact with humans meant death or captivity. That was why it kept away.

The forest landscape was changing now. The path, if it was one, was rising steeply and the trees were giving way to bushes and scrub. The ground too had become stony, so that it was hard to keep up his original fast pace. A little further up, however, he could see that it began to level out. Hopefully, he might then be able to work out where he was.

To his surprise, the view that opened up through the morning mist was a familiar one. He was looking across the flat expanse of thinly grassed meadow land that led towards the escarpment where the cave hermitage lay concealed. Beyond was the Great Protector's Mountain whose summit was just visible from his room in the monastery – the so-called abode of Migo Lopen. After his musings on the migos in the forest he might have guessed that he would end up here. That was somehow the pattern in this country: events had a disconcerting habit of coming halfway to meet your thoughts. Anyway, having arrived here, he decided that he might as well cross the meadow to have another look at the cave. Who knows, perhaps the new occupant, promised by Lama Wangdi, might even have taken up residence by now. As he advanced he was aware that a herd of yaks was stretched out a hundred yards to his left, apparently preoccupied as usual with their never-ending efforts to suck some nourishment from the scanty grass.

Timothy had a natural sympathy for hermits. As a shy person himself, he believed there was much to be said in favour of an occasional retreat from the demands of the world – if only to build up sufficient strength to emerge later, better equipped to face those same demands. In that sense, of course, he realised he was not by nature a fully committed hermit – someone who enjoyed the solitary state for its own sake. His more extrovert friends had also been quick to point out the discrepancy when he had discussed the subject with them. 'You want to have it both ways,' they had said, 'to escape from people when you feel you are losing; but to return when you think you have a chance of winning!'

He had almost reached the middle of the meadow before noticing that the yaks too were on the move, gliding steadily towards the area immediately in front of him. If they got there first he would probably have to thread his way through their ranks to reach the escarpment – a prospect he preferred to avoid even though the monks at Migoling had assured him that the animals were normally docile. Instinctively, he started to jog forward, an action which, as he had simultaneously half-foreseen, only seemed to encourage the yaks to speed up their own advance. There seemed no doubt about it now: they were out to get him, or at least to surround and confront him, unless he could reach the security of the escarpment. Even there he was not sure he would be safe since despite their cumbersome bulk, the beasts seemed to be extremely sure-footed, quite capable of scrambling up the rocks after him.

With less then fifty yards to go, and the leaders of the black herd snorting close behind, he suddenly spotted the entrance to the hermitage. He sprinted the remaining distance and flung himself hard against the door. To his relief, it gave way at once – so easily that he was pitched forward onto the floor. As he lay there panting in the semi-darkness he could make out that there was a dim lamp resting on the small altar in the recesses of the cave, and that a figure was standing next to it. Slowly the figure came towards him. 'You know Timothy,' said a familiar voice, 'we have a proverb here: "Never turn your back on a begging monk or a grazing yak!"'

17

A few minutes later Taranatha and he were sitting together on the rocks outside the cave, watching the yaks grazing quietly again. Timothy found it hard to connect these placid-looking creatures with the wild, foaming monsters which had so recently pursued him. The more he thought about them, the more he began to realise that he had too quickly assumed that their intentions had been hostile rather than just inquisitive or even friendly.

He tried to put the experience out of his mind but was prevented from doing so by Taranatha for whom the episode had evoked an endless stream of reminiscences and stories reflecting in different ways on the vital part played by yaks in the country's economy and culture-stories which he recounted in a slightly sing-song traditional style which reminded Timothy of the accents he had assumed during his London lecture. Local farmers and herdsmen, he intoned, usually had a warm and close relationship with their yaks, valuing their strength and equanimity, and conversing with them in a special language, to which the yaks responded with continuous lively grunts. Folk poems too were inspired by their beauty, and especially by their long horns 'which stretched to the sky!'

Was he putting on this performance to avoid talking about all the real problems: the minister's ultimatum, his recent illness and the reasons for his presence there? Or was it, as Timothy felt more inclined to believe, some sort of light-hearted diversion preliminary to entering those darker areas? In an effort to encourage the Abbot to declare himself, he took advantage of a break in the flow of yak tales to ask the old man about his health.

'Today,' said Taranatha slowly, 'I am feeling a little better. So I decided to walk out here to enjoy the peace and quiet.' He brushed aside Timothy's polite attempts to apologise for his own intrusion.

'I also came here,' he continued, 'to think about the past.'

Timothy began to shake off his effects of yak-shock: 'You mean the history project?'

'That and other things.'

Timothy waited. The Abbot's face gave nothing away but his earlier naive story-telling air had already evaporated, and it was clear that he was now ready to talk more seriously.

'You see, I have secretly nourished many illusions in my life – not small ones either, but fundamental self-deceptions. And for years I would steadfastly deny that I had them.'

'What sort of illusions?' asked Timothy, hardly able to contain himself.

Taranatha's face remained expressionless; he now seemed to be looking not so much at Timothy as straight through him.

'I thought,' he now spoke very slowly, choosing the words carefully. 'I thought people here would want to know about their real past in a way that was different from the myths and legends they had been brought up with . . . that they would want to know more about the outside world, to learn English and so on. That's why, after returning from England, I devoted myself to researching our history and teaching it to students. That's why I then changed my name to Taranatha after the great seventeenth-century historian of Buddhism. That's why I started these language courses in Migoling and elsewhere. But it seems I was quite wrong about all this. Most people here are just not interested in such things.'

Timothy tried to interrupt but the Abbot didn't seem to hear him, though he now began to look at him more intently.

'Then there was another kind of illusion which concerns you—not you personally—but western people, their intellectuals and leaders. You see, I originally thought I could trust them. After all, I had learned so much from my stay in England, not just about history and the historical method but all sorts of other things, freedom and so on. Of course, I also knew about the colonial record – your long denial of freedom to millions of subject peoples. But somehow I imagined that once that period was over, our basic relations would improve. I even believed deep down that you might come to our aid if our progress and liberty were threatened – at least that you would lend us moral support. But now I realise that that too was a sentimental illusion. You are no longer interested in what happens here, and it suits you if we are neatly locked into the Indian security system, whether we like it or not!'

Taranatha paused. Like Timothy it appeared that he had just noticed that the scene around them was rapidly changing. The morning mist had largely lifted, and a shaft of sun-light had broken through the dark clouds, casting an intense yellow glow across the meadow. Following an unseen signal, the yaks too had begun to amble off in search of fresh pastures, grunting and coughing as they went. They were such dumb and harmless beasts really: Timothy could see that now. Why on earth had he allowed himself to panic so easily?

'But most of all,' the Abbot continued in his most sombre tone, 'I was mistaken about my own dharma, history. You have to understand that when I was young, political life here was non-existent – a no-go area. A new group of lamas, with their allies from India and Tibet, had seized power, and that group would tolerate no opposition. If you wanted to survive, you kept out of politics! History, on the other hand, seemed safe since it was categorically different from the concerns of the present. And to a young man like me it was exciting too . . . so much to be discovered that no one had ever suspected. It was exciting too, because in a shadowy kind of way it was also about politics – past politics. But my mistake was to believe that the past tense of history would always protect it, make it a place where one's mind could play freely with knowledge, limited only by the rules of the game – the discipline itself . . . Well, as you know, all that is no longer true, if it ever was! If you try to produce objective history these days—ancient or modern—you soon find yourself in mortal danger.'

For the first time he now smiled directly at Timothy. 'So you see history, like your yaks, has become a dangerous beast. Who would have thought it would turn so nasty?'

Timothy was at a loss as to how to respond to the Abbot's confession. He was certainly moved and saddened by it but at the same time found it hard to take in fully. Too much had happened that morning. It was also as if he didn't really want to hear what Taranatha wanted so much to tell him, since it only seemed to confirm his own sense of helplessness – the feeling that the Tulku's party would be too strong for them, and that his own grandiose plan to uncover the secret manuscript would come to nothing. But that was not all. In one part of his mind he had also to admit to feeling somewhat puzzled by the Abbot's admissions, and even critical of him. True Buddhists, he had been told by Serena and others, were supposed to be without illusions: it was an essential part of their outlook. How was it that Taranatha, a man deeply versed in the philosophy and practice of the dharma, had managed to cling to his illusions—if they were illusions—for so long? He despised himself for having such unsympathetic thoughts when the old man had opened his heart with such candour.

'To tell the truth,' said the Abbot, who had evidently been observing Timothy's reactions carefully, 'I myself cannot fully understand how I could have reached such an advanced age with so many illusions intact! And if you had asked me even a few weeks ago whether I believed the things I have just told you, I would have denied it. It needed the shock of recent events—especially that meeting with the minister—to reveal to me my own hidden assumptions. And for that I am grateful . . . But something else seems to have happened in the process, for which I am not so grateful. You see, in losing those illusions, I also seem to have lost the ruling interest of my life – my passion, if you like, for History itself. It no longer seems to matter. I think it is dead.'

For a few minutes Taranatha closed his eyes and said nothing. 'I'm sorry,' he said at last in a quieter voice. 'For some reason I was suddenly remembering something, a strange incident that took place a long time ago soon after I first arrived in London . . . I was alone in a lift in the university, coming down, I think, from the fourth floor where the library was. Instead of stopping at the ground floor, for which I had pressed the button, the lift jerked past and dropped down very fast to some basement zone. It stopped there with a tremendous jolt. Fortunately, the doors then opened, and much shaken, I stepped out into a sort of dark underworld . . . full of old machinery, huge twisting pipes, like dragons, and vast oblong tanks that looked to me like the tombs of ancient kings. I couldn't find the light or the stairs and the lift refused to return. So I must have stayed down there in that limbo for nearly an hour, hearing all kinds of strange and terrifying sounds. It reminded me of a sort of annex to one of the hells depicted on our temple walls. Eventually a workman found me. In my monk's robe, I think he at first thought I was some kind of ghost, and I myself had begun to feel like one!'

Timothy stared at the Abbot, at his weary, wrinkled face and sunken jaw. There was indeed something ghost-like about him now, or at any rate like a man who had been close to death. Whatever the nature of his recent illness, it must have been very severe. Timothy's earlier state of emotional detachment had now totally gone, and another very different feeling had replaced it. This man, he sensed, thinks I can help him; he hasn't actually said it, but this is what he thinks.

'That must have been very frightening,' he said at last. 'But at least you got out of it. And I'm sure we will find a way out of the present problem.' Aware that his words sounded banal, he searched hard for a better, more convincing way of putting it. 'When I'm really depressed about something,' he found himself saying, 'I usually begin to feel better if I can only manage to face the fact of it and feel the emotion at the same time. It looks as if you have already done that – I mean reached that rock-bottom state, that ground of being.' He felt happier with that expression, it even sounded more Buddhist.

'Not bad,' said the Abbot, suddenly brightening, 'except that since there is no being, only becoming, I'm afraid there can be no ground of being either . . . Anyway,' he continued with growing zest, 'you don't really want to hear any more about my troubles. You want to know about how we are going to cope with the minister's ultimatum, don't you?' Timothy nodded, hardly able to keep up with the old man's lightning change of mood.

'Well,' he said, now brisk and businesslike. 'First of all, you and I will finish the English translations of those pathetic documents they gave me. Then I will send them to the minister confirming that a full account of the late Shar Lama's life and death cannot be constructed from these fragments. Hopefully, if my health permits, I will do that by the end of this month when the deadline expires. And then for a few days we will celebrate the festival of the Protectors, as we do every year at Migoling.'

'And then?' asked Timothy nervously.

'Then,' Taranatha hesitated for only a second. 'Then I will return to this place to continue with my meditations on History, on the Spirit of Time, if you prefer it.'

'You mean you will remain inside this cave . . . indefinitely?' Timothy could hardly bring himself to say the word.

'Certainly,' said the Abbot cheerfully. 'What else can I do? But there's no need to think about that yet. Let's think about the festival. I hope you will enjoy it. And I tell you what! I will invite that Indian girl from Himjin whom you like. What's her name?'

Timothy felt blocked for a moment – by a mixture of hope and expected disappointment. 'Huma,' he said at last, as blankly as he could.

18

It was late afternoon when Timothy arrived in the Warden's office on the first floor of the administrative block. Having looked for him earlier without success, he was glad to find Norbu seated at his desk, anxiously leafing through what looked like an old ledger book. Dozens of similar books were piled up in the open cupboards behind him. On seeing Timothy, Norbu's face lit up. 'What can I do for you, Dr Tim?'

'Nothing in particular. I was just wondering about the protectors' festival. I met the Abbot this morning and he mentioned it briefly but didn't really explain it.'

'It's a wonderful occasion when we remember our dharmapalas, our protectors, with all sorts of ceremonies, processions and masked dances. With all the troubles we are having these days, many of us are very much looking forward to it.'

'Good,' said Timothy, lapsing into a hesitant silence.

'Yes, it is very good, but is that all you wished to ask?'

'Well, no, it's just that there's someone I know whom the Abbot is going to invite to the festival, and I was wondering where she could stay – I mean I gather that women are not allowed to stay overnight in the monastery.'

Norbu's eyes opened with a dawning sense of comprehension mixed with sympathy. 'Dr Tim, please do not worry about such arrangements. You and your friend are very welcome to sleep in my home in the village. My wife and I will be greatly honoured.'

'That's very kind of you. But actually it's only her I was concerned about . . . I can still stay here, of course . . . .' He trailed off, looking decidedly uncomfortable. He knew that people in Kalapur were considerably more down to earth about sex than one might have expected, but was Norbu really assuming his relations with Huma were that close?

'Dr Tim, perhaps I have shocked you . . . you didn't realise that I had a wife and family in the village?'

'Yes, well, it did come as a bit of a surprise. But I would be very pleased to meet your wife and, of course, I'm not shocked.' Timothy seized with some relief on the diversion, and also felt genuinely glad that the Warden was at last able to confide his secret.

Norbu took his hand in both of his and squeezed it hard. 'You are my friend as well as my guest,' he said, 'and so is your girlfriend!' Then, reaching between the ancient books in the cupboard behind him, he drew out two bottles of chang, one of which he presented to Timothy.

Having settled the drinks, Norbu seemed eager to explain more about his marital status. In the old days, it transpired, many monks in Kalapur had been unofficially married despite their vows of celibacy, and the authorities had usually turned a blind eye. The 'married ones', as he termed them, would spend most of their day at the monastery, joining in the various assemblies and rituals, but would return to their village homes in the evening. But now all that had changed.

The government disapproved strongly of the old practice and were doing their best to eradicate it by pressurising the married ones to give up their family life or resign from the order. Only the venerable Abbot's liberal compassion had so far shielded the Warden.

A sudden loud barking from the monastery's guard dogs distracted them. From their window view, a line of twelve monks carrying heavy bundles was visible trudging slowly up the path towards the gatehouse. The Warden muttered something in the local dialect. 'They have returned,' he explained nervously, 'the Reconverted Ones – those who have been on the pilgrimage to the Indian holy places.' Timothy peered down curiously as the monks approached the courtyard. Some of them seemed to be making a conscious effort to straighten up and even swagger a little as they prepared to be greeted by their colleagues; others could not disguise their weariness. All of them, he noticed, had yellow scarves tied round their right arms, giving them an air not so much of enlightened triumph but of being somehow packaged and labelled.

'Dr Tim, you will be amazed at the quantities of food and drink I have had to order for tonight's welcome feast for these people, not to mention the money we have had to raise or borrow to fund their pilgrimage. It has nearly soaked up our limited resources for the protectors' festival. Do you know what I was doing with these old lists when you arrived? I was checking on all the villages where our monks come from – what the Tulku calls our sponsors. He says we must ask the villagers to increase their donations to the monastery, give us more crops, more labour, more money so that we can cover our costs and pay for more pilgrimages. He says we have to change our old ways and become more modern and businesslike, tell the villagers frankly that their future lives—their rebirths if you like—will depend on the merit they gain from giving to us!'

The Warden paused and covered his face with his hands: he had clearly come under a lot of strain. 'Only the Reconverted are invited this evening,' he continued in a subdued tone. 'And then they will become more and more proud and troublesome. There are nearly forty of them now – almost half the monks at Migoling. And tomorrow we have this big public debate about a subject which divides the two sides most bitterly . . . and it will not end there . . . it will only get worse! That is what usually happens here just before the protectors' festival. We go so far on the path to division and self-destruction hoping our protectors will somehow come to the rescue.'

'Sorry to interrupt, Norbu,' said Timothy, emboldened by the chang and warmer thoughts of Huma, 'but there are a couple of points I wanted to check with you. You know I'm working with the Abbot on the history of this place, but I can't keep asking him to explain things all the time, especially when he's ill. . . . So I wanted to ask whether it's true that the previous Shar Lama used to spend much of his time here at Migoling?'

'Indeed he did. It was his favourite place. In fact, it is said that he used to sleep in what is now your guestroom. You see despite his position he was a very humble man.'

'Good heavens! I had no idea,' said Timothy. 'That would explain why the Spirit of Time mandala is there! But there's another thing,' he continued, elated by the discovery. 'Those old records behind you,' he pointed towards the ledgers in the cupboard, 'do you think they could help us trace the monk who acted as the chronicler for the last Shar Lama? Nobody seems to know his name . . . I guess he would have been active here fifty or sixty years ago during the 1940s.'

Norbu looked doubtful. 'It will not be easy,' he said slowly. 'First we will have to work out the years in our own calendar. Next we will have to search for the right book – and they are not always kept in order. And then we will have to look carefully through the monk lists for each new year, and try to find monks who were then of about the same age as the last Shar Lama. You see, according to the custom here, the monk who is chosen to record the life of the Shar Lama has to be of the same age so that, if possible, he can follow his master through life, year after year. That's why we call him the

Lama's Shadow! So even if we succeed in finding the right lists, we may also end up finding three or four possible shadows!' For the first time that afternoon he began to laugh.

As the Warden had foreseen, the monk list for the year corresponding to 1944, which they eventually discovered in a dusty cupboard in the next room, showed three monks who appeared to be about the right age, but with no indication of which one might have been the Lama's Shadow. Their names were Sonam Norbu, Tashi Tsering and Tsewang Dorje. Out of curiosity, Timothy also tried to find Taranatha's name in the list before remembering what the Abbot had told him earlier. He kicked himself for not having asked him for his original name.

'Is there no other way we can identify the Shadow?' Timothy enquired, his earlier confidence beginning to ebb away.

Norbu was unusually silent.

At last, when Timothy had almost given up all hope he got up from his desk. 'There is just one possibility,' he announced cautiously. 'Our most senior monk is aged about eighty. His name is Tenzing and he has a very good memory. He will almost certainly remember the Shadow's name. But unfortunately there is one problem: due to a recent stroke he cannot speak properly or write. But still we can go and see him in his room, and perhaps. . . . . also I must tell you he is looked after by his nephew who strongly supports the Tulku's party.' He thought for a moment. 'The Reconverted Ones will be resting after their journey. Let's go now while it's still quiet.'

Like most of the monks, Tenzing and his nephew occupied rooms in the second courtyard near the guesthouse. Since their main living room was quite well-furnished with rugs and curtains, it appeared that the two belonged to a fairly well-off local family able to look after their needs. While the nephew busied himself in the adjoining kitchen in making tea for his unexpected visitors, his uncle lay back on some cushions, nodding and smiling as the Warden made a number of polite enquiries after his health, using the Kalapur dialect. Timothy waited in suspense for him to say something in reply, but he continued to just nod and smile. At last when they had all been served with salty butter tea, Norbu began to broach the subject of the old Lama's Shadow. Did Tenzing by chance remember him?'

'La, la,' said the old man quietly. Did he recall his name? Again came another 'la, la'. Was it Sonam Norbu? 'La, la.' Tashi Tsering? 'La, la.' As the fruitless interrogation continued Timothy noticed that the man's nephew sat back with a complacent expression.

'I'm afraid you are wasting your time,' he said, resorting to English.

Norbu made one final effort: 'Was it Tsewang Dorje?' he asked doggedly.

'La, la, la, la, la, la!' shouted the old man with such gusto that Timothy nearly let go of his cup. Though the nephew now looked distinctly discouraging, Norbu kept his nerve. There was, he added apologetically, just one more question to ask: did he remember anything else about Tsewang Dorje? For example, how and when he died? The old man clasped his head in an effort to recall something, whilst Timothy, who couldn't see much point in Norbu asking that kind of question, took a long sip of his tea. To everyone's amazement his action seemed to have an electrifying effect on Tenzing. Slowly, unsteadily but very deliberately, he began to raise his own empty cup to his mouth and drain its imaginary contents. Then, after shaking his head violently, he closed his eyes and laid back his head. 'La, la, so!', he announced with impressive finality.

'I'm sorry, my uncle is very tired now,' said the nephew trying to regain control of the situation.

'No, I don't think so,' said Norbu with surprising firmness. 'I think he's trying to tell us that Tsewang Dorje, the late Lama's Shadow, died by drinking poison!'

19

On the following day Timothy arrived in the third courtyard just before four-thirty to find a large crowd of monks already assembled for the debate. Most of them were squatting on the ground on the shady side of the courtyard in front of a strip of open ground evidently intended for the two contestants. Beyond this, a few steps led up to a small verandah adjoining the far side of the courtyard. Here several seats had been arranged presumably for the senior lamas and other high officials. Down in the courtyard there must have been nearly eighty monks of all ages, and their number were still increasing.

Timothy stood gazing at the throng, not knowing where he should sit. As yet there was nobody he could recognise. In fact, seen from behind, the mass of crouching figures, with their shaven heads and dusty red robes, had a dreary anonymous look – more like convicts in a prison yard. Suddenly he realised that someone was waving to him from the other side of the courtyard: it was Chime, the older of the two young novices whom he had not seen for some time. With difficulty he pushed his way through the crowd to reach the boy, who promptly insisted on leading him up to one of the chairs in the verandah, explaining that the Warden had instructed him to find Timothy a place of honour. He then slipped off to rejoin his friends.

Timothy felt decidedly awkward and conspicuous sitting there all by himself, his long legs dangling over the edge of the verandah. His incongruous appearance also seemed to trigger a fit of convulsive giggling amongst a group of teenage monks occupying the front rows of the audience. Pretending not to notice them, he tried hard to concentrate on forming an impression of the rest of the crowd.

From his new vantage point, it was apparent that far from being dozy and depressed—as their rear view had suggested—the monks were decidedly boisterous and at times even rowdy, not unlike the spectators at a football match, with rival supporters of the two contestants exchanging taunts and insults. Also, scattered throughout the crowd were a number of police monks or disciplinarians – rough-looking men holding long wooden staves, which they would raise threateningly whenever groups of supporters were judged to be exceeding the permitted bounds of decorum. After a while Timothy also noticed that the disciplinarians regularly seemed to turn a blind eye to the antics of one particularly large and vocal band of monks sitting together at the back, with the yellow silk scarves of the 'Reconverted' tied rakishly round their arms. Rewarded and encouraged by last night's special banquet (sounds of which had kept Timothy awake), it was plain that they had little to fear from the authorities.

Meanwhile he became aware that something else had caught the attention of the crowd, diverting the rival groups from their recriminations. The small figure of a young novice had appeared on the roof of one of the surrounding buildings, holding a mysteriously ornate gilt instrument, which he then slowly raised to his mouth. A second later, as the sun flashed across the surface of the instrument, three high sonorous notes rang out across the courtyard, at once reducing the clamour of the monks to a low expectant murmur. Simultaneously several robed figures, wearing high lama's hats, entered the verandah from the rear and slipped quietly into their seats. Neither the Abbot nor the Tulku were amongst them, but one of these figures, whom Timothy belatedly recognised as Lama Wangdi, leaned down to tell him that the debate would be about the Buddhist view of history, and that following the Abbot's instructions it would be conducted in English.

By this time the two contestants had appeared in the debating arena, and were prostrating themselves before the senior lamas, one of whom acted as examiner and referee. These officials, who had not appeared before, then called out their names, though Timothy was unable to catch them. But as the two men rose to face each other, he was able to take a good look at each. Both were probably in their middle twenties, but in physical appearance they could hardly have been more different. The one standing on the right was of less than medium height, but thickset and built like a wrestler. His opponent on the left was tall, thin and narrow-shouldered, his most striking feature being his piercing eyes. With the crowd of spectators now palpably excited, the whole scene had so much the atmosphere of a physical contest that Timothy almost expected the referee to step down to deliver a last-minute cautioning homily to both contestants. Instead Lama Wangdi again leaned forward to explain that the man on the right would open the debate by asking a series of questions designed to force the other to concede the validity of his thesis.

As he spoke, Timothy saw that the wrestler was advancing slowly towards his opponent, all the while twisting and turning a rosary round his right wrist in a rather menacing fashion. 'Is it true,' he began in a cool voice, 'that our scriptures foretell the gradual decline of the dharma after its first period of strength and purity?'

'It is true,' replied the other, taking a step back.

'And do the scriptures also foretell that this decline will continue till the advent of Lord Maitreya?'

'They do.' The sharp-eyed man answered calmly, taking a further step backwards. As he did so the wrestler moved forward rapidly to occupy the abandoned ground.

'So,' he continued with a gleam of anticipated triumph, 'we can agree that the scriptures tell us all that is spiritually important about the past, present and future?' His fingers snapped roughly in the other's face.

'Certainly they tell us what is spiritually important,' replied the sharp-eyed one, still outwardly calm. 'But equally on most ordinary matters of history they are silent. For example, they neither record the deaths of our grandparents nor reveal when you and I will die. In short, the scriptures are scriptures, and history is . . . history. I hope we can agree on that?' This time he did not step back but smiled ironically at his rival, finally compelling him to retreat to his original position.

A ripple of surprise and appreciation passed through part of the audience, though Timothy also noticed that the 'Reconverted ones' at the back remained stony-faced. Refusing to show any emotion at his apparent reverse, the wrestler demonstrated his sangfroid by retreating still further back, before embarking on a new line of questioning.

'Please name the process through which all spiritual and worldly developments take place.'

'It is the Spirit of Time.'

'And who is the true representative and embodiment of the Spirit of Time?'

'The Shar Lama.'

The wrestler stood very still for a moment, slowly turning his rosary. Suddenly he flung himself forward with tremendous force, stopping within inches of his opponent, who however remained unmoved. 'So,' he hissed, 'the Shar Lama is the supreme interpreter of the Spirit of Time. Answer yes or no.'

'The Shar Lama,' returned the other quietly, 'can represent to us the events of the past. But his duty is to recognise those events in the way they happened, not to interpret them according to his or our desires. He is the servant not the master of time, and the true voice of history.'

'You speak of recognition not interpretation,' replied the challenger scornfully, 'but these are mere word games. The truth is—is it not?—that the Shar Lama speaks with absolute authority on these matters.'

'He does indeed . . . but his authority derives precisely from the mirror-like quality of his perceptions – no more no less.'

The two contestants faced each other in tensely hostile silence – neither moving from his position. From somewhere on the other side of the courtyard, a solitary drumbeat brought the first part of the debate to a close.

Timothy, who had sat spellbound throughout the debate, tried to stand up, only to find one of his feet had developed an agonising cramp. The spectators in front of him also appeared to be in varying states of confusion: some laughing wildly, others—the Tulku's supporters—looking angry and disappointed: they had expected their man to do better. It seemed to Timothy, however, that the majority were plainly bemused by the whole performance, having had presumably great difficulty in following the language.

As he looked round for Lama Wangdi, a young monk thrust a wooden bowl into his hand, which another proceeded to fill up from a can of steaming hot tea. As the tea distributors worked their way through the crowd, the monks gradually recovered themselves and the steady hubbub of their voices raised in laughter and argument soon filled the whole courtyard. Still looking unsuccessfully for Wangdi, Timothy found himself confronted by the stern-looking young monk who had earlier handed him the bowl. Rather to his dismay, he also saw that the man had one of the yellow scarves of the Reconverted wound round his arm. 'You like it?' he enquired in broken English.

Timothy assured him that he had, and was especially impressed by the contestants' excellent grasp of English. Instead of looking pleased, the monk's frown deepened. 'That is bad,' he said. 'It is bad because the monks must speak in Tibetan or Sanskrit when they speak the Dharma.' Perhaps, suggested Timothy, they had only resorted to English out of consideration for him.

'No,' insisted the other. 'It is because the Khenpo (the Abbot) likes English. He makes all monks learn English in crush programme!' He again shook his head with disapproval and looked up at the sky. 'Very bad thing,' he repeated. 'Lord Maitreya is angry!'

Timothy followed the direction of his gaze, half-expecting to see some sign of the future Buddha's celestial anger. But though the late afternoon light was beginning to fade, the sky was still cloudless and clear, except for a thin line of crows circling high overhead. When he looked down again to resume his rather difficult conversation, he found that the frowning monk had vanished.

A few moments later, the boy with the conch reappeared on the opposite roof to herald the resumption of the debate. But instead of sounding high-pitched and floating, the note he produced this time was long and low, like a deep growl, which lapped its way across the courtyard at ground level, gathering and subduing the monks till they gave up their chatter and came together in a quiet but expectant huddle. They all knew it was now the turn of the sharp-eyed monk to take up the offensive or questioning role. How he performed would determine the outcome of the contest.

To Timothy's surprise, he did not begin by squaring up to his rival in the centre of the arena, as the latter had done, but took a seemingly neutral position directly facing the crowd. This had the effect of visibly discomforting his opponent; it also increased the already rising tension of the spectators. His voice, when he spoke, was neither truculent nor provocative but patient and reasonable, and his gestures were sparing. 'I wish to begin,' he said, addressing the wrestler obliquely through the audience, 'by clarifying your basic position. You believe that history, conceived in the form of the Spirit of Time, has an overall meaning and direction that is uniquely known to its representative, the Shar Lama. Is that true?'

'Most certainly it is true,' replied the wrestler.

'You further hold that the special insight of the Shar Lama extends not only to knowledge of spiritual phenomena but to all past lives and events.'

'Yes, I believe that, as must all true believers in the Shar Lama and the Mandate of Maitreya.' A wave of approval and stamping of feet from the Reconverted greeted this sally.

'Good,' said the challenger. 'Now I wish to consider how far your position is compatible with our traditional Mahayana doctrines.' His voice was now louder, and for a moment he half-turned from the spectators to look directly at his rival. 'Our scriptures tell us,' he continued, 'that Reality is empty, being has no essence, perceptions have no essence, concepts have no essence. True or false?'

'True,' said the other, uneasily.

'So, since History is a concept, it too must be empty and devoid of essence.' The wrestler remained silent.

'And yet you maintain that it has meaning and can be known through insight?'

Timothy's attention now began to wander. It was not that he failed to recognise the significance of the debate. He could see that it was amazingly focused on the very issues that had brought him to Kalapur; that it had obvious, if coded, relevance to the Shar Lama's claims to authority and legitimacy, and the dilemmas facing Taranatha's history project. But despite all this, he had begun to feel tired and found it hard to concentrate, mainly because last night he had slept little, what with the noise from the banquet for the Reconverted, and his excitement at finding out about the murder of the last Shar Lama's Shadow. Also, he could not help thinking that though the contestants' arguments were all very well on a doctrinal plane, it was highly unlikely that any of the metaphysical points being made by this clever, sharp-eyed monk would have any effect on the current power structure in the country. In the ultimate Buddhist analysis, that power might be empty and without essence but in the hands of the Shar Lama and the Tulku it was still alarmingly real.

In another part of his mind he was also aware that all the talk of emptiness and essence had reawakened his memories of Serena. How she would have enjoyed this show! Her liquid green eyes would have taken it all in with that dreamy but attentive gaze . . . Of course, Huma also had beautiful eyes but they were different . . . bright and amusing. Perhaps Buddhists were right about essences—human beings not having them and so on—but it was strange how the quality of a person's eyes could persuade you to the contrary.

A loud hand-clap from one of the contestants, followed by a surge of approval from the crowd, brought Timothy back from his daydreams. Clearly the sharp-eyed monk was still winning the argument, steadily exposing the logical flaws in his opponent's position by a skilful deployment of traditional Buddhist dialectics. Not only was it meaningless to look for overall meaning in history, he was saying, but it was also downright unethical to do so, since the constant reiteration of such claims to grasp at meaning invariably led to the strengthening of the belief in the ego and all the related illusions which the dharma sought to dissolve. In place of that, he himself was content to offer a simple, but far more challenging view of the nature of the Spirit of Time.

'What is that?' his opponent had asked with heavy sarcasm.

'The past is extinct, the future has yet to come and the present lasts only a minute.' That is what our own scriptures say. Do you deny it?'

The wrestler could find no reply.

By now the sun was slipping behind the mountains and it was gradually becoming cooler and darker. Surely the debate would have to end soon, and it must have been obvious to most spectators, whatever their viewpoint, that the wrestler had lost. Yet there was also something about his demeanour and sheer physical audacity that left open a crack of doubt. Was it still possible that he could do something to reverse the verdict? For most of the second round, he had been outmanoeuvred intellectually and sidelined physically – unable to confront an opponent who had insisted on facing the audience throughout. Even now, from his position to the rear of the victorious challenger, he looked a pretty ineffectual figure, almost irrelevant to the main centre of action between his rival and the spectators – someone whose essentially physical challenge had never been accepted.

As if realising that only the most desperate gambit could save the day, the man seemed to will himself free from his previous failure and frustration, and without warning literally leapt forward like an acrobat past his opponent to take over his position directly in front of the audience. 'That one,' he shouted, 'tells you to despise the Spirit of Time, to humiliate the Shar Lama, to spit in the face of Maitreya . . . !'

For a moment the crowd seemed too stunned to react to his challenge. Then, as the chord struck home, the mass of the Reconverted heaved to its feet to roar back its anger. All over the courtyard the monks began to struggle with each other, their robes rippling like a sea of crimson cross-currents in the gathering twilight. Several men ran round the edge of the crowd in an effort to seize the monk who had defeated their champion, only to find themselves confronted by another group who had formed a protective ring around him. In the verandah Timothy caught sight of several lamas quietly slipping away through the rear exit, while others, led by Lama Wangdi, vainly tried to restore order, with only half-hearted support from the police monks, their batons waving symbolically in the air. Somewhere in the heart of the monastery, a drum was beating to announce the debate's conclusion.

Taken aback by the sudden eruption of violence, Timothy tried to push his way to the rear exit through which the lamas had fled. But someone had already caught hold of his arm and was pulling him away in the direction of the courtyard. 'Follow me,' the man shouted. 'The Tulku will protect you!' Timothy could not make out the man's face clearly, but he recognised his voice: it was the frowning young monk with the yellow scarf who had spoken to him in the interval.

20

To his increasing alarm, Timothy found himself being firmly propelled by half a dozen teenage monks towards the first courtyard. 'Don't be afraid,' their frowning leader kept assuring him. 'We won't hurt you – we are your helpers! We are Buddhists!' Having just witnessed their ferocious response to their opponents in the History debate, he was not exactly reassured.

The group finally came to a halt outside a small two-storeyed building in the corner of the courtyard known as the Geshe house. Until recently this had been used by advanced students in philosophy and Tantric studies, but with the spread of the new reform movement such traditional subjects were being discouraged, and the building had now been taken over by the Reconverted as a centre for their special training programmes.

'Please wait inside,' said the leader, 'the Tulku will come soon.' Timothy stepped inside into a kind of classroom, still accompanied by his escort.

'Look,' said Timothy, beginning to recover. 'I know you mean well, but wouldn't it be better if I just went back to my own room and waited for the Tulku there?'

'No,' said the six monks altogether in a well-drilled, almost liturgical response. 'You must stay here. Outside is not safe!' An awkward silence ensued.

How, he wondered, would the monastic authorities deal with the breach of discipline that had just occurred? Would all the monks involved be punished in some way, or only the Reconverted who had clearly started the fracas, provoked by the wrestler's desperate challenge? It seemed to depend on who was now actually in charge – Taranatha who was still sick, or the Tulku who was supposed to be on his way. Most probably the 'authorities' would eventually react like most divided institutions tended to do in such circumstances, including his own London college: they would promulgate some compromise orders that would satisfy neither side. In any case, having observed the recent half-hearted response of the police monks, it was highly unlikely that the Reconverted would be given anything more than a token rebuke.

In an effort to establish some sort of dialogue with his captors, Timothy began to question the youths about why they thought the debate had gone wrong. At first they seemed reluctant to say much, rather like his London students from whom on certain days it was extraordinarily difficult to elicit anything more than a monosyllabic response to the questions he would pose. Here, however, he sensed that the whole group was now in a confused and depressed state, conscious that their spokesman had been unexpectedly worsted in the debate and gone on to break the rules. Eventually their frowning leader did his best to sound more positive. The attack on the Shar Lama's authority had been so shocking, he claimed, that they had been left with no alternative but to respond in the way they did. How else could such seditious talk be silenced? How else could their country be made into a 'Pure Land' except by complete and courageous devotion to their spiritual leader?

His efforts encouraged others to speak out. It was not they who were to blame, they argued, but the monastic officials who had given permission for such an improper subject to be debated in the first place, and then fixed it for the day after the Returned Ones' welcome feast when their representative, the wrestler, had had insufficient time to prepare his case. They sensed too that evil spirits and migos were in the vicinity, intervening against them, and poisoning the minds of their opponents.

'What sort of migos do you mean?' Timothy asked, seizing the opportunity. 'Wildmen and yetis or rebel fighters?'

A tense silence seemed to grip the youths as they turned instinctively to their leader for guidance. 'Both,' he replied tersely, 'both are the enemies of the Shar Lama.'

Before Timothy had a chance to continue his questions, all the members of the group had suddenly thrown themselves down full-length onto the classroom floor. For an instant he wondered: is it possible that the mere naming of the Shar Lama could trigger such a response? – before realising that an imposing figure wearing American camouflage fatigues and heavy boots was now standing in the doorway. 'Rinpoche!' breathed the prostrate students in unison: the Tulku had come at last.

'Good to see you again Dr Curtin,' said LJK in his usual masterful tones as he led Timothy back towards the guesthouse. 'I'm sorry we've had this spot of trouble. But at least I'm glad my students have taken care of you. Anyway,' he continued briskly, 'you must be quite used to this in England: student riots, sit-ins and that sort of thing! As you see, we also have our own trouble-makers and extremists, even in the monasteries!'

'What will happen to them?' Timothy asked.

'Well, we'll decide that tomorrow in our assembly of senior monks. You probably don't realise, do you, that our monasteries have a long tradition of resolving such issues democratically? But I would guess that the assembly will decide to expel the culprit. We must after all maintain basic law and order.'

Timothy looked surprised and relieved; it seemed he had somewhat misjudged the Tulku and his party.

'Yes,' LJK continued, 'as soon as that young man began to cast doubt on the Shar Lama's knowledge and authority—so my colleagues who were there assure me—they realised he was out to make trouble, though they didn't realise just how far the scoundrel would dare to go. No, Dr Curtin, you can't take risks with young extremists like that. As your own government understands very well, such people are a threat to civilised values.'

Taking Timothy by the arm, the Tulku led him up the stairs to his room. 'Please sit down,' he said, pointing to the only available chair, while he himself, after removing his army boots, assumed a Buddha-like posture on the rug beneath the mandala. The irony of the situation was not lost on Timothy: here was a leading supporter of the present Shar Lama sitting under a sacred image specifically dedicated to his predecessor.

'Dr Curtin, I must be frank with you. Our little country is in a state of emergency – that's why I'm dressed like a soldier, to bring home the fact that we have a fight on our hands to defend the dharma! And how we handle it will determine our future progress. For the first time, you see, because of our new policies, our material and spiritual economy is beginning to improve. New opportunities for employment are being created in sectors like tourism, the army, technology, and business, and our enemies are opposed to all that because their interest lies in keeping the country poor, backward and spiritually unmotivated. And so they appeal to the atavistic forces of conservatism and ethnicity to try to persuade people to resist change. That's why we can't allow that reckless debater to challenge the very basis of our movement. It would, as your own government might say, simply send out the wrong message.

'Now, this also brings me to something that concerns you directly, Dr Curtin. I don't, in any way, wish to be censorious, but I cannot see that the enquiries you have been making into the death of Tsewang

Dorje more than half a century ago, can be of any relevance to your current assignment. But what I do know is that, if knowledge of such matters falls into the wrong hands it can do great harm here. Do you understand?'

Timothy, who had remained silent throughout the Tulku's lecture, for the first time felt the spirit of Gabbinger rising hotly within him. Huma, he remembered, had warned that LJK could not just be laughed off as a rich and amusing character: beneath his suavity lay an interfering and dangerous arrogance which was now being deployed at full force to block his own efforts to uncover a past that had never been allowed to surface.

'Rinpoche, I was officially invited by your government to assist Abbot Taranatha in his historical investigations into the recent "Lives of the Lamas". Are you saying that I am not, after all, going to be allowed to do this?' He himself was surprised by the speed and fluency of his own response

'No, of course, I am not saying that,' the Tulku replied calmly. 'But I must remind you of the minister's instructions which you yourself heard less than two weeks ago. These were that the Abbot was to prepare, with your assistance, a narrative account of the last years of the late Shar Lama's reign based upon the source materials he had specified.'

The Tulku paused to align his boots more neatly together on the rug beside him. 'Now please try to be a little more reasonable about this. We have to prepare and publish a national statement about an important period of our past – something that people can accept as authoritative, and which will hopefully contribute to our own process of truth and reconciliation. We cannot lose sight of these main objectives by allowing you to follow up all sorts of minor historical side issues, however intriguing they may appear to be.'

LJK assumed a slightly superior smile. 'And again I must remind you of the need to adopt a more Himalayan perspective,' he said.

'This has to be seen as part of our national history, not something that the ex-colonial power—or its representative—can dictate to us as to the form it should take. Just imagine, what people in England would think if Prince Charles were to commission a Tibetan lama to write his biography. They would be puzzled, to say the least, and of course the prince would never do such a thing.'

'He might!' said Timothy, 'in fact, according to our newspapers, it's just the kind of thing he might do.'

'Rinpoche,' he continued, roused out of his normal polite caution by the other's air of condescension. 'Can I also ask you to try to appreciate the situation a little more from my point of view? I have now been here more than a month, and so far I have made hardly any progress in my assignment. In fact, I don't seem to be getting anywhere at all. The Abbot has been ill and I have not as yet been given any substantial materials to work on. Very soon I will have to start thinking about leaving.'

'Of course, of course, I perfectly understand your position,' said the Tulku, now soothing and reflective. 'I'm afraid we both have to face the truth that Abbot Taranatha is not the man he once was. He is old and very sick now, and finds it hard to cope. It's sad, he used to be so dynamic and made such a significant contribution to our culture. Have you read that early essay he wrote after returning from his studies in England? It was called "Hegel and Maitreya". It compared the historical concept of Hegel's absolute spirit with the role of Maitreya in our Mahayana cosmic historiography, and it helped to lay the intellectual foundations for our present national movement. But now, I'm afraid, he has lost his way . . . '

Timothy felt distinctly confused. How was he to take this? He had never heard about Hegel and Maitreya before, and what LJK was telling him about Tarantha hardly fitted with his own understanding of the Abbot's philosophy. He sensed that his earlier bold expression of feelings had not helped but had given the Tulku the opening he was looking for.

'Look, Timothy,' said LJK now assuming masterful intimacy. 'I'm going to make you a new offer. And it's completely new because I realise I had become too attached to our old solution to these problems; and as someone who tries to apply Buddhist principles to daily life, I am always very aware of the dangers of inflexibility and attachment. Now what I suggest in view of the Abbot's indisposition, you should take over full responsibility for preparing the narrative and the documents. We will extend your assignment and we will go more than half way to meet your requirements as an independent historian. With flexibility on both sides, I feel sure we can manage. For example, your researches on the last Shar Lama's Shadow can be easily accommodated in a small footnote somewhere, and so on. Of course, I don't expect you to give me a definite answer immediately. But just think it over!'

Timothy felt the trap closing. 'I don't think I could do that,' he said hastily, 'I don't know enough about the subject, and it wouldn't be fair on the Abbot.'

'Are you sure?' said LJK, in hot pursuit of his quarry. 'Are you sure he wouldn't be relieved? All I'm asking at this stage, Timothy, is that you give careful consideration to this idea.' For the first time he leant back to relax against the wall.

'In fact, the more I think about it, the more I think it will be better for you and us. After all, it will give you a unique opportunity to see all sorts of secret documents you would never otherwise get to see. That's how much we are prepared to trust you! And, of course, at the same time the whole conservation project would need to be reorganised on a more ambitious scale.' Though looking at Timothy, he seemed to be thinking aloud. 'And that would also mean extending Miss Hassan's contract so that she can stay on longer in Himjin . . . but, of course, those are just administrative details that don't concern us now.'

The Tulku began to ease on his boots, and rose to his feet. 'I'm afraid you must excuse me now, Timothy. I have urgent business to attend to. But I'm very glad we've been able to have this useful chat. And do please give careful thought to my suggestion.'

As he was about to leave, he appeared to notice the mandala on the wall for the first time. 'I must ask our manager to get that thing wiped off,' he said casually. 'It doesn't give the right impression to our guests. It suggests we are still lost in daydreams. One of our new Dharma Development calendars would look much better.'

'But I thought it represented the Spirit of Time!' Timothy protested.

'Maybe,' said the Tulku, only momentarily disconcerted. 'But as you know, time itself always moves on!'

21

As usual when he woke up in the morning, Timothy's eyes gravitated towards the mandala. He couldn't explain rationally why this happened but ever since he had first arrived, part of him had got used to treating it as a kind of mystical website – a medium through which messages extracted from the secret world of Kalapuri Tantra seemed to mingle with the contents of his own imagination. In fact, out of all the things that the Tulku had said on the previous evening, it was the final casual threat to destroy the mandala that had in a strange way most upset and affronted him. And looking at it now in the morning light, the mandala itself seemed to reflect his feelings, with the tiny animals and delicate figurines depicted in its inner sanctums no longer seemingly sheltered and protected by the strong outer perimeters but trapped and oppressed within them.

There was no point in pretending otherwise: he too had been trapped – trapped into suggesting that it was the Abbot who was to blame for the lack of progress with their work on the manuscript sources for the last Shar Lama's reign. But even that wasn't quite true either. The fact was that he himself had been so infuriated by the Tulku's air of complacent superiority that he hadn't realised that in referring to the delays connected with Taranatha's illness, he had actually played straight into the other's hands, giving him the opportunity to imply that they both really agreed the fundamental fault lay in the Abbot's weakness. As for LJK's suggestion that he should take over the project, it was clear that this was a calculated move prompted by the Abbot's failure to co-operate in the way the government required, and the presumption that the Timothy could probably be bribed, tricked or cajoled into doing so; and, if he didn't, well, they could ditch him easily enough. Just as back in London, when it had all begun, he had been outmanoeuvred by Hoadley and Sharir Singh, now as the end approached, and in different circumstances, he was being fooled and humiliated by LJK.

And that was about it, he suddenly realised: the whole bungled project was now fizzling out before it had even got properly started. To accept the Tulku's offer was out of the question: even if that might rescue Taranatha from an intolerable situation (as LJK had subtly suggested), it would also amount to an act of betrayal. On the other hand, if he continued to hang on and wait for the Abbot's recovery, and try to follow up on his own the few accessible clues as to what had really taken place half a century ago, then the chances were that he would end up finding nothing of value or importance. It was, for instance, highly unlikely that sources such as the old monk registers Norbu had shown him—which had helped to open up the tantalising story of the assassination of Tsewang Dorje—would continue to be available to him: the Tulku and his spies would almost certainly see to that.

And what about Taranatha himself? Since Timothy's unexpected meeting with him in the cave hermitage he had once again been confined to his rooms. Perhaps he would never recover. And, even if he did, could Timothy still trust him after what LJK had told him about his earlier apparent involvement in the reform programme and the mandate of Maitreya? Perhaps, he really was 'a duplicitous old lama', as he himself had once jokingly put it, and that the fascination he exercised was as much a product of deception as profundity.

No, the best course was to get away from Migoling now before the tensions in the community grew even worse and themselves effectively ruled out the possibility of further investigation. That would at least give him the satisfaction of stealing a march on LJK, who would lose face from the resignation of his tame foreign expert – something which would certainly discomfort the otherwise invulnerably arrogant Tulku. There was nothing else to keep him in Kalapur – except, of course, Huma, who was supposed to be coming to the protectors' festival. But then, she had already clearly shown that she was not interested in him; to pretend otherwise and stay on for her sake would only hurt him more.

Timothy was disappointed to find the Warden's office closed, with no signs of Norbu. He desperately felt the need to communicate his frustration, and, if possible, start to make arrangements for his departure. Of course, he would eventually have to find a way of informing Taranatha before he left but that could wait till later. Meanwhile as he looked around, it was apparent that something else was going on. Small groups of monks were talking together anxiously in corners and passage-ways, but as he came nearer they either drifted off or became silent. Was their behaviour connected with the authorities' reaction to yesterday's violence? He decided to see if Chana was still at work outside the Maitreya chapel; he would know what was going on, and in any case, in Timothy's present mood, the prospect of encountering Chana's abrasive spirit was somehow enticing.

He found Chana on the landing apparently in the process of packing up all his equipment—brushes and paints, etc.—into a holdall. His work on the giant figure of Migo Lopen had apparently come to a stop, and indeed he seemed to have just blotted out much of the top half of the figure.

'They've shot one!' he announced laconically, as Timothy approached.

'What on earth do you mean?'

'I mean that the Tulku's followers claim to have shot a migo and probably killed it. They say, it got away but won't survive long.'

'Good God! Was it really a migo?'

'Well, that's what they claim. But, of course, some people here think it was one of the human variety – a resistance fighter who had strayed too near the monastery. As you know, it suits the authorities never to admit the existence of these rebels. They always refer to them as migos, which to add to the confusion, is also what the fighters call themselves.'

'Will anyone believe that they've shot a real wildman?'

'Oh yes! Some of the superstitious monks and villagers will certainly believe it. In fact, I'm told they will be holding a special—what do you call it?—séance tonight in the gonkhang to find out what has happened to his spirit. They will ask the oracle to tell them.'

'You mean that sinister old man who stared at me when we had lunch that day with the Warden?'

'Yes. That's the guy. Anyway,' Chana shrugged, 'things are getting too hot here for my sort of work. If I try to finish off old ML in this atmosphere,'—he pointed up at the truncated figure—'there will be another explosion from the Reconverted, and they may target me as well. So, I figure I'd better quit now.'

'But if they can't stand your painting of Migo Lopen, how come they still seem to put up with those images in the gonkhang, and the regular worship of the Protectors?'

'I guess they have to tolerate it for the present – until they win over the majority. Once they do that, then the Tulku will act. It's already happened like that in other monasteries. I no longer get asked to do representations of migos or politically incorrect Tantric protectors in those places. All they want is Superman Maitreya!'

Timothy said nothing for a few moments: a new possibility had just occurred to him.

'When are you thinking of leaving, Chana?'

'Very soon, I guess. As soon as I can hitch a lift to Himjin. Why?'

'Well, I thought I might leave with you.'

Chana stopped fiddling with his holdall, and faced Timothy directly. 'Man, that wouldn't be right,' he said. 'You won't get harmed here and you've still got important work to do.'

'But that's exactly the problem. I've got stuck, completely stymied. I'm getting nowhere . . . so I might as well pack up and leave.'

'But that's a good situation Tim. It's when you get totally blocked here that things start to move – like the Spirit of Time.'

Timothy became silent again. Chana, he thought, is beginning to sound too much like an aging Himalayan hippy. He'll be warning me about my karmic vibes next.

'Look,' said Chana firmly. 'You have an opportunity tonight to witness an extraordinary event in Kalapuri life when the spirits of the dead are made to speak. At least stay and watch what happens. Who knows, you may learn something, and if you still feel like leaving tomorrow, well leave then!'

It was late evening when Timothy found himself climbing the steep stairs that led up to the gonkhang. Part of him had not wanted to witness the séance, if that's what it was. He had read several accounts of how Himalayan oracle priests entered into their trances and uttered vague prophecies, and in his present disillusioned state, it seemed only too likely that they were more often powered by alcohol and drugs than genuine psychic gifts, whatever those were. And yet here he was, persuaded to attend by Chana, and—he had to admit—at once drawn to, and disturbed, by the prospect of a challenge to rationalism.

The gonkhang seemed smaller than he remembered, perhaps because although it was generally dark inside, he could make out that the whole available floor space was filled with crouching monks. Directly ahead stood the giant snarling images of Migo Lopen and the other wrathful protectors of the monastery, their fantastic torsos woven with light from the scattered butter lamps below. A little to their right, and likewise partially illumined, rose the austere, reflective image of Manjushri – a reminder presumably of the inherent connection between wisdom and fear.

As he stumbled his way through the crouching monks, several dim figures in the front signalled him towards an empty space, as if it had been specially reserved for him. It was so bizarrely like trying to find your seat in a darkened cinema or theatre that he began to smile, before realising as his bottom reached the floor, that whatever he was about to witness had already begun.

It was starting, he could now see clearly, with a tableau of strange figures positioned in a stage-like space a few yards in front of him, and immediately to the left of the protector images. Odd how these key characters had hardly been visible till now! There was the oracle himself, quietly seated on a sturdy-looking chair, his eyes closed, his hands on his knees, legs wide apart and bare feet pointing outwards. His unkempt hair was tied up in a tuft and partly covered by a red cap, and he seemed to be wearing some sort of animal skin trousers, with the top of his body enveloped in a short fur cloak. On either side of him stood two small skinny monks, optimistically entrusted with the responsibility of somehow supporting his bulky frame if he should stumble or collapse, while a third monk was busy blowing white incense from a censer into his face.

Placed next to the oracle's chair was a long ornate table filled with ritual cakes apparently made out of decorated barley and butter and shaped into flowers and figurines which at a distance seemed to twinkle like exotic fairground toys. There were other offerings too, including cups filled presumably with tea and milk or—especially if Timothy's earlier surmises were correct—large quantities of beer. Beyond lay a long stool on which were piled various weapons associated with the protectors, a quiver and arrows, a spear, and what looked like a pile of stones.

The tableau was completed by an elderly lama (whom Timothy had never seen before) sitting in front of the oracle, whose function was evidently to guide him through the several stages of the performance. Such were the four characters in this drama, the purpose of which was to conjure up a fifth, Migo Lopen himself! Timothy's efforts to analogise and tame the event began to falter: it was not a play, nor was he a sophisticated anthropologist.

Gradually becoming more accustomed to the dark, he looked around vainly for a familiar face. These were monks whom he didn't know – and not surprisingly, the yellow scarves of the Reconverted were notably absent. In the midst of his growing unease, another comforting resemblance unexpectedly suggested itself: the gonkhang was almost the same shape and size as the old lecture room where the Himalayan Centre used to hold its meetings in London, and he began to imagine Hoadley caught in the oracle's chair and hypnotised into disclosing the true story of the old Shar Lama's flight.

The beginning of a low rhythmic chant from the old guiding lama drew his attention back to the mysterious tableau. This, he knew from the anthropological accounts, was the formal invocation to the protector to descend from his mountain abode and take up temporary residence in the oracle's substantial form. At first the chant was slow and coaxing but almost imperceptibly it became faster and more insistent, its message regularly reinforced by a clash of cymbals held high by one of the skinny supporting monks. As the tempo increased and the smoke from the censer kept swirling towards him, the oracle lost his previous quiescence: he seemed to gasp greedily at the smoky fragrance and his whole body started to shake continuously. Several times he tried unsuccessfully to rise from his chair, his face red and puffy, only to collapse back with a withered, drawn expression. Timothy found the whole process unpleasant to watch; though it could not have lasted more than five minutes, it seemed that the man's whole metabolism had become permanently locked in a timeless reflex of desire and pain.

At last the chant ended, and though the oracle's face remained red and occasional spasms still shook his body, it was clear that a transformation had taken place. Slowly he got to his feet, and swaying slightly, bowed three times to the image of Manjushri. As he returned to his chair, Timothy saw that the whole expression and even structure of his face seemed to have altered: his jaw looked more massive and his eye ridges more prominent, whilst across his darkened lips spread the fixed and savage smile of Migo Lopen.

In recognition of his new identity, the guiding lama now tried to present the oracle with his insignia – first the quiver, which he held for a second, only to fling it to the floor, and then the spear, which he grasped more eagerly, waved high over his head, and then with no apparent effort snapped into two pieces. As if to underline his anger, he again sprang up and began to stride backwards and forwards at great speed swinging his long arms wildly before finally staggering back into his chair, where he was handed a drink by the presiding lama. The interview, it seemed, was about to commence.

Leaning forward respectfully, the lama spoke close to the oracle's ear. What could he be saying? What on earth did one ask the mountain god of the migos when he came on a visit? Before he could begin to find an answer, Timothy realised that the monk sitting next to him was trying to whisper something into his own ear. 'He is asking the protector if a migo has been killed, and if so, whether his spirit is angry and seeking revenge?' The oracle made what sounded like an affirmative grunt, and Timothy hastily whispered back his thanks to his helpful neighbour. Only then did he belatedly recognise him as

Tenzing's nephew, the monk who had done his best to discourage their enquiries into the fate of the last Shar Lama's Shadow.

'And now he is asking him what the angry spirit will do . . . and the protector is saying he will try to capture the la—that is, the spirit—of a human being and take possession of his body.'

Since the oracle's answers sounded to him more like inarticulate snorts, Timothy began to wonder how his neighbour was able to interpret them so easily. Perhaps he was just guessing or even making up the whole dialogue.

'The lama is now asking the name of the person in danger from that spirit.' Whether that question was really being put Timothy couldn't tell, but it was obvious from the tense atmosphere that all the onlookers were now expecting some crucial revelation. How much the oracle in his Migo Lopen persona was aware of all this was impossible to judge—certainly his eyes remained shut throughout the performance—and some moments passed before he muttered something in reply, which even the guiding lama apparently failed to catch since he appeared to repeat his question. The answer when it came again at first seemed unintelligible – unintelligible because under the circumstances it was almost inconceivable because . . . because it actually sounded as if he had said, 'A B C!' Timothy had read that Himalayan oracles sometimes spoke in riddles and even in foreign languages which they themselves would not normally use or understand, but surely in this case he must have misheard some Kalapuri dialect words. He turned expectantly to his neighbour but for the first time the monk offered no explanation.

Though aware that the oracle had now collapsed exhausted into the skinny arms of his supporters, and would probably soon recover consciousness, Timothy's mind was still preoccupied with the mystery of his last utterance. Assuming he had after all heard it correctly, what could it mean? Had the Abbot's English language lessons somehow percolated through to the oracle's subconscious? For some reason he found himself recollecting Taranatha's London lecture, and how, to convince the Centre's members of the importance of the Migoling chronicle, he had told them the strange story of the two English merchants who had died on their way through the frozen passes of Kalapur, and been mistaken there for wildmen . . . Arbuthnot and Blake. Yes, those were their names . . . A and B. But what about C? Could it be . . . Curtin? Was he himself to be the target of the spirit's malevolence?

Suddenly he felt terribly cold. 'I must be going quite crazy,' he thought. How on earth could the oracle know about Arbuthnot and Blake? And why pick on me? He must, as Gabbinger used to say, try to bring his imagination more under control. In an effort to steady his nerves, his gaze rested on the calming image of Manjushri. It was still there, of course, but somehow not so bright. Maybe some of the floor lamps had given out or been shifted.

As he had expected, the oracle had by now emerged from his trance and was drinking slowly from a cup handed to him by the lama. The fierce, mask-like features of Migo Lopen had somehow dissolved leaving him with a stunned expression like an elderly man who had just been mugged, while in the background the voice of the guiding lama could be heard chanting a short prayer of thanksgiving. And yet the other figures in the tableau had not moved, and Timothy sensed that the drama was soon going to continue, that a second feature was scheduled. To his dismay, he also found that prospect strangely exciting. He wanted to flee, to escape before something unpleasant happened, but part of him also wanted to stay.

Postponing the decision, he turned instead to his neighbour to thank him again for his commentary, adding, 'how did you manage to hear what he said?' Tenzing's nephew gave him an artful smile: 'We just know,' he said. 'We can make out.'

Before he could ask him more about the oracle's final message, Timothy noticed that something else was now taking place amongst the characters in the tableau. It appeared that one of the attendant monks was endeavouring to tie some sort of thread round the fingers of the guiding lama. 'Now the lama is about to request the protector to oblige the malignant spirit to take possession of the oracle and reveal his intentions,' explained his neighbour. 'But to do this he has to be able to tie down the spirit and force him to stay in the oracle's body.' He paused before adding in a confidential whisper: 'Please understand that our reform programme will soon put a stop to these superstitious practices.'

By now the oracle was again sitting motionless, and the thread round the lama's fingers was apparently sufficiently secure for him to embark fully prepared on the second appeal to the protector. This time, however, the initial chant was shorter, and the oracle's response quicker. There was the same febrile inhaling of the incense, reddening of his face, and sudden painful convulsions, but the moment of possession seemed to come sooner, as if the spirit had been hovering close by, or, as Timothy preferred to surmise, the oracle's psychic capacities had probably been well-lubricated during the interval by a liberal intake of chang.

Whatever it was, the results were not at first spectacular. After getting up and bowing in the direction of Migo Lopen, the oracle stood there dazed and hesitant for a while; his features had not changed but he kept blinking and his lips were trembling and frothing. But then without warning he started to fling himself around from one end of the empty space to the other, making strange yelping cries, as if trying to escape, while the old lama clung on desperately to the threads round his fingers. Eventually he slowed down and came to a stop by the weapons that had been left behind on the long stool after the previous performance. Then again without warning he took hold of some of the larger stones and began to hurl them around with tremendous force, hitting some of the onlookers in the process and causing them to cry out. While most tried to duck down in their panic, a few ran forward to help the tableau monks restrain him, but only with the greatest difficulty was he finally dragged, still yelping, back to his seat.

Nothing happened for the next few minutes. The oracle, who still seemed to be in his trance, lay back panting and sobbing, the sweat being wiped from his face by the monks, and in between taking sips from a cup held with difficulty by the lama. At last, the latter appeared to judge that it was now possible to initiate some form of interrogation, this time using not words but gestures. 'Why,' he seemed to ask with his thread-bound fingers outstretched, or, as Timothy's neighbour interpreted it, 'Who?' The audience, now recovered from the earlier panic, held their breath.

The oracle's response was unexpected: after a spasm of blinking he simply opened his eyes and looked around—something that rarely happened in such séances—all the time making a low whistling sound. Timothy saw immediately that his eyes were dark red, glaring like a pair of lanterns in the semi-darkness that meanwhile seemed to have extended its hold over the gonkhang. They looked exactly how he remembered them on that first occasion when the man had stared at him in that peculiar way as he had talked with Norbu and Chana, and, though he fought hard against the notion, he could not help feeling that they were searching for him again.

The spirit of the migo—for it was easy to see him as such—now stood up and, followed at a safe distance by the attendant monks, slowly seemed to slide his way along towards the further end of the front row of onlookers that began under the darkening image of Manjushri. There he stopped and started to peer closely into the frightened faces of the monks, row behind row, as if trying to seek out the one from whose frame he would expel the conscious principle and into which insert his own. The process was excruciatingly slow and deliberate, and the longer it took, the more Timothy became convinced—despite the protests of his rational self—that it would only end when the oracle's eyes met his own. But what was even more alarming was that at some level he seemed to want this to happen, want the oracle's glaring eyes to lock onto his, want to become wild . . .

As the oracle came closer and the sound of his whistling grew louder, Timothy got to his feet. He had to escape from this dark and sinister place at once, with its overpowering stench of rancid butter, even if this meant trampling on the hands and feet of the surrounding monks. Struggling to find his way to the door—and intermittently pursued by his own shadow—he was aware of upturned faces, dim and startled, and for a fleeting moment even thought he caught a glimpse of his friends, Warden Norbu and Lama Wangdi – but, if so, why had they ignored him? As he sprinted across the outside landing and reached the stairs—unable to see anything clearly for there were no lamps here—he tripped on one of the large stones thrown out by the oracle and fell headlong down the stairs into darkness. A spray of tiny illuminated flowers and figurines seemed to fan out in front of him, fragmenting as they rose. 'If this is how they will capture my spirit,' he thought, 'who will free me?' The fragments froze above him and there was nothing more.

PART FIVE

Princess Dekyi

22

'What have you been upto, Abbu?' Huma had always been
frank and direct with her father in moments of crisis just
as he had usually been vague and indirect with her. In fact she had
not expected to find him at home when she called from the Shahs'
bungalow, but now as she had him on the phone they both realised
he would not find it easy to be evasive, whether they spoke in Urdu
or English, or more likely, a mixture of both.

'Look, Beti, I am only trying to help you. I know this young man
very well. He was my student in Delhi a few years ago. He is a very
decent fellow who comes from a good family. I'm sure you will like
him once you get over this . . . this surprise.' He was going to say
'shock' but it was not his way to use a harsh word where a soft one
would serve better.

'But Abbu, you know very well that's not the point. I told you
long ago I would choose my own husband when the time came, and
I thought you had understood and agreed to all that.'

'Beti, I have got to tell you that something else has happened – something I haven't even told your Ammi yet. You see the authorities at my university here are trying to get rid of me and take away my full pension rights. They say I have been spending too much time away in America but the real reason is that they don't like the kind of history I teach: it's not in tune with national feeling. Now if they succeed, I will no longer be able to support you all properly in the future. So . . .'

'But Abbu you never have supported us properly!'

'You are right Huma, I have not been a good father to you.' As usual, he sounded so plaintive that she began to feel sorry for him. 'But now the situation may get even worse, unless you have some other resources to draw upon. That's why . . .'

'I have got my own job in the Conservation Institute,' Huma interrupted. 'But you never take that seriously, do you?'

'Of course, I do, and I'm very proud of you. But that job pays only a pittance. And besides, there's another thing which Ammi worries about a lot. You are twenty-six now, and though you are still a lovely girl you are getting to the age where men will not still be flocking after you . . . Huma, please go back and try and make it up with Sherwani Sahib, for your own sake and ours.'

Huma didn't reply. Her father was not usually so persistent. Perhaps that woman friend of his in America was behind all this. She put down the phone.

For a while she sat and waited, overwhelmed by a familiar feeling of betrayal, and half hoping her father would call back. When no call came she began to feel stronger. It was clear from what he had said that Mr Sherwani must have contacted him—perhaps through his own parents in Delhi—soon after that embarrassing scene in his office. It was also likely that in the next few days all kinds of pressures would be brought to bear to induce her to change her mind. Above all, she would need to keep a cool head to think things over quietly, and to do that, she needed to escape and, if possible, go into hiding somewhere.

But where? If only Abbot Taranatha's invitation to attend the protectors' festival at Migoling could be brought forward a week. Who knows, perhaps it could, if she could somehow convey a personal message to him. The trouble was, as Mr Kelsang had earlier explained to her, the Abbot was still very ill, and on no account to be disturbed. But she also remembered what Princess Dekyi had told her at that reception: that if she ever needed help, or wanted to reach Taranatha in a hurry, she should not be afraid to get in touch with her. Huma did not feel like telephoning her now. Since it was a bright though cold morning, and Mr Kelsang would not mind if she started work later, she could easily walk to Dekyi's house which was somewhere on the northern outskirts of the city. Putting on her thick red down jacket, she managed to slip out of the bungalow before Mrs Shah could appear for what she called their morning chat, in reality a thinly veiled attempted update on all the more personal aspects of Huma's life.

Following her usual route through the Indian colony, Huma realised that her mood had changed. True, part of her was still depressed and anxious as a result of what her father had said, but at the same time he had inadvertently opened up another scenario: the prospect not of merely rejecting Mr Sherwani and remaining single but of actually marrying someone else of her own choosing. Since this idea had entered her mind it proved surprisingly hard to shift, and she found herself daydreaming about whether she might marry Timothy, whose company she had certainly been missing a lot during the past few days. What, she kept wondering, had happened to him since he had returned to the monastery? And was it even possible that it had been hidden thoughts of him that lay behind her rapid decision to look for a way out of her current problems by bringing forward her own visit to Migoling? She again reminded herself of the need to remain cool. There was no sense in escaping from the pressure of her father's machinations only to be carried away by her own romantic impulses.

Suddenly something furry brushed against her leg. It was Rustum, the Shahs' Persian cat, who had recently developed some kind of feline crush on her, unless, of course, he was being trained to spy on her movements by Mrs Shah. He had somehow managed to follow her all this way through the city without her becoming aware of his presence. After a few futile attempts to shoo him back home, she accepted his company. It was like having a familiar, or, as some people here seemed to believe, having one's own spiritual double occupying an animate form.

They were now passing by the Shar Lama's palace on the other side of the narrow river and following a road that would, she hoped, eventually lead off towards Dekyi's house. A small band of monk musicians was stationed outside the palace walls, blowing their long trumpets loudly in what looked like a rehearsal for some sort of state occasion. She knew that there were all kinds of rumours flying around that a special public ceremony was going to be held soon—fifty years after the Shar Lama's accession—in which various sweeping changes would be announced, including a development programme to be funded by the World Bank and a new name for the country itself. It was, according to some sources, going to be called Zhing Kham, the Pure Land – not perhaps the most auspicious rebranding for a South Asian country, bearing in mind the fate of Pakistan which had at its inception laid claim to a Persian version of the same aspiring description. Huma was also, of course, only too aware that the Migoling history project was intended to confer the final seal of legitimacy on the Shar Lama's government as it moved to inaugurate these national changes.

As the road separated itself from the river and began a slow winding ascent through the barley fields towards the mountains, Huma realised that Princess Dekyi's original directions for finding her place had not been very exact. She could see several large farmhouses—impressive half stone and timbered buildings with elegant, gently sloping roofs—scattered around the landscape, any one of which might turn out to be hers. She would probably have to stop at one and ask the way. As she hesitated, she caught sight of a small car coming down the road ahead from the lower slopes of the mountain. It looked very old but shiny, almost glittering, and as it appeared to be travelling towards her at considerable speed, she cautiously stepped aside to the edge of the narrow road. When the car drew closer she could make out that the driver was a middle-aged Tibetan man and that some passenger was sitting behind him. Then without warning the driver braked hard, causing the ancient vehicle to rear up and swerve wildly, barely missing Rustum who, now calmly sitting in the middle of the road licking his paws, had evidently chosen that precise moment to leap out in front of it.

The driver and his passenger, a woman virtually smothered beneath innumerable scarves, emerged slowly, obviously considerably shaken. 'Well,' said the wrapped woman speaking in English, 'at least the cat is unhurt!' Huma swallowed on her apologies. 'Princess Dekyi!' she gasped.

'The trouble with fathers,' said Dekyi, exhaling a benevolent cloud of cheroot smoke, 'is that they either love their daughters too much or not enough. Mine was the first kind!'

Huma and she were sitting on facing cushions in the second floor living room of Dekyi's large converted farmhouse, with Mrs Shah's cat stretched out in front of them before a rusty iron stove. The rest of the room was bare of furniture except for a low table, and a few shelves on one of which stood a cage containing a small green parrot. The other shelves supported numerous framed photos of members of Dekyi's family and various social gatherings. Outside, in the courtyard, they could hear the Tibetan driver testing and re-testing the engine of the Princess's ancient baby Austen.

Huma had meant to explain her predicament coolly with the minimum of essential detail, but the sympathetic warmth of the old lady's welcome and her readiness to drop her previous programme and attend to her, had had their natural effect, and she had found herself almost tearfully pouring out the whole story of her father's betrayal and the agent general's extraordinary proposal. Dekyi had then promised to dispatch her driver—engine permitting—to Migoling in the afternoon, with an urgent request to the Abbot to provide Huma with advanced sanctuary.

'But what exactly did your father do that was wrong for you?' For the moment relieved of her own worries, Huma felt close to her benefactress.

'He was simply too proud of me when I was young, taking me around to all the important people he had to meet, and all the time showing me off. And because he himself was almost the most important person in the country—for many years he was the Shar Lama's chief minister—everybody thought they had to admire and reward me in order to gain his favour. The result was not so much that I thought I was very special, but that my special position was only natural and ordinary. It was part of the way the world was made.'

'What about your mother? What did she think of you?'

'My mother was a very good woman, but she had soon realised that I belonged first and foremost to my father: I was his little doll, and, so being a kind and practical woman, she concentrated on bringing up my brothers. And so you see, held high by father, flattered and comforted by everyone, I floated through my childhood and girlhood with very little idea of what the world was really like.'

'So that's how you became a balloon lady!' Huma's first image of Dekyi as she had appeared at the minister's reception came back to her with such telling immediacy that she could not hold it back.

'Yes. What a good description, especially since I have now put on so much weight!' For a moment Dekyi looked a trifle disconcerted.

'But Huma, at the time I'm talking about, I was very light and slim. In fact, my father used to call me his little Zugma.'

'zugma?'

'Yes. It's what people in India call a dakini – a kind of fairy or wise woman who belongs to the sky, but comes down to help mortals seeking enlightenment. But yes—as you said—a sort of balloon lady!'

'But didn't anybody—any man, for instance—ever bring you down to earth?'

'Oh yes,' Dekyi said. 'Several tried and one almost succeeded . . . But before I tell you about that, let's get some lunch.' She leant out the window and called to her driver: 'Lobzang, leave that car alone now and find us something to eat.'

For the next few minutes Dekyi seemed to withdraw into herself, murmuring mantras under her breath and slowly counting the beads on her rosary. Huma felt bad: perhaps the old lady had been hurt by her tactless evocation of the balloon image.

'Wake up, Princess!' said Lobzang, eventually depositing various bowls and trays on the low table, containing oranges, saffron rice and small cakes.

Dekyi beamed happily: 'These are the kind of things we used to have in my father's picnics,' she said, 'especially those he would arrange for the AG . . . I mean the agent general. You see, Huma, because of his position, my father had to see a lot of the AG in those days and so he tried his best to build up a friendly relationship with him by organising expeditions to scenic spots. Actually these things were quite elaborate. First, he would send out a troop of porters and minor officials on mule-back to find a suitable place, and there they would erect a small tent and prepare the refreshments. And some hours later my father and I would set out in our car followed by the AG in his. That's, of course, if the place could be reached by road, otherwise we would go there on ponies.

'The AG was a young man, not bad-looking, if a little on the plump side. He was really quite attached to our country, and my father liked him. And though I was still an innocent young dakini, I could tell that he liked me too because he was too shy to look at me for long, but then when he thought I wasn't looking, he would dart these intense little glances at me.

'One fine day in early spring my father arranged a picnic for all of us near the monastery at Migoling. We drove out there as usual and the monks staged a special masked dance for us. Then we all walked out to a meadow where my father's men had set up the tent and prepared the refreshments, just like what Lobzang has got us.'

Huma began to feel a bit restive. Dekyi seemed to have forgotten the point of their previous conversation, and to be just randomly recalling picturesque events from her past.

'At first we had a good time that afternoon; I seem to remember we all played rounders. But then, just as we were having our tea, the weather changed abruptly and it started to rain very hard indeed, as it occasionally does at that time of year. Unfortunately our little tent collapsed and all ended in panic and confusion, with some people running back towards the monastery while others tried to find their way through the forest tracks and back to the cars. Somehow in all the confusion I got separated from my father and found myself alone with the AG taking shelter from the storm in a nearby hermitage cave used by the local monks. It all happened very fast then: he began to kiss me wildly and I recall that I didn't try to stop him because I liked him and—as a sort of self-appointed dakini—I felt I had a duty to help him. We ended up making love on the straw floor in front of a rather startled-looking image of Guru Rinpoche.'

'Did anyone find out'? asked Huma, her attention now magically recaptured.

'Fortunately not,' said Dekyi. 'It was all over so quickly, and we each managed to make our way separately through the downpour and back to the cars without anyone else getting suspicious.

'And so Huma, one could say that though our respective fathers may have treated us very differently, we both ended up with an AG in our lives!'

'I know I shouldn't really ask you this, Princess,' said Huma smiling, 'but I'm dying to know what sort of Indian was this agent general? Was he a Sikh?'

Dekyi looked puzzled. 'My dear, he wasn't an Indian at all. He was an Englishman. Really, I thought you had understood.'

'You mean it was . . . Mr Hoadley?'

'Yes, of course, it was Mr Hoadley!'

'And what happened afterwards? What on earth did he do?'

But Dekyi had finished her story. It was, she intimated, now time for Huma to leave. Perhaps if the Abbot sent back the message that she could go out to Migoling tomorrow—and the old car was still working—she would tell her more then. And meanwhile Huma must not leave her cat behind.

'Eh Gee!' screeched the green parrot from across the room as his potential enemy departed. 'Eh Gee!'

23

Princess Dekyi arrived early next morning at Huma's office, having apparently secured the Abbot's permission for her to stay in Migoling village for the week prior to the protectors' festival. But Dekyi's mind seemed to be somewhere else as she waved Huma to join her in the back seat of the car, and for some time she continued to remain silent. Huma didn't mind this because she herself was also preoccupied with her own thoughts. Another letter from her sister Rukhsi had just arrived which she had only managed to read after she had left the bungalow – having first had to tell Mrs Shah that she was going to be away for a fortnight touring the country with a friend. The letter had said:

Dearest Apa, you must by now have heard from Abbu about his plan to marry you off to Sherwani Sahib. I'm afraid it's even worse than you can imagine because I have found out (don't ask me how), that

Sherwani's father is some high-up official in the Ministry of Education, or whatever it's called, and Abbu thinks he will try to intervene to save his university job if his son marries you. I have told Abbu and Ammi that I will go on hunger strike unless they stop pressurising you. Rest is all OK. Love, Rukhsi.

P.S. Please try to get me a pair of those special Kalapuri boots before you leave.

Huma desperately wanted to believe that her sister was mistaken in her suspicions. It had been painful enough to accept that her father had embarked on his plot for the reasons he himself had given her, without having to come to terms with this extra dimension. In fact, since the effort took up virtually all her mental and emotional resources, it was just as well that Dekyi herself also seemed to have retired into her own inner world.

'That's where it happened!' the Princess called out, suddenly emerging from her reverie as they stopped in front of the Himjin High School for Girls. 'That's where I learnt about the invasion plans!'

Huma had been dimly aware in the midst of her own thoughts and anxieties that instead of making straight for the Migoling road, the driver had for some time been criss-crossing Himjin evidently in search of this building away on the other side of the expanding city.

'This used to be the old Agency General building in Mr Hoadley's time,' Dekyi explained. 'Now it has been turned into a school.'

Huma found her own state of self-absorption dissolving fast at this new revelation. 'What invasion plans?' she asked.

'British, of course,' said Dekyi, with the thinly-controlled patience of one who expects others to have full access to their own mental resources. 'Surely you know, Huma, that the British government in India sent an expeditionary force here in 1944, just after the old Shar Lama had disappeared – surely you know about that!' The old lady began to relax more. 'Look,' she added, 'I know you don't want a history lesson. You want to hear what happened to me and the AG. But it just happens that history was an essential part of our relationship; at least that's what the AG thought.' Huma detected a touch of regret in her voice.

By this time, the unusually glittering but antique appearance of the Princess's car was beginning to attract the attention of a number of schoolgirls. 'Are you making a film?' one of them enquired boldly in excellent English.

Dekyi looked distinctly put out. 'Drive on, Lobzang!' she said imperiously.

Once again Dekyi seemed to withdraw into herself, and it was not until they had travelled some way up the Migoling road that she again took up the story, immediately forcing Huma to abandon her resumed meditation on paternal betrayals.

'After what happened that day in the hermitage cave, the AG wrote me a long apologetic letter. He told me how terribly sorry he was, that he had completely lost control of himself, and asked me if I would ever forgive him. Without exactly spelling it out, he also conveyed to me that because of his official position and the duties entrusted to him, it would be impossible for him to ask me to marry him, and he could only beg me to keep it all a secret from my father, and try to carry on as if nothing had happened!'

'And did you keep it a secret?' Huma put in quickly.

'Oh yes,' said Dekyi, 'what else could I do? If I had opened my mouth, there would have been an almighty scandal, a diplomatic incident of Himalayan proportions!' She giggled for a moment. 'But you know, Huma, it was still very hard to bear . . . not so much that he should have done such a thing in the first place—though the possible consequences of that were worrying enough at the time—but that he could then write such a letter: almost like an official communication of apology from HMG's representative.' She waved her head from side to side in still inextinguished incredulity.

'All the same he was taking quite a risk in writing that letter,' Huma pointed out. 'After all, if you had decided to tell your father and an official complaint had been lodged, then he would have given you self-incriminating evidence.'

'Yes, you are right,' Dekyi admitted. 'But there was also something else in his letter that in a strange way did the AG some credit, taking him to a higher plane. You see he ended up saying that he would find a way of trying to make it up, if not to me personally, then to my country. Of course, I didn't understand it properly at the time, but in a peculiar sort of way he appeared to regard what he had done to me as a kind of symbol of how Britain had all too often treated Kalapur itself: as a little strategic toy that existed primarily for its greater neighbour's advantage and convenience. And so he felt he had to pay me back, not so much humanly, or as man to woman, but politically!'

'But how on earth could he do that?' asked Huma, now totally gripped.

'Well, it was quite simple really: he had to betray his own country – at least I think he'd decided on that.'

'You mean you don't actually know for certain?'

'Well, let me tell you what happened next, Huma, and then you can judge for yourself. You see some months later—I think it was around the middle of 1944—relations between my father and the AG were getting more strained with the Japanese invading India and the old Shar Lama extending hospitality to some Japanese monks. The British authorities in India were convinced these monks were spies, though the AG himself was not so sure. One day my father was having some discussions with Mr Hoadley in the old agency office we just visited, and as usual he had taken me with him as kind of secretary, of course, knowing nothing about what had taken place at the picnic. For some reason or other, Mr Hoadley and my father had to go into the outer office, leaving me all by myself in the

AG's private room with his official files piled up on his desk. And I remember that the topmost file was called on the cover "Japanese monks in Himjin", or something like that, and it was marked "Hush – Most Secret!"

'It's time for your medicine, Princess,' said Lobzang interrupting her flow to pass back a bottle of a locally-brewed brandy. Huma noticed that its label depicted two smiling yetis sharing a drink in the snow.

'You must join me, Huma,' said Dekyi, reaching inside her bag for two wooden cups, 'especially now the weather's turning so abominable.'

Looking out of the car window for the first time since the story had started to unfold, Huma was surprised to see how thick the mountain mist had become in a few minutes. They must, she surmised, have now reached the highest point in the pass before the road began to wind down towards Migoling. Recalling how long Lobzang had spent trying to put the engine right on the previous day, she started to feel a little nervous: what if they had a breakdown here on this cold and desolate stretch? How long would they have to wait for help?

'Here, drink up,' said Dekyi. 'It's good for the nerves!'

'Anyway,' she continued, resuming her story, 'there I was all alone with the AG's secret file – and, as you can imagine, it was impossible not to read it. In fact, I recall having the strong feeling that he meant me to read it since he was not the sort of fellow who would carelessly leave something like that just lying around . . . And it was then that I learnt the most astonishing news: overriding the AG's more cautious advice, New Delhi had decided to send a small Indian Army contingent up through the passes to Kalapur, with instructions to the AG to expel the monks and place the Shar Lama under immediate house arrest in his own palace! Can you imagine?' The old lady's eyes opened so wide that Huma felt she was about to be visually consumed.

'But the oddest thing was that I knew at once what I had to do: I would not tell my father, at least not immediately, but I would take action by myself. You see I already had one terrible secret, and this was just another one to add to the score. So, when they came back into the room, I said "Yes, Papa, No, Papa, and Goodbye Your Excellency" as usual, and then at the first opportunity I ran round to the Shar Lama's private secretary (he's dead now, of course, probably murdered) and told him what I had seen in the AG's office. And two days later, very early in the morning, the Lama took off in his little aircraft. And the rest,' said Dekyi, downing the remains of her Two Yetis with a flourish . . . 'the rest is still a mystery!'

'Amazing!' said Huma. 'But surely you must have told the story to others.'

'Only to my father,' said Dekyi, 'in a censored version and a long time afterwards – in fact shortly before he died.'

'So what made you tell me now?' Huma only wished Timothy could have been there.

Dekyi didn't reply immediately. 'I'm not sure I know myself,' she said finally. 'I suppose it was partly because you began by telling me about your father and your own AG story . . . and, of course, you can appreciate that my story is . . . well, so personal, that it is not one I can go round telling people here, especially in the current climate of censorship and conspiracy. But yes, there is another explanation which you may find it hard to follow. You see, believe it or not, I myself could never quite explain or accept what had happened with Mr Hoadley, and because I could not understand it, I decided to bury the memory of it – until now!'

'You mean, somehow my coming here helped you to . . . to come to terms with it.'

'Yes, it did. And that's very important according to our local Buddhist tradition in Kalapur. No, I don't mean that stuff about Maitreya we hear so much about these days; I mean the older, deeper sense of the Spirit of Time (that Taranatha represents) that says that, we must first understand the course of our own lives before we can hope to end the process of becoming and of rebirth, and that we can best do this in direct communication with others who are in a position to benefit from what we know. For me, you are such a person, and that's why I told you.'

They had by now emerged from the mountain mists and descended into the Migoling valley. On the opposite slopes, high above the pine forest, the roofs of the monastery were just visible. Huge white clouds hung low overhead, threatening at any moment to engulf them.

'The village is just around the corner,' Dekyi announced, 'beyond those fields there. The Abbot has arranged for you to stay in one of the farmhouses. It belongs to the family of one of the monastery officials. His name is Norbu.'

24

Huma lay awake in Norbu's guest-room, half-listening to the early morning grunts of the farm animals in the stables below. After four days' stay she now realised that this was almost the only time when she could be alone with her thoughts. At all other times during the day she had already become part of the family, and to an increasing degree, part of the village community as well – expected to answer endless questions, to debate local issues in their regular social gatherings, and in between impelled by her own sense of duty (and despite her hosts' attempts to stop her), to help out in the routine activities of farming, as winter drew to a close. It was not easy in these circumstances to imagine what life might be like with either Ahmed Sherwani or Timothy Curtin – as one cleaned out the mangers of goats and cattle or collected their dung for manure. Only during the hour or so before the family rose—and as her own mind hovered between dreams and full consciousness—could she make the attempt, which after all had been part of her reason for coming here.

In the case of Sherwani Sahib, or the Eh Gee as she now thought of him, the life she could expect, were she to accede to her father's wishes, was not all that difficult to imagine. Above all, it would be a highly social type of life that she would enter. Well, there was nothing insurmountable about being sociable, indeed she rather enjoyed it. And surely if she could successfully adjust to these Himalayan villagers, she should also be able to cope with foreign diplomats and their wives.

Or would she? She had already seen enough of that world to know that she would not find it easy to be natural or remain herself within its confines and conventions: always to be polite to people who bored her, to make endless small talk at her husband's receptions, to be officially stationed in another country without feeling part of it. The more she thought about it, the more intolerable it became. And what would be the purpose of it all – other than to help save Abbu's job and placate her Ammi's fatalism? That it would give her the supreme opportunity of learning to love—or at least live with—a man of whom she knew virtually nothing, who in turn—for this was clearly part of the bargain following the failure of his first marriage—would expect her to give him a son, so that the same pattern might be secured and repeated for the next generation.

But what about Timothy? What would life be like with him? Ever since he had said goodbye and gone back to the monastery, she knew she had become attached to him, and that they had both become quite deeply involved in the same local issues. But she had only known him for a few weeks, so would such feelings last, and would he, and the different lifestyle that would inevitably accompany him, actually be good for her? Back in her home in India, despite their constant insecurities, she had some sense—in her father's absence—of her own position as the main support for the family, and at least until this new and unexpected development, had believed that they had both respected her position and accepted her independence. On the other hand, if she were to marry Timothy and perhaps live in London, might he somehow exploit her readiness to help him, till she ended up being turned into an English housewife, catering to his whims, while occasionally subjected to the racist attitudes and condescension of the ethnic English, who would deny her even that position?

She was again brought back to the present by the sounds from the animals below. Why was it that she had ended up seeing the negative sides of both relationships? It seemed that her experience of her father's constant betrayals was forever casting its shadow over her expectations, that and perhaps also her mother's pessimism unmediated by her sense of resignation. Here at least she had an opportunity to observe a refreshingly different style of family life, a different set of assumptions about what was required of fathers, mothers and their children.

'This,' Norbu had announced to her when they first met, with a mixture of pride and embarrassment, 'this is my wife Sonam.' Huma had barely time to get used to the idea of a married monk before he had gone on to introduce his elder brother Puntzog, who it turned out was also married to Sonam, and (together with Norbu himself) was evidently the co-father of Sonam's two older daughters and two younger sons – the latter attending the primary school attached to the Migoling Monastery, without themselves being enrolled as novices. These first disorientating introductions had ended with Huma meeting Norbu's unmarried sister Yangchen, a rather sad-looking woman who seemed to exist slightly on the margins of the relaxed and cheerful group dynamics of the rest of the family, though fully expected to minister to it. Huma was later to encounter Norbu's elderly parents, who shared the smaller next-door house along with several other relatives whose precise status and connections her mind refused to take in.

As soon as she had grasped the unfamiliar shape of the family, Huma perceived that though Puntzog, as the elder married brother, was nominally regarded as its head, it was really Sonam who occupied the pivotal position, expected to determine and arrange the main business of each day and generally consulted on all other matters of concern. At the same time there didn't seem to be any tightly-fixed gender roles within the family, with all adults happily sharing in agricultural and household jobs as well as taking care of the children, with only the unfortunate Yangchen being treated by all as a kind of unpaid servant.

Above all, what most surprised Huma was the apparent absence of any jealous tensions between Norbu and his brother, and the fact that none of the children seemed to differentiate between their two 'fathers', or display any awareness of truly 'belonging' to one rather than the other. It was difficult to conceive of a set-up and atmosphere more different from her own family life, with her absent father, and her mother still brooding miserably on her failure to bear him a son, and indeed Huma's own preoccupation with his inability to love her as much as she felt she deserved. Was it really any wonder that he'd tried to escape – from the eternal guilt of his wife and the heart-breaking expectations of his elder daughter?

Also very different—and disconcerting too—was the family's frankness about sex, especially the occasional bawdiness of Sonam's conversation when they were joined by neighbours. Huma had had considerable difficulty at the start in persuading Norbu to promise not to reveal her arrival in the village to Timothy, with whom he appeared to have established a close friendship. She had no idea how he had explained this to his wife, but during the previous evening when they had all been invited to another house to join other farming families, Sonam had convulsed the other villagers by apparently hinting at the physical pleasures which Huma was missing by keeping her presence a secret from her boyfriend. Since Sonam could not speak English and Huma's understanding of Kalapur Tibetan was very limited, it had taken her some time to make out what they had been saying, and even then she wasn't quite sure about it, leaving her no alternative but to cover her own confusion with a falsely-knowing smile.

But it was not so much sex as politics and religion that had dominated the conversation that evening, swept along by vast quantitites of chang, for which Huma (who had up till then avoided it) was, under pressure from the family, now acquiring a taste. As she recalled what had happened and what she had said, she could hardly believe she could have lost her cool so badly.

It had started when she had learnt that secret agents sent by the Migo resistance fighters had been recently circulating amongst the villagers, trying to enlist their support for national elections, and warning them against the government's plans to force them to abandon their traditional religion. Most of those present inclined to support the Migo cause but a minority led by a tall eloquent farmer argued heatedly in favour of the government's policies. Huma could only understand about half of what he said but she gathered he was telling his neighbours about the huge international loan that the Shar Lama and his ministers were about to negotiate with the World Bank. This, he assured them, would create much needed hydro-electric schemes and other new sources of power and wealth, such as oil, from which modern hospitals could eventually be built. By contrast, he claimed, the Migos' continuing opposition would only lead to more bloodshed and postpone the material progress that otherwise lay within their grasp.

After a while Huma anxiously noticed that some people were beginning to be swayed by his arguments. 'Just imagine,' said Yangchen, her eyes shining, 'electric lights and hot water all the time!'

'And cars not yaks!' put in one of the Norbu-Puntzog boys.

Apparently detecting some scepticism in Huma's expression, the farmer started to turn his attention to her, switching to fluent English in the process. 'Above all, we must look to India, your country, for help,' he said ingratiatingly. As Huma continued to sip her chang in silence, he went on, trying to get her to declare her opinions: 'As you've just heard, more and more people here want material progress. They want cars and electricity not terrorism and bloodshed.'

'Do they also want despotism and lies?' Huma burst out, unable to contain herself any longer. 'And what about holding elections?' Shouts of encouragement came from several Migo supporters behind her.

'Despotism? I don't know what you mean. Here we expect a government to govern. And what are these lies you mention?' The farmer's eyes narrowed.

'Well for a start, lies about their legitimacy, their right to rule,' said Huma hotly. 'Perhaps you don't know about it, but there's growing evidence that the whole recent history of this country has been distorted to justify their seizure of power.'

'So,' said the farmer sarcastically. 'You think we are interested in these ancient academic debates? I tell you we don't care any more about the past – what we want is a better future!'

'And we also want all our neighbours to celebrate the end of winter peacefully together,' said Norbu arriving late for the party, and adding in an anxious whisper to Huma, as he drew her aside: 'this man is the richest local farmer and a leading supporter of the Tulku. Please be careful what you say.'

Just as well he had rescued her then, she thought. Otherwise, with all that chang inside her, she would probably have gone on to reveal Timothy's search for the lost manuscript, not to mention Princess Dekyi's stories about Mr Hoadley. But the encounter had not just been personally embarrassing: on another level it had also been disconcerting to discover through what the farmer had said a certain naivety about her own approach. After all, in a sense, he was right: what she and Timothy had been investigating had happened half a century ago, and meanwhile the ordinary people around her were still struggling to survive in a bare subsistence economy, and with only the basic remedies afforded by traditional medicine. Could she blame them if they clutched hopefully at the government's promises of a better life?

25

Later that morning, after accompanying Puntzog and some herdsmen down to the stream to water the goats, Huma decided that she could reasonably leave the family to their own devices in the afternoon, and go by herself in search of the hermitage cave where Mr Hoadley had made love to Princess Dekyi. She had always intended to look for the place and today seemed a good enough time to do so, particularly after she had heard Puntzog talking earlier about a bizarre event that had happened during the night.

Apparently, the Tulku's men at the monastery, joined by some villagers, had shot and wounded a migo wandering in the vicinity of the village. Nobody had got close enough to be sure whether it had been of the human or yeti kind, and whatever it was had managed to escape the hunters, leaving a trail of blood visible the next morning. Since Huma guessed that the event would almost certainly come up for debate at the villagers' usual late-afternoon chang party, it might be prudent to absent herself and so avoid getting embroiled in another heated argument about the rights and wrongs of the Migo resistance movement.

Not, of course, that she herself didn't care about what had really happened in the night. In fact, as she set out after lunch across the narrow bare fields—soon to be ploughed for buckwheat—towards the route that Sonam had told her to follow, her mind kept returning to the mystery.

Both she and Timothy had always found it hard to understand the real grounds for the government's negative representation of Kalapur's alleged indigenous wildmen. Instead of protecting and studying them (if they really existed), or even 'advertising' them as potentially money-spinning tourist attractions, they were officially branded as evil, sub-human creatures whose spiritual master, Migo Lopen, had broken whatever original vow he had taken to protect Buddhism. This in turn was part of the regime's wider efforts to persuade people to abandon their traditional Himalayan version of the dharma which, it was claimed, now needed to be thoroughly cleansed of ancient local cults and superstitions.

At the same time, it was obvious that this negative projection of the migos was also politically designed to strengthen the government's stance against the shadowy, long-term opposition movement, which had originally assumed the Migos' name in order to draw upon the country's deep folkloric belief in their awesome power and tenacity. Thus, by asserting every now and then that its own forces had destroyed some indigenous migo, when it had actually killed a rebel fighter, the government sought to create the impression that the very real and human Migo resistance to its authority was largely fictitious. Given the villagers' recent testimony to the presence of Migo agents in the area, that was almost certainly what had taken place last night.

As Huma climbed the steep path that led up through the forest to the hermitage cave, she began to wonder whether she had really chosen the right day for this excursion. Despite all the villagers' jocular talk of the imminent arrival of spring (when their current round of parties would soon give way to gruelling hard work), today it had steadily become much colder, with the sky turning from cloudy blue to leaden grey. Sonam had told her that it would take about an hour to reach the cave, but she had only managed to leave the farmhouse by half-past two. That could mean that if she somehow lost her way or got delayed by a sudden heavy blizzard—as had happened to Dekyi at her picnic party some fifty years before—it could be quite dark by the time she returned, a conveniently suspicious and shadowy target for the Tulku's nocturnal anti-Migo patrols!

All around her the coniferous trees were dark and still, and the white magnolias she glimpsed through the trees looked like exotic refugees caught unprepared in a hostile climate. At one point she even thought she heard the sudden crunching sound of trodden twigs not far behind her, quickly spun around, but saw nothing. To keep up her spirits, she tried to think about the special dances for the protectors' festival in which Norbu and Puntzog had asked her to join in a few days' time. They had shown her all sorts of wonderful costumes and animal or spirit masks, one of which had looked uncannily like a caricature of her father. The authorities would, of course, have liked to have banned such dances, with their associations with Migo Lopen and other undesirable protectors, but they were still far too popular for them to risk confrontations with hundreds of angry villagers and monks.

At last she emerged out of the wood on to a grassy meadow bordered on the far side by a rocky escarpment. Sonam had told her to look out for the prayer flags that marked the entrance to the cave, and sure enough not very far to the right she could make out two white strips against an ocean grey sky – like the thin sails of a boat. A tremor of excitement jerked her cold limbs back to life: it seemed that the story of Dekyi's long-ago adventure with the amorous Eh Gee had touched her more than she had realised.

The cave, when she reached it, had obviously been improved considerably since Dekyi's day. A thick stone wall with a lockable door and a small window had been constructed along the front side, and inside the place had been quite thoughtfully equipped—almost refurbished—with all the basic necessities for a prolonged withdrawal into solitary meditation: a straw mattress, a table and chair, and even a small wood-burning stove with a flue pipe projecting out above the entrance. Rather to her disappointment, it did not immediately look like the right scene for a dramatic sexual encounter except perhaps of the most mystical Tantric type. She recalled that Dekyi had told her that when she had come here the cave had been virtually devoid of furniture, with only a wooden altar on which had stood a small bronze figure of Guru Rinpoche. That had now gone and been replaced by a solitary female figure leaning forward in a poise of graceful tension. Huma felt sure it was a dakini, and the thought brought Dekyi closer.

She at once began to take in the artistic qualities of the image more intently, and was particularly struck by the skill with which the artist had captured the balance and energy of the female body, with the gilt surface investing it with an extra glow of warmth. It was obvious too, that whoever had been using the cave recently had been careful to keep the figure free of dust, though oddly—as she examined its position on the wooden altar more closely—it seemed to be very slightly tilted to one side and not exactly centrally placed either. Huma had always felt uncomfortable with the asymmetric, nonetheless being also cautious, she hesitated before grasping the twelve-inch brass figure gently to restore it to its proper position. As she did so, she could tell that there was some kind of small obstruction underneath that was causing a slight deviation from the horizontal plane. Raising the figure higher, revealed it to be a small paper plug that had evidently dropped out of a deep narrow opening under the base of the image. Huma instinctively poked her finger inside the hole to discover what felt like a thin sharp spool with paper sheets tightly rolled around it. Though it would almost certainly only turn out to contain nothing more than a sequence of prayers, her curiosity was aroused, and so she fiddled and tugged away till the roll finally slipped out on to the altar like a neatly delivered parcel.

With practised deftness, Huma started to unroll the scroll. As she had expected, it was covered with the Tibetan script and was also surprisingly long. The paper seemed quite old, probably more than twenty years by the looks of it, perhaps older still. But why go on further, she thought, there's nothing I can understand here? Just as she was about to give up, the scroll itself suddenly came to an end, to be followed by another which appeared to be more recent and was inscribed in a different script. The light was so poor that it was several seconds before she realised it was in English, and considerably longer before she succeeded in reading the title: 'Account of the last years of the late Shar Lama prepared by the monk Tashi Rigzen for Tsewang Dorje, the Lama's Shadow.'

For a moment she stood transfixed. Then, in a sudden move that would have deeply shocked her mother and surprised even Huma herself, she flung herself in full length gratitude before the golden image of the nameless dakini. At the same time, her mind began to race forward: first she must read through the account, then she must somehow contact Timothy. She quickly got to her feet and ran towards the front of the cave, waving the scroll aloft like the vajra held by a Tantric adept. Standing next to the small window, the text should be easier to read. But even here the light was not sufficient, so she decided to open the door, only to find that it had somehow got jammed. She pushed hard against it with her shoulder. It moved a fraction before meeting the solid metal arm of the closed padlock.

'In this account I have faithfully set down the story of the last years of His Holiness in so far as it is known to me from my own experience: how he came to learn of the British plan to imprison him; how he set out with four companions in his personal airplane to take refuge in

China but was forced from lack of fuel to make an emergency landing in the remote mountains of the eastern border; how he thereupon resolved to give up his worldly powers and live the life of a humble unknown hermit in a simple hut constructed and protected by his four followers; how the author of this narrative found him there in the course of his own wandering spiritual itinerary, and for a short while became his fifth protector; and how His Holiness finally died in 1948, having declared his sacred lineage—the embodiment of the Spirit of Time—to be now defunct.

'And I have further set down this account, conscious of the facts that the Shar Lama's wishes have been subsequently disregarded, his own life story distorted, and his other faithful followers killed (I alone surviving), that the true history of these events be in due course properly recorded according to our custom, and that the present writer may acquire merit thereby.'

Huma carefully placed the scroll on the ground beside her where she lay, stretched out on the mattress, her head propped up against the altar. She had read through most of it now, skipping a few passages, till she reached the end. Not a bad achievement, she reckoned, after the shock of suddenly finding herself locked in, with no other means of escape. It was not, of course, the first time this had happened to her: in some ways her childhood punishment by the Sisters of Inordinate Mercy and her father's failure to secure her release had seemed worse. Well, she had survived that and hopefully she would also somehow evade the fate now planned for her by the Tulku's men – if they were indeed responsible. Perhaps she had been right in feeling that someone had been following her on her way through the wood . . . perhaps that farmer, whom Norbu had warned her against the other evening, had decided to try to teach her a lesson. Anyway surely, whatever monk had been using the cave recently—maybe it was the translator of the scroll—would turn up, or more likely Sonam and her family in the village would soon come out in search of her once she was found to be missing. Meanwhile whoever had been here earlier had thoughtfully left a pile of basic provisions: fuel for the stove, matches, a bucket of water, some candles and some tsampa.

But what an extraordinary story it had been, told very simply, but with a suppressed depth of feeling that pointed to its essential truth. But who was this Tashi Rigzen, not to mention the Lama's Shadow for whom his account had been intended? And who on earth was responsible for this unsigned English translation that looked as if it had only been completed a short while ago? The Abbot himself perhaps? Huma desperately longed to share her discovery with Timothy who would almost certainly think up all sorts of exciting hypotheses. But right now, having had a restless night, she was beginning to feel very sleepy. Outside some kind of snowstorm had already started when she had peered through the tiny window, after vainly trying to force the door open. It must be quite thick on the ground now and very cold, though inside the cave it felt almost pleasantly warm. She could even take off her down coat and rest her head on it. But she must try to stay awake in case anyone came and called for her. If only Timothy would come . . .

And now it seemed he had come . . . She felt his presence . . . beside her at the stern of a little sailing boat as they pulled away from the shore where her father stood waving and smiling. She waved back and heard herself calling '*Khuda Hafiz*'. The wind was blowing hard on the thin strip sails of the boat and the sky was leaden grey; in no time they had left the shore far behind, though she could just make out her father's tiny figure still waving in the distance. All this time she was also aware of Timothy's stiff presence beside her, for some reason unable to turn and look at her. Only when she poised her body, and felt herself warm and glowing like the dakini, did he free himself to face her . . .

Huma woke with a start. It was cooler and darker in the cave now. How long had she dozed off? She got up, put on her coat and walked over to the door. A stream of cold air surprised her body. She pushed hard at the door and fell out onto the snow.

Outside all was white and still – like entering a scene in an old silent film, except for a huge orange moon hung high above the trees. But Huma saw quickly that the scene was not quite as undisturbed as had first appeared, for running up across the snowy meadow between the forest and the cave lay two parallel tracks of footprints already half covered. I don't care who or what have left those tracks, she thought, I have had enough adventures for today and I'm going back to the village.

For a second, she completely forgot about the manuscript scroll she had left in the cave at the foot of the altar. She rushed back inside to fetch it but it was no longer there.

PART SIX

Taranatha

26

'What is your father's name and profession?'

It was some time before Timothy could focus on the words, let alone make sense of the question. Was he dead and this was some kind of preliminary check on his identity to determine his fate in the next life? An intense pain throbbed deep inside his head, and he had difficulty in hearing the words properly through the continuous hissing in his ears. The rest of his body seemed to be still there though; only his right ankle and foot felt stiff, swollen and very sore, as if set in concrete. Very cautiously he opened his eyes.

To his relief he found he was lying on his mattress in the monastery guest-room, and was being carefully observed by a man in a white coat whom he had not seen before. That at least meant that there was no need to ask the conventional question in such circumstances: 'Where am I?' But beyond that, what did he know and remember? And what on earth was his father's name and profession?

All kinds of scenes and sensations—answers to other questions he had not yet even consciously formulated—began to invade and overwhelm his aching head: the startled faces of the monks as he struggled to find a way out of the gonkhang, his own extended shadow hovering on the wall, the stars that rose above him as he fell . . . And with the images came all the unwelcome associated thoughts: they must have thought he was completely mad, rushing out in that wild way, either that or scared out of his wits. It was all an appropriately pathetic end to his failed mission to recover the hidden history of Kalapur. But perhaps even that was not the end of it, he thought, as he recalled the weird disturbing feeling that the oracle had been out to capture his spirit. Perhaps he had succeeded, and he would soon discover that he could no longer speak properly but only make yelping cries!

'His name was Roy,'—with some relief he heard his normal voice—'and he was a British diplomat. He died nearly fifteen years ago.'

'It doesn't matter now,' said the doctor, gauging his condition. 'We can fill in this strange form later. The main thing is to help you get some rest. Here drink this. I'll come back and examine you properly in the morning.'

'Hello, Mr Curtin, you remember me? I am Dr Urgyen and I am the personal physician to Abbot Taranatha. He sent me to you last night as soon as he heard of your accident.' The doctor smiled. 'Now if you are feeling a little better, I would like you to tell me exactly what happened.'

Timothy hesitated. It was not that he didn't remember: he now remembered only too clearly, and even his aching head felt slightly less painful after several hours' sleep. But could he bring himself to admit to this man the state of mind that had led him to flee from the gonkhang, and which had in effect also led to his fall? Was it medically necessary to tell him all that?

'Look,' said Dr Urgyen, continuing to observe him in a close but kindly fashion, 'before you explain, perhaps I should tell you a little more about myself . . . I was born in this country, and I first went to study western medical science in India. But in the end it left me dissatisfied, and I decided to come back here and study our traditional Himalyan medicine instead. That took another nine years. But I don't regret it because it has taught me to rely more on my own skills, especially in observation and diagnosis, and to understand a little more about the relations of mind and body. You see I carry no instruments, no charts, no x-rays. And the motivating spirit in our tradition is not ambition or competition but compassion.'

'So, why were you wearing a white coat when you came to see me last night?' Timothy asked. 'Surely that's the standard uniform of the western scientific doctor?'

'Yes, yes, you are quite right, and very observant too, especially for someone who has been through such a traumatic shock. And the reason why I wore that coat was to give you immediate confidence when you first opened your eyes and saw me – the feeling that you were not just in the hands of some tricksy Himalyan healer.' He laughed. 'You see sometimes compassion requires a spot of cunning too.' He paused. 'Now, tell me what happened.'

'It's very hard to explain in the clear light of the day,' said Timothy, 'and it all makes me feel very stupid. You see, while I was watching that séance I somehow got the feeling that the oracle was out to get me, I mean to capture my psyche and make me act out my own wildest impulses. And part of me wanted to experience that, whilst the rest of me could imagine nothing worse. And in the end I couldn't handle the situation, and so I just freaked out and ran away, hardly aware of where I was going.' Timothy felt relieved: it seemed that the words were telling the story for him and he didn't have to intervene or control them. In any case, he thought, this doctor is the kind of person who will work it out anyway, so why try to disguise things?

'Then when I reached the top of those steep steps I tripped on some large stones which the oracle had chucked out earlier and just fell headlong. I don't remember anything after that.'

Looking a little puzzled, Dr Urgyen asked: 'Are you sure that someone didn't come up behind and push you – is that possible?'

'Well, I suppose it's just possible, but at the time I wasn't aware of anyone following me – only my own huge shadow on the gonkhang wall! Anyway, you must think I'm crazy to have reacted like that!'

'No, not at all,' said Dr Urgyen in a matter-of-fact tone. 'No doubt your case expresses some personal features of your own psychology, but in general the state of mind you describe is quite common here. People here get these anxieties like people in England get depression. In fact, the conditions are not so dissimilar. But to set our minds at rest—and see whether you have suffered anything more serious than a sprained ankle and a sore head—I am going to give you a thorough examination.'

For the next hour Dr Urgyen carried out his careful survey of Timothy's body: noting all his symptoms and sensations, checking his tongue, examining his urine, gently pressing his head and limbs, and above all taking his pulse, not once but many times, and with a subtle variety of digital pressures. For much of this time he remained silent, his head inclined, just listening, observing, concentrating. Timothy felt that at no time in his life had anyone so personally yet objectively, explored all the secret rhythms of his veins and organs. It was a curiously reassuring experience.

'As far as I can see,' said Dr Urgyen, at last summing up the results of his investigations, 'there is some slight imbalance between bile and phlegm especially in your head and limbs, but you are young and it is not serious. I will give you some pills which should make you feel better in a few days. But I am just a little concerned about that deep headache. If that doesn't clear up soon I would suggest that you go to see a good doctor in Delhi.'

'And you can see no signs of spirits and demons?' Timothy now felt he could put the question like any normally disturbed inhabitant of Kalapur.

'That is not something I can easily determine since such interventions can sometimes function as secondary causes of humoral imbalance. But, as I said, there appears to be nothing very serious in your physical condition. Of course, if you would like to pursue it, there are plenty of specialists around here—monks and exorcists—who will be only too happy to perform all sorts of complex rituals to eliminate such possibilities. For instance, they might tell you to gain merit by paying some local butcher to free a goat about to be slaughtered. Or—rather confusingly—somebody else might advise you to have the same animal sacrificed as a literal scapegoat. Or again you might arrange with a lama for various small effigies to be made of you and the suspected demon, and for someone wearing your clothes to stand in for you in a special ceremony to expel any evil forces. Oh yes, and in that case you would also have to change your name afterwards!' Dr Urgyen paused for breath. 'No, Mr Curtin, on the whole, I think you would find it easier to consult that doctor in Delhi.'

After Dr Urgyen left Timothy began to feel slightly better. It seemed he had not suffered any serious physical injury, and he had found the courage to admit the state of panic that had seized him during the séance. But what was more, his mind had suddenly become much clearer. Up till now he had been unable to understand what had happened and why he had reacted in the way he did: he had only felt shame, pain and embarrassment. But Dr Urgyen, with his matter-of-fact air of compassion, had somehow shown him the way to approach his experience. Had the oracle really intended to mount some kind of psychological attack on him? He realised he would probably never know for certain, but given the man's earlier strangely sullen glare—which Chana had also noticed—and the possibility that he might even have come under pressure from the Tulku's party to try to frighten Timothy into leaving the country, it was not wholly irrational to suppose that he had intended to harm him.

But what about his own contradictory reactions to the experience: his deep fear of revealing his animal instincts versus his equally strong desire to do so? No doubt it was all connected with sexual frustration, and even to that unfortunate episode with Lucy Gabbinger long ago, but more specifically he now realised that it had more to do with the apparent collapse of his relationship with Huma. Indeed, the more he thought about her, the more obvious it became that things had started to go wrong for him ever since he had left her in such a miserable and confused state, feeling that he was somehow responsible for her last cold reactions, but unable to make out exactly what he had done or not done. And because he had been so upset by the experience he had tried hard to forget about her. But, of course, he hadn't succeeded. People like Norbu, Taranatha and even the Tulku had for one reason or another mentioned her in contexts that indicated that they knew about his relationship and assumed it was still continuing. And each time he had heard her name he had felt a mixture of elation and depression, before again vainly attempting to drive her from his memory. Even during the séance she had been present in her absence, his confused feelings obscurely reflected in the distortion of his conflicting impulses.

But why had he always taken it for granted that he was to blame for her cold reaction, that he had somehow failed to live up to her expectations? Couldn't the explanation be different, related perhaps to her own confusion and difficulty in accepting the extent to which she had come to depend on him, which he in his turn had been too self-centred to recognise? Perhaps she needed more time to come to terms with her feelings for him, time to make adjustments about which he knew little. Maybe she did after all care for him a little. Well, in a day or so she should arrive for the festival. He would find out then – provided she came. His calm clarity faltered for a moment.

It faltered partly because he had also become aware that something unusual was going on outside. Monks below in his own courtyard were calling to each other, responding apparently to the deep hypnotic growl of horns being blown somewhere at the other end of the monastery. Soon the long horns were joined by other instruments: the squawking of the short trumpets, the fast fluttering of cymbals, the low beat of drums. The whole ensemble seemed to be aimed at expelling something, first expelling, then cleansing. Timothy tried to get out of bed to see what was going on, only to feel a excruciating pain in his ankle as his foot touched the floor. Hopping his way to the window, he was just in time to see the last few monks hurrying through to the first courtyard and then out of sight. Almost immediately the music itself ceased, as abruptly as it had begun. Perhaps it was part of a rehearsal for the protectors' festival. He limped back to bed.

He found himself wondering whether Taranatha would be well enough to make an appearance during the festival as he had promised when they had last met in the hermit's cave. If so, it would probably be the last time they would meet since he had already decided before his accident that there was little point in continuing with his historical investigations on the Tulku's terms, and in any case Dr Urgyen was now urging him to fly back to Delhi for a check-up as soon as possible. At the same time he felt bad as he remembered that he had been so totally preoccupied with his own problems that he hadn't even thought to ask Dr Urgyen about the Abbot's health, even though Taranatha—sick as he was—had sent his own personal physician to take care of him. He recalled how ill the old man had looked when they had last sat together outside the cave.

Taranatha. It was such an unusual and memorable name, Sanskrit in origin and not Tibetan, like the names of almost all the other monks he had met, except of course, for the Tulku who had chosen to keep the classical name of the alleged founder of his dubious spiritual lineage. Presumably, the Abbot had assumed his name at some turning-point in his youth when he had decided to follow in the path of the original Taranatha, the great seventeenth-century historian of Tibetan Buddhism. Timothy remembered how disappointed he had been when Norbu had failed to identify Taranatha in the 1944 list of monks, and wondered whether the Abbot would now be willing to reveal his real name.

Outside the sounds of the horns and cymbals, which had earlier ended so abruptly, had started up again, only this time the whole orchestra was much much closer – a deafening Tantric serenade almost beneath his window. If anything could shift his headache, he thought, it would be these blasts and clashes, breaking and dispersing the illusions of hostile reality. The noise was in fact so deafening, that he completely failed to hear the softer sound of rapid footsteps ascending the stairs that led up to his guest-room. In the next moment the door burst open, and a mysterious masked apparition in a floating terracotta gown stood shimmering before him in the first spring sunlight.

'Timothy!', said Huma, throwing off her mask, and reaching forward to cup his face in her hands, 'what have they done to you?'

'They tried to change me into a migo,' said Timothy, giving her a dazed kiss. 'But what have they done to you?'

'Oh, I've become a dakini – at least for today!'

27

Hands clasped, Timothy and Huma gradually managed to convey to each other the gist of what had happened since their last dismal meeting in Himjin: the AG's proposal of marriage ... Timothy's encounter with the Abbot ... Princess Dekyi's story ... the riot that followed the debate ... Huma's stay in the farmstead and her discovery of the manuscript ... the séance in the gongkhang and Timothy's final flight and fall. And somehow, as all the separate scenes fast-forwarded and meshed together, they felt their two lives seemingly bound into a single narrative – a complex but shared experience.

'Oh, and it was Norbu who told me where you were,' said Huma. 'He was in quite a state and couldn't stop apologising for having been called away on the very day when you had your accident ... '

She was interrupted by an urgent knock on the door. 'That must be him,' she said, frantically trying to tidy her hair and restore an air of unruffled calm to her dakini gown. 'He insisted on coming to see us as soon as he was free.'

'Mr Tim, Miss Huma, how can you forgive me?' It was with some difficulty that Huma succeeded in blocking the space beside the bed where the Warden seemed intent on prostrating himself.

'On the very day when you were both in the greatest danger I could do nothing to help you. And the Abbot told me that above everything else, I must see that you came to no harm, and I failed!'

'Look Norbu, it really doesn't matter, the Abbot heard what had happened and sent his own doctor to take care of me. And as you can see, I'm all right now – I've somehow survived, and so has Huma!'

'Yes, we are both fine – even a little ecstatic!' Huma smiled. 'But tell us what happened in Himjin. You said something to me about being suddenly summoned there by the ministry. What was all the fuss about?'

It was some time before Norbu could bring the words out. 'They said I've got to leave the monastery,' he gulped it out at last, 'either that or leave my wife and family. They chose their timing very carefully: just when the Abbot is too weak to protect me.'

'And what will you do?'

'I have no choice. I will close my accounts and leave the monastery tonight.'

'But what about the Abbot? Is he really that desperately ill?' Once more Timothy was being forced to confront the reality of Taranatha's condition, the man he had always imagined to be indestructible, but even now he sought to evade the issue, saying, 'I thought his illness was partly diplomatic, that understandably he was sort of using it to avoid the minister's ultimatum on the history project.'

'There may have been some truth in that earlier,' said Norbu ruefully, 'but now I'm afraid his condition is far worse. You see, for some mysterious reason he decided to go out last evening and got caught in that blizzard. When he returned, his servants say that he was half-dead.'

Huma stared hard at Timothy. 'My God!' she said, 'that explains it. He must have come out to collect the manuscript in the cave, and then taken it away while I was asleep.'

'I know nothing about that,' said the Warden, 'but you will soon have the opportunity to judge his condition for yourselves. You see, when I returned early this morning, I went to him straightaway. He was too weak to say much, except that he wanted to see you both as soon as possible. He said it was urgent.'

'OK,' said Timothy. 'Give us a few minutes and we will come.'

Huma and Timothy had never actually visited the Abbot's rooms before: all visitors had been strictly forbidden for the past few weeks, and it was only, of course, by chance that Timothy had encountered Taranatha that day in the hermitage cave. After Huma's dramatic discovery of the manuscript, they were now both convinced that despite his illness he had all this time been hard at work translating the account by Tashi Rigzen, and that it was even possible that he himself was Tashi Rigzen! But given a lifetime's dissimulation, and the dangers that still threatened him, would he now be ready to acknowledge this unequivocally? The Abbot was nothing if not unpredictable, and as Timothy, supported by Huma, hopped and hobbled, slowly and painfully, towards the first courtyard, they knew they had to be ready for anything.

When they finally reached the door that led to the Abbot's apartment, Timothy stopped for a moment to recover himself. It felt surprisingly hot in the morning sunshine, and his head was still throbbing badly. Till now he had hardly noticed that the whole monastery was deserted, presumably because most of the monks had left to join the villagers' procession to celebrate the protectors' festival.

'Never mind!' said Huma, also perspiring from her efforts. 'I expect they can manage with one less dakini!'

'And one less migo!' muttered Timothy, as they pushed open the door and began with difficulty to negotiate the stairs. From somewhere out of the shadows a monk appeared to assist them.

The large room they entered at the top of the stairs was, without doubt, the Abbot's study. Closely stacked tall racks of books filled up almost all the area around the door, largely excluding the light that seemed to come from an opening on the other side. As they advanced awkwardly in single file down the narrow aisle that led between the racks, the light became stronger, till they found themselves standing in an open space in front of a wide window that overlooked the path winding down to the village. Three people were in the room, none of whom moved as they approached. Seated in a high-backed armchair immediately facing them was Taranatha himself, while standing behind him and looking down, they recognised the austere figure of Lama Wangdi. Another elderly monk sitting beside the Abbot on a cushion, finally acknowledged their presence: 'Please take a seat,' he said, pointing towards a vacant sofa.

Sensing that something had just happened, they instinctively looked again at Taranatha. It was only then that they noticed that his head was thrust back and his eyes were closed, and that though his whole expression was peaceful and serene, his face looked grey and very still, in strong contrast to the deep vibrant maroon of his robe. Taranatha, it seemed, had just died.

At almost the same moment they became aware of a low chanting voice, as Lama Wangdi bent down to touch the Abbot's shaven head: 'When the journey of my life has reached its end, and since no relatives go with me from this world, I wander in the bardo state alone. May the peaceful and wrathful Buddhas send out the power of their compassion and clear away the dense darkness of ignorance.'

With a numbed shock, Timothy recognised the same Bardo prayer which the Abbot himself had recited at his London lecture. Well, he couldn't help thinking, you've escaped us all in the end, escaped with your final secrets, just when we were about to catch up with you. But then, as you yourself used to say, you were a bit of a duplicitous old lama, someone who uniquely survived on mystery, and when the mystery went, it seems you also had to go. And what an exit, to the strains of the Bardo prayers, English-style!

Feeling oddly detached, Timothy gazed around what had been the Abbot's home for so many years. This part of the room was almost bare of decoration, only a small print of what looked like the British Museum hung on the far wall, whilst on the larger wall space behind the sofa, he recognised the faded outlines of the same Kalapur version of the Spirit of Time mandala that decorated the wall of his own room. It all seemed very appropriate, symbolic even of the Abbot's own life: the classical concrete powerhouse of history alongside the ultimate abstract distillation of its saving value. How the old man must have suffered, knowing what had happened half a century ago but compelled to stay silent!

Timothy became aware of Huma nudging at his arm. He had been so lost in his thoughts that he had not noticed that the old monk, who had been sitting on the cushion, was coming towards them holding a rolled-up scroll. 'It's the translation,' Huma whispered. 'Can't you see he's going to give it to us?'

Timothy took the scroll and passed it to Huma. Was this the end of their quest? Lama Wangdi's interminable chant continued but Timothy now began to distinguish another voice, as if superimposed on it. It sounded frail and a bit crackly but somehow familiar, as if pre-recorded:

'Don't be too hard on me Timothy,' the voice seemed to say. 'I wanted to tell you all what you wanted to know; but you took a long time to come, and I had to go. It was a great pity really, since, as you should know by now, our tradition values the communication of one man's truth to another: it can release and enlighten both. Still you will find all you need to know about my past life in the translation of my original account. Yes, Huma was right, I am (or was) Tashi Rigzen. So take the translation away with you—and the original as well—and show it to the United Nations or World Bank or anyone who can help to restore peace and justice to this country. And please try to understand that I am asking you to do this because I have complete trust in you. Oh, and Timothy, could you do something else for me? Please tell Wangdi and his friend not to pull such long faces. Can't they see the pain has ended?'

The voice faded leaving only the steady drone of Lama Wangdi's chant.

'Did you hear something?' Huma asked. 'Did the Abbot speak to you?'

'I don't know,' said Timothy. 'Well, yes . . . I think so. At least I heard what he might have said!'

28

'Our flying time to Delhi will be approximately one and a half hours.'

Timothy was reassured to hear again the familiar pukka tones of Captain Feroze as he and Huma waited anxiously for take-off. They had decided to leave for Delhi immediately after the Abbot's death, first for Timothy to consult a local doctor, and then to contact the World Bank officials to make them aware of the deep-seated political and religious crisis within Kalapur, resulting from the original seizure of power carried out in the name of the present Shar Lama more than fifty years ago. With Taranatha's unique narrative in his possession—and not for the first time he checked it was still safely packed in his brief case—it should be possible to demonstrate to the officials that the government whose loan they were in the process of approving, was neither legitimate nor stable. In such circumstances, he would try to persuade them – it would be prudent to make the loan conditional on the holding of free and fair elections in the country. Though far from feeling confident of success, for almost the first time in his life he found himself actually looking forward to a formidable challenge – fortified by the trust that Taranatha had seemed to place in him in his dying moments.

In the seats behind them the small party of middle-aged Japanese tourists who had originally travelled with Timothy on his outward journey were themselves returning home, evidently one of the first groups invited to come on an extended tour of the country as part of the new tourist development programme. 'Six weeks in Shangri-la' was the title of the English version of the shiny brochure they were still clutching. He had greeted them earlier like old friends when they recognised him in the departure lounge, and happily waved their brochures. Had they encountered any migos during their stay? His enquiry had only elicited torrents of giggles.

Since the plane still showed no signs of leaving, he again took out Taranatha's manuscript. Though it certainly rang true as a personal testament, and made sense of so much that had previously baffled him and Huma, it was perhaps inevitable that it also raised further questions. For instance, Taranatha said that his encounter with the old Shar Lama and his protectors in the remote eastern part of the country, had been a matter of pure chance – something that had just happened in the course of his own wanderings in search of spiritual knowledge. But given the widespread disturbances in Kalapur that followed the Lama's mysterious flight, it seemed more likely that the young Taranatha would have been actively searching for the lost leader rather than merely practising meditation.

All this time Huma had been quietly sitting beside him, her head resting on his shoulder but saying nothing. Her decision to join him on the trip to Delhi, she could now see, amounted to a decisive step in their relationship, though it had not at first seemed like that at the time, but rather as a natural and spontaneous act. It was as if the Abbot's death and his final decision to reveal his past to both of them had somehow given her courage to move forward in her life – that and Princess Dekyi's earlier confiding of her secret.

'Tim, I can tell you are still busy talking to Taranatha inside your head,' she said, nudging him gently, 'and so was I! But as it looks as if we are going to be delayed a bit longer, I'm going to write a note to my sister.' She had now got used to calling him Tim, apparently as a way of appropriating him, and she also noticed that he seemed to like it.

'Dear Rukhsi,' she wrote, 'I think I have now found the answer to Abbu's plots and plans: I have found someone else for myself! If you can somehow meet us at the Delhi YWCA on Tuesday afternoon, you can tell me what you think. Love, Huma.'

'What's Rukhsi like?' Timothy asked.

'Like me, only more so!'

'I'd like to meet her then.'

'You will, maybe quite soon! But right now I'm going to try and get some sleep. You can carry on thinking about the Abbot.'

Why had Taranatha chosen to remain silent for so long about what he knew about the previous Shar Lama's survival? Timothy's continuing attempts to make sense of the Abbot's life kept coming up against this central mystery. Of course, to have spoken out would almost certainly have led to his own death, and surely in the circumstances nobody could blame him for preferring to live. All the same, Timothy could not help thinking of alternative options, like, for example, staying on in Britain after completing his research, and exposing the illegitimacy of the new Shar Lama's regime from a safe distance. Why had he decided to return to Kalapur?

Instinctively, he felt that the answer had something to do with the Abbot's personal commitment to researching his country's history: to do that work properly he had to be in Kalapur. After all, he himself had spoken eloquently of history as being the ruling passion of his life, and as such it may have counted for more than the personal pressures to reveal the truth about the old Shar Lama (even though, paradoxically, that too was part of history). But perhaps other considerations had played a part in maintaining his silence. It was clear, for instance, that Taranatha took the pacifist side of his Buddhist commitment very seriously, that he was as critical of the Migo resistance movement as he was of the Shar Lama's government, since both had caused the loss of life. For him to have spoken out to challenge the government's legality would probably have made things worse.

At the same time, Timothy could not help thinking that it was also possible to put forward another very different, even 'duplicitous', explanation of the Abbot's conduct. Perhaps the Kalapur authorities had all along known about his youthful activities, but had decided not to pursue him either in return for his silence or because they derived advantages from his academic reputation abroad. Was it even possible that they had been able to use (or misuse) some of his more speculative writings, such as the essay on Hegel and Maitreya, to boister the ideological and cultural basis of their own 'reform' movement (as LJK had hinted)?

But the more he explored these negative possibilities, the less likely they became. Everything the Abbot had told him about the government's policies, not to mention his courageous stand against the minister's ultimatum, seemed to rule out the idea that he had entered into any secret deal with the regime. But just as the mental journey out from the central kernel of the Spirit of Time mandala could lead you into all kinds of traps and blind alleys, it was only to be expected that the Abbot's own explanation would not explain everything. Even that last message that had seemed to reach Timothy's consciousness in the moments following the old man's death could hardly be verified.

Perhaps after all, only one thing mattered: that in the end, and in keeping with his own tradition, Taranatha had decided that the time had at last come to reveal his secret, hopefully to the eventual benefit of his country and more immediately for the benefit of those to whom he had disclosed it: Huma and Timothy!

He placed Taranatha's manuscript carefully back inside his case. Behind him the Japanese tourists were still happily laughing together despite the continued delay in their departure. What, he suddenly wondered, would he say if they were to ask him about his stay in Kalapur: what had he got out of it?

At various times, during the past few days, he had found himself recalling the words of Lama Wangdi when they had first met outside the hermitage cave. Apropos the monks' retreats, Wangdi had explained how some of those who set out on the Tantric path first sought to discover their own yidam, and to do that they needed both the skilful instruction or example of a guru, and the loving insight of a dakini. Well, he himself could never claim to have seriously sought to follow the insights of Tantric Buddhism – much as those paths had intrigued him ever since Serena had first described them. But in a weird way, and lost as he had been in his own fears and confusions, he had yet contrived to find a kind of guru in Taranatha (for all his ambiguities), and in Huma surely the nearest he would ever get to a dakini. And with their help and inspiration, maybe he had already started to construct a kind of yidam for himself: a vehicle and persona for his future life. And the surprising thing was that, even the Abbot's unexpected death did not change the position or how he felt. Was he beginning to understand what was meant by 'emptiness' – still the most baffling concept in Himalayan Buddhism?

If so, he was not yet ready to pursue it fully, for his indirect awareness of others soon reminded him that what he had just thought about, was hardly the sort of conventional touristic success story that the Japanese or any other travellers would want to hear. Other things that had happened might impress them more: that he had uncovered the hidden history of Kalapur, escaped from demons, seen death, found love . . .

At last as the little plane began to move in readiness for take-off, Huma, still half-awake, reverted to her previous train of thought: 'And I'd also like you to meet my father sometime,' she said.

In a few moments they would be gazing down over the scene of their adventures. Of course, Timothy reminded himself—as it were, to keep his feet on the ground—there were some things he had failed to do. Most obviously, like the Japanese tourists themselves, he had not succeeded in finding the migo. True, he had in a sense located the source of its fascination in his own psyche, but despite all the stories and rumours of its presence, the actual creature (if it was there) had finally eluded him.

They were now ascending rapidly up over the narrow Himjin valley; soon the wings of the plane would almost seem to brush against the dense trees that clustered on its higher slopes. Somewhere in those recesses, he instinctively felt, the few remaining migos still defied their dangerous, would-be discoverers – those who would turn them into scientific objects or circus freaks, and either way almost certainly destroy them. How much longer could nature itself protect them? As if to answer hopefully, a dense cloud completely enveloped the plane, ending for the time being at least all hopes of finding them.

Glossary

Avalokiteshvara	:	The Bodhisattva of compassion.
Bardo	:	The intermediate state between death and rebirth.
Bodhisattva	:	A Buddha-to-be dedicated to helping others to attain enlightenment.
Chang	:	Light beer.
Chorten	:	Buddhist monument containing relics or religious texts.
Dakini	:	In Tantric practice a female deity or force inspiring and challenging seekers after enlightenment; also (more loosely) an enlightened woman.
Dharma	:	The Buddha's teaching.
Dharmapalas	:	Fierce deities protecting Buddhist teachings.

Dhritarashtra	:	Guardian king of the Eastern direction,
Emptiness (Sunyata)	:	In Tibetan Buddhism signifies the ultimate absence of inherent or individual nature in all phenomena.
Five Precepts	:	The basic moral injunctions for Buddhists, viz., not to destroy life; not to steal; not to commit adultery; not to lie; not to drink intoxicating drinks.
Geluk	:	Leading sect of Tibetan Buddhism, dominant from the fifteenth century.
Geshe	:	Doctor of advanced Buddhist philosophy.
Gompa	:	Monastery.
Gonkhang	:	Monastic temple dedicated to protective (and terrifying) deities.
Guru Rinpoche	:	Title given to Padmasambhava (see below).
Hemadatsi	:	Chilli and cheese dish.
Kalachakra	:	The Wheel of Time (a Tantric text and tutelary deity).
Kangyur and Tengyur	:	Tibetan translations of the corpus of Sanskrit Buddhist texts and commentaries.
Karma	:	Actions viewed as having inevitable consequences.
Khenpo	:	Abbot.
Kira	:	Skirt or dress.
Kudun	:	Master of discipline in monastery.
La	:	Spirit.
Langdarma	:	Ninth-century Tibetan ruler who persecuted Buddhists.
Lhakhang	:	Monastic temple.
Lopen	:	Master.
Maitreya	:	The future Buddha.
Mandala	:	The world or mode of being of a deity

		represented as a complex symmetrical pattern.
Manjushri	:	The Bodhisattva of wisdom.
Mantra	:	A group of syllables symbolising the qualities of a deity.
Migo	:	Wildman or yeti.
Padmasambhava	:	The Indian Tantric sage responsible for introducing Buddhism into Tibet and the Himalayan region in the eighth century.
Rinpoche	:	Title conferred on distinguished lamas, especially tulkus.
Senma	:	The ogress from whose union with Avalokiteshvara sprung the six kinds of beings in the universe.
Sha	:	Meat.
Shambhala	:	Mythical Buddhist kingdom somewhere north of Tibet and prototype for the Western idea of Shangri-la.
Tantra, Tantric	:	Esoteric Buddhist teachings emphasising spiritual development introduced into the Tibetan region where they were further refined and extended; also known as Vajrayana.
Tara	:	Female Bodhisattva representing feminine qualities of the Buddha.
Thangka	:	Tibetan-style banner or icon, painted or embroidered.
Tsampa	:	Roasted barley flour .
Tsenyi Lopen	:	Master of Philosophy.
Tulku	:	A distinguished lama recognised as the reincarnation of a previous great lama or as the present representative in a long line

of reincarnated lamas all bearing the same name as the founder of the lineage.

Vajra : A pronged sceptre (literally a diamond or thunderbolt) used in Tantric rituals.

Vajrapani : The Bodhisattva of power.

Yidam : In Tantric practice an aspect of one's own nature visualised as a Buddha quality.

Zugma : See Dakini.